The Heir of Mist and Memory

Echoes of Eirene: Awakening the Kingdom's Legacy

Evelyn Northwood

Copyright © 2024 by Evelyn Northwood

First Edition: May 2024

Table of Contents

Chapter 1
Dreams of Mist

In the twilight of sleep, the boundary between the real and the imagined blurs, as it often did for Serena, a simple village girl whose nights teemed with visions far more vivid than her quiet life in ThistleDown would suggest. This particular night, as the soft glow of the moon filtered through her window, casting long, whispering shadows across her humble room, Serena found herself again in that misty, surreal landscape that both terrified and beckoned her.

The world around her was a tapestry of silver and shadows, an ethereal realm that seemed spun from the threads of otherness. Shapes formed and dissolved in the mist—a broken column here, a statue's plinth there, all adorned in the creeping verdure of oblivion. The cool air brushed against her skin like a forgotten memory, carrying whispers of a life she could not recall, a song of longing that pulsed in the rhythm of her own heart.

Suddenly, the mists parted, and there it stood—a creature as integral to her dreams as the mists themselves. Whisper, the ethereal mist fox, its fur a cascade of cloud and smoke. It regarded Serena with eyes like amber moons, bright with an intelligence and sadness that pierced her to the core.

"Serena," it seemed to say, though no sound broke the silence, its voice a melodic echo in her mind, "follow me."

Compelled beyond reason, Serena moved through the fragmented visions of grandeur, her feet guided by a path she could not see but felt—instinctively knowing that this was the way. Whisper led her to the ruins of what her heart told her was once a palace, its mighty arches now but whispers of their former glory, shrouded in the ever-shifting veil of mist.

Here, amid the ruins, Whisper's form shimmered with a clarity that made the fox seem more present than ethereal. "This was Eirene," Whisper conveyed, not through words but through a rush of emotions and images that flooded Serena's senses. "Your kingdom, lost but never forgotten, veiled by the very mists that now cloak your legacy."

The revelation struck Serena with the weight of destiny. Eirene, a realm of mist and memory, a kingdom that was hers by birthright but hidden behind layers of enchantment and secrecy. Her inheritance, lost to the whims of those who feared what she might one day become.

As dawn's first light breached the horizon of her dream, the ruins and the mist began to fade, but Whisper's eyes held hers, anchoring Serena to the fading dream. "Remember," it urged, a plea from the very soul of the kingdom that stirred within her, a flame rekindled by the promise of revelation.

Serena awoke with a start, her room bathed in the pale light of morning, the remnants of her dream lingering like the echo of a distant melody. She lay in silence, the weight of her dreams pressing upon her with the urgency of a newfound purpose. Outside, ThistleDown was waking, the familiar sounds of the village stirring beneath the soft sigh of the morning breeze. But for Serena, the day held a different call, a whisper of adventure and discovery that promised to unveil the truths of her birthright and the mist-shrouded legacy of Eirene.

Morning draped its gentle light across ThistleDown, painting the modest cottages with hues of gold and amber. Birds chirped a lively chorus, yet for Serena, the quaint sounds of awakening seemed distant, muffled by the echoes of her revelation-filled dream. As she rose, the images of mist and ruins clung to her, a haunting veil over her senses.

She made her way to the kitchen, where the familiar, comforting scent of fresh bread and herbal tea brewed by her Aunt Mara filled the small space. The elder woman noted Serena's distracted air with a perceptive glance, her eyes narrowing slightly with concern.

"You're quiet this morning, dear. Another dream?" Aunt Mara asked as she placed a steaming cup before Serena. Her voice was soft, a soothing balm that somehow made it easier for Serena to anchor herself back to reality.

Serena nodded, her fingers wrapping around the warm cup, the heat grounding her. "Yes, but not just any dream, Aunt Mara. It was... vivid. There's a fox made of mist, calling itself Whisper. It told me of a place called Eirene, said to be my kingdom." She paused, gauging her aunt's reaction to the fantastical elements of her confession.

Aunt Mara's face remained impassive for a moment before a sigh escaped her lips, and she sat down opposite Serena. "I knew this day might come," she began, her tone tinged with a mixture of sadness and resolve. "Your dreams are memories, Serena. Eirene is real—or it was, long ago. You are descended from its last rulers. This village... it's not just your home; it was your sanctuary, a place to hide you from those who'd wish you harm."

Serena's heart raced, her mind a whirl of disbelief and awe. "Why me? Why hide a kingdom?"

"Because, my child, you are the heir to a legacy stolen and forgotten in the mists of time and magic. The truth was meant to surface when you were ready... perhaps that time is now," Aunt Mara explained, her hands clasping Serena's.

"But how can I believe all this? A kingdom? It sounds like a fairy tale," Serena protested, her voice a mix of fear and wonder.

"Fairy tales often stem from truths long buried, dear. Your parents wanted you to live freely, away from the burdens of the crown until you were old enough to choose," Aunt Mara said, reaching for an old, leather-bound book from a high shelf. She flipped through it until she found what she was looking for—a faded map of a land shrouded in mist. "This is Eirene."

Serena leaned in, studying the map with an intensity that surprised her. The names of forests, rivers, and mountains whispered to her, tugging at strings she didn't know her heart possessed.

"How can I reclaim something I don't understand, Aunt Mara? How do I even begin?" Serena's voice trembled with the weight of her destiny.

"You start by believing, Serena. Trusting in who you are, and who you're meant to be. Whisper, that fox in your dreams, might be the key to unlocking your past and Eirene's secrets," Aunt Mara encouraged, her gaze steady and reassuring.

"And what if I fail? What if I'm not the ruler Eirene needs?" The doubt in Serena's voice was palpable, the fear of the unknown a heavy cloak around her shoulders.

Aunt Mara reached across the table, squeezing her hand. "You will never know unless you try. And remember, you are not alone in this journey. You have me, and now, you have Whisper."

Their conversation was interrupted by a soft, almost imperceptible sound outside—a rustling that was not quite like the wind. Serena's senses sharpened, her recent dreams having heightened her awareness of the unusual.

"Go, Serena. Start your journey. Find Whisper, and find yourself," Aunt Mara said, standing to clear the table but pausing to add, "And no matter what happens, you are loved. You are meant for great things."

With a heart both heavy and light, filled with dread and determination, Serena stood. She packed a small bag with essentials, the weight of her aunt's trust and the pull of her destiny guiding her hands. As she stepped outside, the cool morning air brushed against her cheeks like a promise. The village of ThistleDown, with its quaint charm and hidden depths, seemed to whisper farewell to its daughter, now set upon a path that would lead her into the mists of her forgotten kingdom, towards a fate intertwined with the very essence of memory and mist.

Stepping beyond the familiar bounds of ThistleDown, Serena's boots crunched softly against the morning frost, each step a beat in the newfound rhythm of her destiny. The village, with its waking murmurs and curling smoke from hearths, receded behind her as she ventured toward the edge of the enchanted forest that skirted the village—a boundary between the known and the veiled worlds she was now drawn to explore.

As the trees began to thicken, enveloping her in their ancient embrace, the air grew tangibly cooler, the mist seeming to rise to greet her. It was here, beneath the boughs heavy with the weight of unspoken secrets, that she found Whisper waiting, its form more substantial in the dim light filtering through the leaves.

"Whisper," Serena called softly, her voice tinged with a mix of reverence and uncertainty. The fox's ears twitched at her approach, and it turned to face her, its eyes glowing with a soft, otherworldly light.

"You have come," Whisper said, its voice not heard but felt within her mind, a melodious echo that resonated with the rustling leaves and whispering winds.

"I... I had to come. Aunt Mara told me of my heritage, of Eirene," Serena replied, her words faltering under the weight of her awakening reality. "She said these dreams... these visions... they're memories?"

"Yes, memories of a past woven into the very mist that shields your kingdom. You are the heir, Serena. The last of your line, and Eirene calls to you," Whisper conveyed, its form shifting slightly as if blurred by the very air around it.

"But how can I reclaim what I do not know? How do I even begin to understand my own legacy?" Serena's voice cracked, the enormity of her task looming like the shadows that danced between the sunlit patches on the forest floor.

"By learning, by remembering. Your journey back to Eirene begins with understanding the Veil of Mist that protects it. This mist is not just a barrier; it is a bridge," Whisper explained, circling around her before facing her again, its tail flicking thoughtfully.

"A bridge to what? To the past? To my memories?" Serena asked, her curiosity piqued despite her reservations.

"To both, and more. The Veil holds back the memories of Eirene, keeping the kingdom hidden from those who would seek to destroy it. But for you, it will part," Whisper assured her, its confidence a stark contrast to her own uncertainty.

"And if I can part the Veil, retrieve these memories, then what? What awaits me in Eirene?" Serena's gaze was fixed on Whisper, seeking not just answers but reassurance.

"Restoration, renewal. The crown of Eirene has been dormant, its power untouched since the great betrayal. You must awaken it, as you awaken the land," Whisper responded, its voice a gentle chime in her mind.

"But I am no queen. I am... I was just a girl from a village, with nothing but dreams too large for her," Serena confessed, her shoulders slumping under the invisible weight of her future crown.

"Every queen begins as something else—a girl, a dreamer. You carry within you the blood of rulers and the heart of the mist. Eirene does not need the queen you will become; it needs the girl you are, with all your doubts and dreams," Whisper reassured her, moving closer, its form almost caressing her as the mist swirled around them both.

Serena took a deep breath, letting the cool air fill her lungs, the essence of the mist seeping into her, lending her a strength she had not known she possessed. "And will you guide me, Whisper? Through the mist, to Eirene, to all that I must become?"

"Always. I was born of the last queen's hope, her love for you, her daughter. I am here to protect you, to guide you. Together, we will walk the paths lost to memory, and find the way home," Whisper promised, its voice now a comforting anchor in the swirling uncertainty that surrounded her.

With a nod, a silent acceptance of her fate, Serena stepped forward, her hand reaching out to touch Whisper. As her fingers brushed against the fox's ethereal fur, a warmth spread through her, a connection to the land of her ancestors, to Eirene, solidifying in her heart.

Together, they turned toward the heart of the forest, where the mist grew thicker, weaving through the trees like a river of forgotten stories. With each step, Serena felt the weight of her legacy, not as a burden, but as a bridge to the kingdom she was meant to reclaim, her doubts slowly dissolving into the mist, replaced by a burgeoning resolve to uncover the truth of her past and the future of Eirene.

The forest grew denser, a labyrinth of ancient trees wrapped in veils of cascading mist, each breath of wind whispering secrets of forgotten lore. Serena, guided by Whisper, moved with a cautious awe, her senses attuned to the subtle shifts of the world around her—a world that seemed to breathe and watch with unseen eyes.

The path they followed was less a path than a suggestion, marked only by the occasional clearer space between the trees or a slightly smoother stretch of ground beneath the tangled roots. The deeper into the forest they ventured, the more Serena felt the presence of the mist not just around her but within her, filling her with a sense of connection to this hidden land that pulsed with magic.

Occasionally, Whisper would pause, its ethereal form shimmering more brightly for a moment, as if to assure her or perhaps to listen more deeply to the murmurs of the mist. "We are close now," it would tell her, its voice a comforting echo in her mind. "The threshold approaches."

As the morning waned into afternoon, the light dimming under the thickening canopy, they came upon a clearing. It was a sudden openness in the embrace of the forest, where the mist rolled gently across a mirror-like pool that lay at its center, surrounded by a ring of ancient stones. Each stone was carved with intricate symbols that seemed to shimmer slightly with a light of their own, despite the overcast sky.

"This is the threshold," Whisper said, its voice barely above a whisper, blending with the rustle of the leaves. "The gateway to Eirene lies across this water. The pool reflects not just the light, but the truth hidden within the mist."

Serena approached the edge of the water, peering into its depths. The pool did not reflect her face but instead showed a montage of images—a city of splendid towers and wide, bustling streets filled with people of all kinds, markets overflowing with goods, children playing in the sunlight. It was a vision of Eirene in its glory days, as if the pool remembered and yearned for the past.

"The Eirene you see was," Whisper intoned solemnly, "but it can be again. The mist preserves not just the memory of what was, but the potential of what might be. Your will, your desire to reclaim and restore, shapes the mist."

With a deep, steadying breath, Serena closed her eyes, reaching out with her senses to feel the mist swirling around her, through her, within her. When she opened her eyes, the images in the pool had changed. Now it showed a city partly in ruins, the echoes of grandeur marred by decay and neglect, yet still noble, still proud.

"This is the Eirene that is," Whisper continued, its tone somber yet not without hope. "And the Eirene that awaits your care, your rule."

Serena's heart swelled with a mix of grief and resolve. Here was her heritage, her responsibility—a kingdom both beautiful and broken, waiting for her to lead it back to its former glory. She looked at Whisper, her guide, her guardian, her first subject, and nodded.

"How do I cross into Eirene? How do I begin?"

Whisper nudged her gently towards the pool. "Step into the water. Let it carry you across the threshold. Trust in the mist, Serena. Trust in yourself."

Taking another breath, filled with the scents of earth and magic, Serena stepped forward. The water was cool, almost cold, lapping gently at her feet as she walked into the pool. With each step, the water rose, taking her deeper, yet she felt no fear, only a profound peace.

As the water reached her waist, then her chest, she realized she was no longer moving forward but being gently pulled. The mist thickened around her, obscuring her vision, and for a moment, she was blind. But she felt Whisper's presence, reassuring and solid in the world of shifting shadows.

Then, as suddenly as it had enveloped her, the mist cleared, and Serena found herself standing on the shores of a great lake, the city of Eirene spread out before her, its towers catching the light of a setting sun that painted everything in hues of gold and amber. She had crossed over; she was home.

The day closed around her with a soft, whispering sigh, the shadows lengthening as the light faded. Serena stood at the edge of her future, the weight of her past a gentle hand on her back, pushing her forward into the destiny she was born to fulfill. The journey had just begun, but for the first time, Serena felt ready to embrace whatever challenges it might bring, for Eirene was her burden, her privilege, and, ultimately, her home.

Chapter 2
Whisper's Revelation

The city of Eirene stretched before Serena, its once-majestic architecture now marred by the passage of time and neglect. The streets, though empty, whispered of past bustling life, each cobblestone and cracked wall telling a story of glory and downfall. Serena walked alongside Whisper, their steps echoing in the hollow expanse of the deserted market square.

"What happened here, Whisper? How did Eirene fall to such ruin?" Serena's voice broke the eerie silence, her eyes scanning the faded frescoes and overgrown fountains.

"It was a gradual decline, born from forgetfulness and betrayal. When the mist was summoned to protect the kingdom, it also obscured it from the outside world and from itself," Whisper explained, its tail flicking with each step. "Memories faded, and without memories, so too did the power and will of the people."

Serena paused by a fountain, its basin cracked and dry. She ran her fingers over the intricate carvings of mythic creatures now eroded by time. "And my family? The rulers before me?"

"They fought as long as they could. But as the mist thickened, so did the confusion and fear. Your mother, the queen, was the last to rule before the veil of oblivion became too dense. She hid you away, hoping one day you'd return to restore Eirene."

"And so I have returned, but to what? Ruins and shadows?" Serena's words carried a weight of sorrow, her gaze lingering on a statue of a lion, its once fierce demeanor now softened by moss.

Whisper nudged her gently, encouragingly. "To opportunity, Serena. To possibility. Ruins are merely the soil in which the future can be planted."

Serena smiled faintly, bolstered by Whisper's unwavering faith. "Then let us begin planting. What is the first step in lifting this veil, in restoring the memories and the glory of Eirene?"

"The Crown of Remembrance holds the key. It is not merely a symbol of rule but a vessel of Eirene's collective memory. If you can find and restore the Crown, you can awaken the city's memory, its spirit, and its people."

"And where is this crown?" Serena asked, her resolve hardening with each new piece of the puzzle laid before her.

"Lost in the heart of the palace, protected by spells and the shadows of the past. It will not be an easy journey, nor a safe one. The path to reclaiming the Crown of Remembrance is guarded by those who have forgotten their loyalty to the true heir."

Serena's determination grew as they walked through the archways leading to the royal palace, its towering gates closed and overgrown with ivy. "Then we will remind them. Lead on, Whisper."

As they approached the gates, a chill breeze swept through the square, carrying with it faint whispers—echoes of the past or perhaps warnings. The gates creaked ominously as they pushed them open, the groan of metal on stone resonating like a mournful cry through the halls beyond.

Inside, the palace was a labyrinth of shadows and whispers. Dust motes danced in beams of light that sliced through the gloom, illuminating scenes of bygone opulence now laid to waste. Serena's heart ached for the home she never knew, each step deeper into the palace reinforcing her purpose.

Whisper's form glowed softly, casting a gentle light around them. "This was once the heart of Eirene. You can restore it to that glory, Serena. Not the glory of power and dominion, but of hope and memory."

"I will," Serena affirmed, her voice echoing slightly in the vast emptiness. "I will restore Eirene, for my mother, for my people, and for all that we have lost to the mist."

Their voices gradually faded into silence as they delved deeper into the palace, the weight of history bearing down upon them, yet buoyed by the light of hope that Whisper carried forward into the dark.

Serena and Whisper ventured deeper into the heart of the dilapidated palace, their footsteps muffled by the thick carpet of dust that blanketed the floor. The once resplendent halls, now dim and shrouded in cobwebs, seemed to close in around them, heavy with the scent of decay and the burden of forgotten eras.

As they approached the grand throne room, the air grew colder, and the silence seemed imbued with a spectral expectancy. The massive doors, adorned with fading gold leaf and the crest of Eirene, stood slightly ajar, as if inviting them to uncover the secrets held within.

Serena pushed the doors open with a resolute push, her heart pounding with a mix of fear and anticipation. The throne room, vast and shadowy, was illuminated by shafts of light piercing through the broken ceiling, casting long, eerie shadows across the floor.

"This... This was where your ancestors ruled, where destinies were forged," Whisper intoned softly, its voice resonating in the quiet, a stark contrast to the stillness.

Serena stepped forward, her gaze drawn to the throne at the far end of the room, a solitary silhouette against the backdrop of a tattered royal banner. "It's so desolate now, Whisper. Can this really be brought back to life?"

"It can, and it will," Whisper assured her, moving to float beside her as she walked slowly towards the throne. "The Crown of Remembrance is here, somewhere hidden in this room. It awaits its true heir—to awaken and restore."

Serena approached the throne, running her hand along its carved armrests, the wood cold and rough under her fingers. "How do we find it? Where do we even begin?"

Whisper's form shimmered, casting a soft glow that seemed to pulse in tune with Serena's quickening heartbeat. "Listen, Serena. The crown is ensconced in magic, bound by the royal bloodline. It calls faintly to those who belong to it."

Closing her eyes, Serena focused, reaching out with senses she barely understood. At first, there was only silence, a void as empty as the room seemed. But slowly, a hum, soft and almost melodic, began to fill her ears, a sound that seemed more felt than heard.

"Do you hear it?" Whisper asked, its voice a mere whisper itself against the chorus of the calling.

"Yes, I think I do. It's like... like a song, almost forgotten," Serena replied, opening her eyes and looking around, trying to pinpoint the source of the sound.

"Follow it, Serena. It will lead you to the crown."

Moving through the throne room, guided by the haunting melody, Serena felt the weight of centuries slip away as the song grew stronger, more insistent. It led her to a tapestry behind the throne, faded and worn but still depicting the glorious history of Eirene—a tapestry that seemed to pulse with a life of its own.

"The crown is behind this," Serena said, reaching out to touch the fabric. The moment her fingers brushed against the tapestry, the melody crescendoed into clarity, and the fabric parted, revealing a hidden alcove.

Inside, set upon a pedestal, was the Crown of Remembrance. It was less a crown and more a circlet, simple yet elegant, crafted of silver and set with a single, large gem that shimmered with an inner light. As Serena stepped closer, the gem glowed warmly, responding to the proximity of its rightful queen.

"This is it? This is what I came for?" Serena's voice was a mix of awe and disbelief.

"Yes," Whisper confirmed, its light reflecting off the silver of the crown, casting prismatic colors across the dark walls. "This is the Crown of Remembrance. Take it, Serena. Claim your heritage."

With a trembling hand, Serena lifted the crown from its resting place. The moment it touched her fingers, a rush of warmth filled her, visions of Eirene in its heyday flashing before her eyes—laughing children, bustling markets, vibrant festivals—all the life that once filled these now silent halls.

"This is Eirene," Serena whispered, tears of hope and resolve mingling in her eyes as she slowly placed the crown upon her head. The room seemed to breathe with her, the shadows receding as if bowing before their queen.

With the crown upon her brow, Serena felt not just the power of the artifact itself but the responsibility it carried. She turned to Whisper, her expression one of newfound determination. "We will bring Eirene back, Whisper. We will restore it to what it was, and more."

Together, they turned to leave the throne room, the crown secure, the first step in Serena's quest to revive her kingdom completed. The journey was just beginning, but Serena was no longer just a girl driven by dreams; she was a queen, guided by the echoes of her ancestry and the hopes of her people.

With the Crown of Remembrance now resting upon her head, Serena stepped out from the shadowy confines of the throne room into the corridors of the palace, her steps imbued with a newfound sense of purpose. The crown not only symbolized her rightful rule but also seemed to resonate with a subtle power, its presence alone beginning to stir the dormant energies of the palace.

As they navigated through the winding hallways, the air around them seemed to shift, the oppressive gloom retreating ever so slightly with each step Serena took. Whisper floated beside her, its light casting serene glows against the walls, illuminating faded tapestries and portraits of long-dead monarchs who watched silently as their descendant passed.

"With the crown, the palace awakens," Whisper said softly, its voice blending with the subtle sounds of the building's reawakening—the distant echo of stone grinding against stone, the murmur of the wind through cracked windows, the gentle shift of earth as though the palace itself were stretching from a long slumber.

Serena's touch seemed to breathe life into the surfaces she grazed; the once dull and tarnished fixtures began to gleam faintly, reflecting back the light of Whisper's glow. The heavy air started to clear, revealing the true grandeur of the palace's architecture, its intricate masonry and sweeping arches now visible beneath the years of neglect.

As they reached the grand atrium, the center of the palace and the heart of its magic, the impact of the crown was unmistakable. Here, the air was clearer, almost vibrant. The large, stained glass window that dominated the atrium's far wall, previously obscured by centuries of dirt and grime, now let in streams of light, coloring the floor with hues of amber, jade, and sapphire.

Serena paused in the center of the atrium, closing her eyes to feel the pulse of the palace, the gentle thrum of life returning. She could sense the Crown of Remembrance working through her, its magic intertwining with her will, reaching deep into the foundations of the palace and beyond, whispering promises of renewal to the land that lay waiting beneath the layers of fog and decay.

"The crown and you are now one, Serena. Through you, Eirene will rise anew," Whisper affirmed, its tone filled with reverence and awe.

Opening her eyes, Serena looked around, her heart swelling with hope and determination. She could feel the connection, not just to the palace but to the entirety of Eirene, a bond forged through centuries, anchored in the present by the weight of the crown upon her brow.

"I feel it, Whisper. I feel the kingdom's heart beating with mine," Serena murmured, her voice a testament to the profound connection she now experienced. "We will restore Eirene, bring back its glory and its people. We will make it a kingdom remembered not just in history, but in the lives of all who will call it home once more."

With a deep, steadying breath, she lifted her gaze to the window, the light casting her shadow long and queenly across the atrium floor. It was time to plan, to act. The restoration of the palace was just the beginning. The cities, the villages, the people of Eirene—all awaited the touch of their queen to awaken them from their enforced slumber.

Serena and Whisper moved on, leaving the atrium behind, their path now clear. Each room they entered, each hall they traversed felt the influence of the Crown of Remembrance, the stirrings of life returning, faint but steady.

The journey of restoration was fraught with challenges, Serena knew, but with the crown's power and Whisper at her side, she felt ready to meet them head-on. Eirene's revival was at hand, and she, its queen, was the herald of its dawn.

Emerging from the atrium, Serena and Whisper continued their journey through the palace, now approaching the library—a vast room rumored to house ancient texts and scrolls, some of which held the secrets and spells that once protected and prospered Eirene.

The heavy wooden doors creaked ominously as they pushed them open, revealing rows upon rows of shelves laden with books, their spines coated in dust and cobwebs. The air was thick with the musty scent of old paper and forgotten words.

"Here, Serena, lies the knowledge of your ancestors," Whisper intoned, gliding ahead and illuminating the shadowy recesses of the library with its ethereal light. "These texts hold the wisdom of ages past, and perhaps, guidance for the future."

Serena followed, her eyes wide with awe and a spark of curiosity. She reached out, touching the spine of a particularly ancient-looking tome. "Can these really help us restore Eirene?"

"Yes," Whisper confirmed, floating close to a large tome on a central pedestal. "But the knowledge here is guarded, not just by locks or wards, but by the will to seek it. You must show your intent, prove your worthiness to glean the secrets held within."

"How do I do that?" Serena asked, her voice echoing slightly in the vast chamber.

"Start by opening this book," Whisper suggested, indicating the tome before them. "It is known as the Codex of Regnum, written by the first rulers of Eirene."

Serena approached the pedestal cautiously, her hands trembling as she opened the cover. The pages were yellowed with age, but the writing was still clear, glowing faintly as if reacting to her touch.

"Read, Serena. Read and understand," Whisper urged gently.

Serena began to read aloud, her voice growing steadier with each word. "'In the heart of Eirene lies not just the power of land, but the spirit of its people...'"

As she read, the words seemed to lift from the pages, swirling around her, each syllable imbued with a power that resonated deep within her soul. The library responded, the very air pulsating with a dormant energy that now stirred to life.

"This... This is magic, isn't it?" Serena whispered, awe-struck.

"Yes, the magic of your lineage, the magic of Eirene itself. It recognizes you, Serena, as its rightful heir, as its queen," Whisper replied, its light brightening with each passing moment.

"What do these words mean, then? How can they help us?" Serena asked, turning the page to continue her reading.

"They are spells and incantations, but also lessons. They teach us that the strength of the kingdom lies not in its fortifications or weapons, but in its heart, in its people," Whisper explained. "You must unite the people, rekindle their spirits as you have rekindled the magic of this place."

Serena nodded, absorbing the gravity of Whisper's words. "Then we must go to them, to the people. We need to bring them back, show them that Eirene lives, that their queen has returned."

"Indeed, but remember, the journey is perilous. The lands beyond these walls are filled with remnants of the past, some forgotten, some twisted by the same forces that sought to bury Eirene in obscurity," Whisper cautioned.

"I am ready," Serena declared, her voice resolute. "Eirene calls to me, and I must answer. We will begin at the heart, in the capital. We will rebuild from there, spreading hope and restoring the land."

"Very well, Serena. Then let us prepare. Gather what knowledge you can carry, and we shall set forth at dawn. The path of revival is long and fraught with shadows, but with the crown's guidance and the Codex's wisdom, you shall illuminate the way," Whisper concluded, its tone imbued with solemnity and encouragement.

Closing the Codex, Serena looked around the library, now a beacon of light within the palace, a symbol of the revival that awaited the entire kingdom. The shadows receded further as she took up several scrolls and books, arming herself with the knowledge and power needed to face the challenges ahead.

Together, they left the library, stepping back into the corridors that now seemed less foreboding, more hopeful. The journey to restore Eirene had truly begun, and Serena, with Whisper by her side, was ready to lead her people out of the shadows and into the light.

Chapter 3
The First Steps

As the first light of dawn crept over the horizon, casting a gentle glow across the landscape, Serena stood at the edge of the palace grounds, her gaze fixed on the city below. It was time to venture forth, to see the realm that lay beneath the veil of mist and memory, to meet the people of Eirene whom she was destined to lead.

Whisper, ever present at her side, shimmered in the early morning light. "The journey begins, Serena. Are you prepared to see your kingdom as it is?"

"I am," Serena replied, her voice steady despite the flutter of nerves in her stomach. "It's one thing to read about Eirene's plight and another to witness it. I need to see the lands, to understand what must be done."

"Very well," Whisper said, leading the way down the winding path that descended into the valley. "We will first visit the village of Elderglen. It lies on the outskirts of what was once the royal forest. The people there are simple but hearty, likely unaware of your return or even your existence."

As they walked, the path narrowed, flanked by towering trees whose branches intertwined above, forming a natural archway. The air was cool, filled with the scent of pine and earth, a whisper of nature's enduring watch over the land.

"Will they accept me? After all, I am a stranger to them, appearing from the mist," Serena mused aloud, her hands clasped tightly in front of her.

"It is not your lineage alone that will win their loyalty, but your actions. Show them their queen has returned not just to reclaim a throne, but to restore a kingdom," Whisper advised, its tone gentle yet firm.

As they approached Elderglen, the sounds of daily life reached their ears—chopping wood, laughter, the distant bleating of sheep. The village appeared, nestled in a clearing, its cottages made of stone and wood, smoke curling up from chimneys into the clear morning sky.

Stepping into the village square, Serena saw the villagers pause, their curious eyes turning toward her, expressions mingled with caution and curiosity.

"Good people of Elderglen," Serena began, her voice echoing slightly in the still morning air. "I am Serena, your queen, returned to reclaim the throne of Eirene and to restore our kingdom to its former glory."

The villagers exchanged looks, whispers buzzing among them. An elderly man stepped forward, leaning on a carved wooden staff. "Your Highness, if it truly be you, why come now? We've been left to the mercy of the mist and the hardships it brings for generations."

Serena met his gaze, her resolve clear. "I was hidden away for my safety until the time was right. I have returned to lift the mist, to bring back the prosperity and peace that once defined Eirene. But I cannot do it alone. I need your help, your trust."

"And what of our struggles? Will you ease the taxes that burden us? Will you rid us of the bandits that prey on our roads?" another villager called out, a young woman holding a child.

"Yes, I will address all these issues," Serena assured them. "But I need to understand the full extent of your troubles. Speak freely, and together, we will find solutions."

The villagers began to voice their concerns—one by one, they spoke of failed crops, of young ones lost to illness, of the fear that pervaded their nights. Serena listened, Whisper at her side, her heart heavy with the weight of her people's suffering, yet also filled with determination.

"This is but the first step," Serena said as the assembly drew to a close. "I will return, and I will bring aid. For now, know that you are not forgotten, and hope has returned."

As Serena and Whisper left Elderglen, the villagers watched, some skeptical, others hopeful. The path ahead was long and fraught with challenges, but Serena felt a fire kindling within her—a fire to fight, to lead, to heal.

Her journey to reclaim Eirene had truly begun, and though the road was uncertain, her heart was steadfast. With each step, each village, each soul she touched, she wove the threads of the future—a future where Eirene would rise, remembered and restored, a realm of light reborn from the shadows.

Leaving Elderglen behind, Serena and Whisper ventured further into the heart of Eirene. The path meandered through a landscape draped in the silver tendrils of mist, which seemed less a barrier now and more a veil to be drawn aside, revealing the kingdom's hidden wounds and whispered secrets.

As they walked, the land began to change, the trees thinning out to reveal rolling fields that should have been lush with the harvest. Instead, the fields lay barren, the soil dry and cracked, the aftermath of neglect and the suffocating presence of the mist that blanketed the kingdom for too long.

"This land... it's dying," Serena murmured, her gaze sweeping across the desolate expanse. "How can we restore it, Whisper? The damage seems beyond repair."

"It will take time and effort, and the will to see it through," Whisper replied, its voice a gentle chime amidst the sighing of the wind. "The land reflects the state of the kingdom. As you heal one, so too will the other begin to recover. Your connection to the crown and the land is deep; you must draw on that strength."

They continued their journey, reaching a small farming community by midday. The people here were few, their faces etched with the lines of hardship and resilience. As Serena approached, a middle-aged man stepped forward, his posture wary but his eyes reflecting a cautious hope.

"You are the queen they speak of, returned from the mists?" he asked, his voice gruff but not unkind.

"Yes, I am Serena, your queen," she replied, meeting his gaze firmly. "I have come to see the troubles of the land for myself and to seek your aid in restoring Eirene."

The farmer nodded slowly, then gestured towards the barren fields. "We've tried to cultivate the land, but nothing takes hold. The soil... it's as if it's lost the will to give."

Serena walked to the edge of a field, kneeling to let her fingers sift through the dry earth. "I feel the pain of the land, as if it mirrors the sorrow and loss of its people. But there is hope still. With care and magic, we can revive the earth. Whisper, is there knowledge in the Codex that might aid us?"

"There are spells of renewal and growth, ancient magics bound to the royal line. Used wisely, they can bring life back to this land," Whisper explained, floating closer to Serena as she stood, dusting off her hands.

"Show me," Serena said, determination lighting her features. "Let's begin here, now."

Whisper guided her through the incantation, a series of delicate, flowing words that Serena spoke aloud. As she did, the air around them shimmered, the mist responding, swirling as if agitated. Gradually, the soil beneath her hands began to warm, the first signs of life stirring within.

The farmer watched, awe and hope dawning on his face as faint green shoots began to break through the soil's surface. Around them, others gathered, whispering in amazement as the field slowly transformed before their eyes.

"It's working," Serena breathed, a smile breaking over her face, the first true smile since her return. "The land remembers, just as the people must."

"It does, and they will," Whisper replied, its light glowing warmly. "With each patch of earth healed, with each heart mended, Eirene will rise again."

The community murmured their approval, their earlier resignation now replaced by a budding enthusiasm. "Tell us what we must do, Your Majesty," the farmer said, his voice strong and hopeful. "We will work, learn, and fight alongside you."

"We will start by restoring the farms, one by one," Serena declared, standing tall among them. "We'll bring back the harvests, and with them, the prosperity and joy that once defined this land. I will seek your counsel, learn from your experiences. Together, we will heal Eirene."

As they discussed plans and shared knowledge, the connection between Serena and her people strengthened. The road ahead was long and fraught with challenges, but the queen and her subjects were united in purpose, their spirits lifted by the tangible signs of recovery in the once-barren field.

With renewed vigor, Serena and Whisper left the farming community, heading towards the next village, each step a testament to the burgeoning hope that perhaps, just perhaps, Eirene could indeed be restored to its former glory.

The road to Stonegate wound through a dense copse of elder trees, their branches heavy with the history of Eirene. As Serena and Whisper approached the village, they could hear the river that divided the town churning over stones worn smooth by time and constant flow. The village itself was built around this river, the lifeblood of the community, with cottages and small shops perched along its banks, all crafted from the local gray stone that gave Stonegate its name.

Upon their arrival, the villagers eyed Serena with a mixture of curiosity and reserve. Among them, a stout woman with streaks of gray in her hair stepped forward, her demeanor as sturdy as the stone of her surroundings.

"Good day to ye, stranger. What brings ye to Stonegate?" she inquired, her gaze flicking briefly to Whisper then back to Serena.

Serena met her gaze, her posture confident yet open. "Good day. I am Serena, your queen, returned to reclaim and restore our kingdom. I wish to understand the challenges you face here in Stonegate and how I might aid in addressing them."

The woman eyed her for a moment, then nodded slowly. "Well then, Your Majesty, we welcome ye. I'm Mira, the miller of Stonegate. Our main trouble is the river—it's been flooding more each year, worse than any can remember. It's eroding the banks and threatening our homes."

Serena walked with Mira to the river's edge, observing the fast-moving waters and the erosion clearly visible at the riverbank. "I see. This river sustains you but also threatens your safety. Whisper, do we have knowledge in the Codex that could help control the waters?"

"Yes," Whisper responded, hovering over the rushing river. "There are spells for channeling and calming waters. Properly cast, they could mitigate the flooding and protect Stonegate."

"Then let us do it," Serena decided, rolling up her sleeves. "Show me, Whisper."

Together, they performed the incantation, Serena's voice steady as she spoke the ancient words. Gradually, the river's rush began to ease, the waters slowing as if listening to her command. The villagers gathered, watching in awe as the water level slowly receded, revealing more of the riverbank previously hidden under the turbulent flow.

Mira, watching the transformation, her eyes wide, turned to Serena. "By the gods, ye truly have the power. Ye've calmed the river!"

"It is my duty and my honor to serve the people of Eirene," Serena replied, her eyes on the now gently flowing river. "But this is only a temporary measure. We will need to work together to fortify the banks and manage the water flow sustainably."

"Aye, that we can do," Mira agreed, her initial skepticism giving way to respect. "With yer help, we can make Stonegate safe again."

"I will send aid from the palace to assist in reinforcing the banks," Serena promised. "And I will return to ensure that Stonegate thrives, not just survives."

Gratitude spread among the villagers as they discussed plans with Serena for the improvements needed. Through the exchange, Serena felt a deepening connection to her people, each interaction teaching her more about the kingdom she was determined to rebuild.

As the sun began to set, casting long shadows over the village, Serena and Whisper prepared to leave Stonegate, their spirits buoyed by the success of the day. The path ahead remained daunting, but with each step, Serena's resolve deepened, fueled by the tangible changes she could bring about.

"Today was a good day, Whisper. We made a difference," Serena said, looking back at the village.

"Yes, and there will be many more," Whisper replied. "Each step forward strengthens you and the kingdom."

With the fading light guiding them, they continued on their journey, leaving behind a village that had a little more hope than it had that morning, and a queen more determined than ever to restore her realm.

As the sun dipped below the horizon, casting a golden sheen over the land, Serena and Whisper continued their journey, the shadows of the elder trees stretching long and thin across their path. The air grew cooler, the scent of damp earth rising to meet the evening breeze, a reminder of the day's transformations and the power of concerted effort and will.

Their next destination was the hamlet of Clearwater, a small community known for its weavers and dyers, skilled artisans who once colored the fabrics of the kingdom with vibrant hues drawn from nature itself. As they approached, the sight of abandoned looms and vats, long since dry and cracked, spoke of a craft nearly forgotten and a way of life greatly diminished.

Serena paused at the edge of the village, her heart heavy with the weight of seeing yet another facet of her kingdom in decline. Whisper hovered beside her, its glow soft under the twilight sky. "Each place we visit, we see the need for revival, for a return not just to former glory but to a sense of purpose and community," it said softly.

"Yes, we bring back more than just material wealth or safety; we revive the spirit of these places," Serena responded, stepping forward into the heart of Clearwater. She walked through the quiet streets, her presence a silent promise of attention and care.

The few villagers who remained watched her approach with cautious optimism. An elderly woman, her hands stained with the faint remnants of dyes, approached Serena, her steps slow but steady. "We have heard whispers of a queen who walks the mist, who brings hope," she said, her voice trembling not just with age but with emotion.

Serena knelt beside her, taking her hands gently in her own. "I am Serena, and I am here not just to bring hope but to make it real. Tell me, how can we help you bring life back to Clearwater?"

"It's the water," the old woman explained. "The springs that fed our vats have run dry. Without water, there is no dye, no cloth. Our art is dying with the springs."

Serena felt a surge of resolve. "Then we will find a way to bring back the water. Just as we calmed the river in Stonegate, so too can we seek the springs here."

With Whisper's guidance, Serena performed a ritual, calling upon the ancient magics bound to her crown. She spoke words that echoed with the force of her will, her voice blending with the whispering winds. Slowly, moisture began to gather in the air, condensing into droplets that seeped into the ground, seeking the hidden veins of water beneath.

The ground beneath their feet grew damp, and then wet, until finally, a small trickle of water began to flow once more through the village. It was a modest beginning, but it was a start, a sign of potential and of hope.

The old woman wept openly, her tears mingling with the newfound wetness of the earth. "Bless you, my queen," she said, her voice thick with gratitude. "You have given us more than water; you have given us back our lives."

Serena helped her to stand, feeling the weight of her crown not as a burden, but as a beacon—a source of light and life. "This is but the start," she promised, her gaze sweeping over the village. "I will send experts from the palace. We will learn about water management, and we will ensure that Clearwater lives up to its name once again."

As night settled fully around them, Serena and Whisper left the village, the sounds of renewed activity beginning to stir behind them. Small steps, perhaps, in the face of so much need, but each step was a victory, each act of magic a stitch in the tapestry of a restored kingdom.

With the stars beginning to sparkle in the clear night sky, they moved on, their hearts lighter, buoyed by the day's successes and the promise of tomorrow. The journey was far from over, but with each village visited, each problem addressed, Serena grew into her role, her resolve hardening like the jewels in her crown—unbreakable and bright.

Chapter 4
The Ruins of Remembrance

Under a sky brushed with the soft colors of dawn, Serena and Whisper made their way to Myrtlewood, a village once famed for its storytellers and bards, whose tales were said to weave history and magic into tapestries as vivid as any painted scene. As they approached, the silhouettes of derelict buildings and the overgrown paths spoke of a splendor that was now muted, the stories faded into whispers.

As they entered the village square, a lone figure awaited them, an old man whose eyes sparkled with a hint of the knowledge of yore. He was perched on a crumbling stone wall, a thick book resting in his lap.

"Greetings, Your Majesty," he called out, his voice resonant, echoing slightly off the stone around them. "I am Eldric, the lorekeeper of Myrtlewood. I've been awaiting your return, foretold in prophecies woven by the bards of old."

Serena approached him, intrigued. "Lorekeeper Eldric, I am here to listen and to learn. What prophecies speak of my return?"

Eldric closed his book gently and stood, his movements belying his age. "The prophecies spoke of the Veiled Queen who would emerge from the mist to reclaim the forgotten throne. They said she would bring back the light of old, the stories, and the glory of Eirene."

"And how do we bring back these stories, the culture that once thrived here?" Serena asked, her gaze sweeping over the quiet desolation of the village.

"By restoring the Great Hall of Myrtlewood, where the storytellers gathered. It lies in ruin now, but it was once the heart of our village," Eldric explained, motioning towards a large building whose roof had partly caved in. "Restore the hall, and the people will gather once more. The stories will return, and with them, the soul of our village."

Serena nodded, understanding the importance of such a place. "Then we will begin here, restoring the Great Hall. Whisper, do we have the means?"

"Yes, Serena. With your magic and the will of the people, you can raise the hall from its ruins," Whisper responded, its form shimmering with potential energy.

Serena turned to Eldric. "Will you help us, Lorekeeper? Will you guide us in this task?"

"I will, Your Majesty. And I will begin by recounting the tales that must not be lost, to inspire those who will help in the rebuilding," Eldric agreed, his voice steady and inspiring.

Together, they approached the Great Hall, and as Eldric began to speak, reciting lines of ancient verse that spoke of heroes and heroines, of magic and everyday miracles, Serena felt the power of the words in the air around them.

"Now, let us weave magic with these words," Serena declared, lifting her hands as she began an incantation taught to her by Whisper. The magic flowed from her, guided by her voice, her will, and the stories that filled the air, seeping into the stones of the Great Hall.

Slowly, the rubble began to shift. Stones rolled back into position with the sound of grinding earth, and timbers lifted, reassembling into the skeleton of a roof. The magic wove itself into the very fabric of the building, fortified by the power of the tales being told.

As the sun climbed higher in the sky, the villagers of Myrtlewood, drawn by the sound of Eldric's voice and the sight of their queen wielding ancient magics, came to watch. They saw the ruins rise and reform, saw their history being rebuilt before their eyes, and one by one, they stepped forward to help.

"Your stories are your strength," Serena told them as they worked alongside her, lifting beams and fitting stones. "They bind you to this land and to each other. They are as vital as the waters of the river or the soil of the earth."

By the time the evening shadows began to creep across the village square, the Great Hall stood once more at the heart of Myrtlewood. It was not just reconstructed; it was revitalized, imbued with the magic of the crown and the spirit of the village's own history.

"This is only the beginning," Serena proclaimed as they stood before the restored hall, the villagers gathered around, their faces alight with newfound hope. "Together, we will write the next chapter of Eirene's story."

And as the villagers cheered, Serena felt the weight of her crown not as a burden, but as a profound honor. The path forward was clear, paved with the stories of the past and the endless possibilities of the future.

Inside the newly restored Great Hall of Myrtlewood, the air buzzed with the excitement of the villagers as they prepared for the first storytelling evening since Serena's return. Tapestries depicting the legends of Eirene were rehung, and torches lit, casting a warm glow over the faces of those gathered. Serena, dressed in simple yet regal attire, sat beside Lorekeeper Eldric, her presence a beacon of hope and revival.

Eldric, his eyes twinkling in the firelight, cleared his throat and addressed the assembled crowd. "Tonight, we begin anew. With our queen here, let us weave the tales of old with the threads of the future we hope to build."

Serena leaned forward, her interest piqued. "Lorekeeper, would you share with us one of the tales? Perhaps one that speaks of resilience, something that mirrors our current journey?"

"Of course, Your Majesty," Eldric replied, his voice strong and clear. "Let me tell you the story of Aelwyn the Wise, a ruler of Eirene who faced great adversity but led our kingdom to a golden age of peace and prosperity."

The villagers leaned in, their expressions a mix of curiosity and nostalgia.

Eldric's voice rose and fell with the rhythm of his tale. "Aelwyn came to power in an age of turmoil. The kingdom was fractured, its people divided. But Aelwyn knew that the strength of Eirene lay not in its fortresses, but in the hearts of its people."

Serena nodded, absorbing every word. "And what did Aelwyn do to unite the people?"

"He traveled to every corner of the kingdom, just as you are doing, Your Majesty. He listened to the troubles of the people, shared in their joys and their sorrows. He helped them see that their differences were nothing compared to what they could achieve together."

A young girl in the audience, her eyes wide with wonder, piped up, "Did Aelwyn use magic, like Queen Serena?"

Eldric smiled at her. "Aelwyn had many skills, little one, but his greatest magic was his wisdom and his compassion. However, he did wield a staff, carved from the Elder Tree, which was said to calm storms and bring rain to parched lands."

Serena's gaze swept over her people, feeling a kinship with this character from their past. "It seems Aelwyn and I have much in common. But tell me, how did the people respond to his efforts?"

"They rallied behind him, for they saw in him a leader who truly cared for their welfare. Under Aelwyn's rule, Eirene flourished like never before. Fields bore harvests richer than any in living memory, and the arts—much like our storytelling tonight—prospered," Eldric explained, gesturing around the hall.

An old man, his voice seasoned with age, asked, "But what of the challenges, Lorekeeper? No rule is without its trials."

"True enough," Eldric conceded. "Aelwyn faced dissent, even betrayal. But he met each challenge with a steady hand and a clear heart. He believed in justice tempered with mercy, and in leading by example. In doing so, he not only preserved the kingdom but enhanced it."

Serena reflected on this. "His story is indeed inspirational. It teaches us that the path of a ruler is fraught with difficulties, but also filled with the potential for great deeds."

"Yes, Your Majesty," Eldric agreed. "And like Aelwyn, you have begun your reign by touching the hearts of your people, by reviving what was lost, and leading with empathy and courage."

The crowd murmured their agreement, their faces alight with a renewed sense of unity and purpose.

As the tales spun on, weaving the past with the present, Serena felt a profound connection to the lineage of rulers whose blood flowed in her veins. She understood now that her journey was about more than restoration—it was about rekindling a collective spirit, a shared identity.

The evening waned, and as the last story was told, the villagers of Myrtlewood left the Great Hall with spirits lifted and hearts full. Serena remained seated, pondering the tales and the tasks that lay ahead.

With each story shared, the fabric of the community was stitched tighter, and as Serena rose to leave, she knew that her story, one day, would be woven into the rich tapestry of Eirene's history, told and retold in the very hall that echoed now with the laughter and whispers of a people coming back to life.

The morning after the storytelling, Serena convened a council in the Great Hall. The villagers of Myrtlewood, representing a broad swath of the community from farmers to weavers, gathered around a large, rough-hewn oak table. The hall, still echoing with the remnants of last night's revived spirit, served as a fitting backdrop for discussions of the future.

Serena, seated at the head of the table, began, "Thank you for joining me today. Last night, we rekindled the flames of our heritage. Today, I ask for your counsel on how we can continue to rebuild not only Myrtlewood but all of Eirene."

An elder, his beard as gray as the morning mist, nodded in approval. "Your Majesty, it's heartening to see you embrace our traditions. For rebuilding, we need to ensure that our crafts—especially our weaving—can find markets. Our products are fine, but without trade, our skills are wasted."

Serena responded thoughtfully, "A valid point. We must establish trade routes. But first, we need to ensure our roads are safe and passable. Banditry has been a problem, not to mention the disrepair due to neglect."

A middle-aged woman, her hands stained with dye, interjected, "Safety is a concern, yes. But there's also the matter of attracting traders. If we restore the annual Festival of Tapestries, it could draw merchants from across the land."

Whisper, materializing beside Serena, added, "The festival could serve as a showcase of not only Myrtlewood's talents but also a symbol of Eirene's resurgence. It's an excellent opportunity to foster community spirit and economic revival."

Serena smiled, "Indeed, Whisper. We will reinstitute the Festival of Tapestries. Let's plan for it to coincide with the completion of road repairs. This will give us time to prepare and also ensure that travelers can reach us safely."

A young man, a carpenter by trade, spoke up, "What of the roads, then? Many bridges are in disrepair, and the paths are overgrown. We will need support in materials and manpower."

"I will allocate funds from the royal treasury to support this," Serena declared. "Furthermore, I will send a contingent of engineers from the palace to assist in the planning and rebuilding efforts. Myrtlewood will serve as a model for what we can achieve across the kingdom."

A weaver raised her hand, her voice eager, "And education, Your Majesty? Our children need to learn the crafts, yes, but also reading, writing, history. Our traditions must be passed on, not just in stories but in schooling."

Serena nodded firmly, "Education is the foundation of a prosperous society. I will instruct the royal scribes to establish a curriculum that includes not only practical skills but also our rich history and arts. We will build a school here in Myrtlewood."

The room buzzed with approval and renewed energy. Plans were made, tasks assigned, and the community's hope, once dimmed by years of neglect, now brightened with each new decision.

As the council concluded, Serena stood, addressing the room, "Your engagement today assures me of our path forward. Together, we are weaving a new future for Myrtlewood and for Eirene. Let this council be just the beginning of our dialogue and our action."

The villagers, inspired and invigorated by the morning's decisions, dispersed to begin their tasks, each person carrying a piece of the collective dream they were building together.

Serena and Whisper remained behind, surveying the hall that had, in mere days, transformed from a relic of the past to a beacon of the future. The queen's heart was full as she contemplated the journey ahead, her resolve as steadfast as the ancient stones of Myrtlewood. The path would be long and filled with challenges, but with each step taken together, Eirene would rise, renewed and resilient.

The newly paved road leading out of Myrtlewood glistened under the afternoon sun, reflecting the collective effort of the villagers and the royal engineers who had worked side by side. As Serena walked along the path, inspecting the progress, she was accompanied by Arden, the chief engineer sent from the palace.

"Your Majesty, the roads connecting Myrtlewood to the neighboring villages have been reinforced," Arden reported, his eyes scanning the horizon. "We've also set up patrols to ensure the safety of those who travel these routes, particularly merchants and traders."

Serena nodded, her gaze following the winding road. "Excellent work, Arden. Safe and reliable roads are the arteries of a thriving kingdom. They bring trade, news, and unite us in more ways than one."

As they walked, they approached a bridge overlooking a serene river, recently restored. "This bridge was one of the first projects we completed," Arden explained. "It's vital for the upcoming Festival of Tapestries. We expect many visitors."

Serena leaned against the new railing, looking down at the flowing water. "It's more than just a bridge, Arden. It's a symbol. A connection between our past struggles and our future triumphs."

Arden smiled, appreciating the sentiment. "Indeed, Your Majesty. There's a similar bridge we plan to construct over the eastern pass. It's been neglected for years, but once restored, it will open up trade routes to the eastern provinces."

"I'm pleased to hear that," Serena said, turning to face him. "Let's ensure that project is prioritized. The eastern provinces have felt isolated for too long. Reconnecting them will bring much-needed stability and prosperity."

"Absolutely, Your Majesty. I'll adjust our schedules accordingly," Arden assured her, noting down the directive.

Their conversation was interrupted by the arrival of a messenger, breathless and dusty from his journey. "Your Majesty, news from the capital," he said, handing her a sealed letter.

Serena broke the seal, scanning the contents quickly. Her expression remained composed, but her eyes lit up with interest. "It seems that word of our efforts here in Myrtlewood has spread. There are delegations from the northern territories who wish to learn from our model of revitalization."

"That's encouraging," Arden remarked. "Your leadership is inspiring many, Your Majesty."

"We should prepare to host these delegations soon," Serena said, handing the letter back to the messenger. "Inform them that they are welcome to visit at the conclusion of the Festival of Tapestries. It will be a perfect opportunity to showcase the progress we've made."

"Yes, Your Majesty," the messenger replied, bowing before departing swiftly.

Serena turned back to Arden. "Let's continue this momentum, Arden. The festival is just the beginning. Each successful project adds another layer to our foundation."

"Understood, Your Majesty. I'll coordinate with the local leaders to ensure everything is in place for the festival and the arrival of our guests," Arden said, his tone full of resolve.

As they continued down the road, the shadows of the afternoon stretched long across the land. The air was filled with the sounds of construction and conversation, a melody of progress and promise.

Serena felt a deep satisfaction in the work being accomplished, in the visible changes that were taking root. Myrtlewood, once a forgotten village, was now a beacon of hope and a testament to what could be achieved when a kingdom worked together toward a common goal.

The road back to the palace lay open and inviting, but for Serena, the journey through her kingdom was far from over. With each village revitalized, each road rebuilt, she was not only reconstructing Eirene but also redefining what it meant to be its queen. And as the sun dipped below the horizon, casting a golden light over the land, the path ahead promised even greater challenges, matched only by the potential for unprecedented renewal.

Chapter 5
The Enchanted Forest

The Festival of Tapestries was a riot of color and sound, celebrating the revival of Myrtlewood and the skills of its artisans. The village streets, once quiet and somber, now thrummed with the energy of bustling crowds, music, and the laughter of children. Stalls lined the market square, displaying vibrant tapestries and textiles, each a testament to the craftsmanship and renewed spirit of the people.

Serena, wearing a simple gown that echoed the colors of the earth and sky, walked among her people, her presence reinforcing the bridge between royalty and commoner. Her eyes gleamed with pride as she observed the fruits of their collective labor, the tangible results of the revitalization efforts that had transformed not only the landscape but the hearts of the populace.

As she approached a stall showcasing particularly intricate weavings, the artisan, a middle-aged woman with deft fingers and a keen eye, greeted her warmly. "Your Majesty, it's an honor. These designs are inspired by the stories you helped preserve, the legends of Eirene that once again echo through our village."

Serena admired the tapestries, her touch gentle on the threads. "They are beautiful, truly. It is I who am honored to see such artistry. It's a reminder of what we can accomplish when we draw on our heritage and work together."

Further along the street, children darted between legs, their laughter mingling with the melodies of flutes and drums. Performers, dressed as characters from Eirene's lore, reenacted scenes from ancient myths, their dramatic flourishes captivating the audience.

Serena paused to watch a play depicting the tale of Sirion, the Winged Guardian, who protected the ancient forests of the kingdom. The performers, young and old, delivered their lines with a passion that spoke of deep connection to their roles, their history.

As the play concluded, Serena clapped along with the crowd, her applause sincere and enthusiastic. Turning to Whisper, who floated discreetly by her side, she remarked softly, "Seeing them embrace their past like this, it gives me hope that Eirene's future is bright."

Whisper's glow shimmered in agreement. "It is not just the past they embrace, but the possibilities of the future. You have ignited a spark, Serena, that grows stronger with each passing day."

The festival continued into the evening, the setting sun casting long shadows over the village square. Lanterns were lit, and the festivities took on an even more magical quality. Serena found herself drawn to a quieter corner of the square, where an elderly man sat carving small figurines from wood.

"Your Majesty," he said, looking up with a smile that crinkled the corners of his eyes. "Would you care for a figure? I carve them in the likeness of Eirene's protectors."

Serena selected a figurine, turning it over in her hands. "It's lovely. Your skill is remarkable."

"It's my way of giving back," the man replied. "Each figure is a protector for the home. It's a small thing, but it's part of keeping our culture alive."

As night fell and the stars began to twinkle above, Serena felt a profound connection to everything around her: the people, their crafts, and the land itself. The Festival of Tapestries was not only a celebration of art but a symbol of unity and strength.

The air was cool and crisp as she made her way back through the village, the sounds of the festival fading behind her. Each step was a reminder of the journey still ahead, of the work to be done and the promises to be kept. But tonight, under the starlit sky of Eirene, Serena knew that each step was also a step toward a reawakened kingdom, vibrant and alive with the hopes and dreams of its people.

As the festival continued to flourish, the arrival of delegations from neighboring territories added a new layer of complexity and opportunity. Under a canopy of vibrant tapestries in the village square, Serena met with leaders from the northern territories, their discussions aimed at forging stronger ties and encouraging mutual support.

"Welcome to Myrtlewood," Serena began, her tone warm yet commanding. "It's an honor to host such esteemed guests at our Festival of Tapestries. This festival symbolizes the rebirth of our culture and the strength of our community."

Lord Teryn, a robust man with a keen strategic mind, nodded in appreciation. "Your Majesty, we've heard of your efforts to restore Eirene. Seeing it firsthand is truly inspiring. We're interested in learning how we might apply similar strategies in our own lands."

Serena smiled, pleased by his interest. "I believe that our successes can be replicated. It starts with revitalizing our cultural heritage and ensuring the prosperity of our people. How are your own territories faring?"

Lady Arila, representing the eastern provinces, leaned forward. "We face challenges, Your Majesty. Our lands have been isolated, the roads unsafe. Trade has suffered, and with it, our economic stability."

Serena listened intently, her mind already weaving together potential solutions. "Safety and accessibility are foundational. We've been focusing on rebuilding our infrastructure and enhancing security. Perhaps we could extend these efforts into your territories, starting with joint patrols and engineering projects."

Lord Teryn seemed intrigued. "A collaborative approach could benefit us all. And what of trade? We have goods to offer, but reaching markets has been our greatest hurdle."

"Let's consider a trade pact," Serena proposed. "By guaranteeing safe passage and mutual benefits, we could open new routes and increase commerce. We could start with a trial market day here in Myrtlewood, inviting traders from all our lands to participate."

Lady Arila nodded thoughtfully. "That sounds promising. It would give our artisans and merchants a chance to showcase their goods and test the waters."

"And it would strengthen our bonds," Serena added, her gaze sweeping over her guests. "Our unity can be our greatest strength. Together, we can ensure that our regions not only survive but thrive."

Lord Teryn raised his cup in agreement. "To unity and prosperity. Your vision, Queen Serena, gives us hope for a brighter future."

The conversation shifted towards logistics and specifics, with each leader expressing their concerns and hopes. Plans were drawn for road constructions, shared defense strategies, and cultural exchanges.

As the meeting drew to a close, Serena stood, addressing the group. "This is the beginning of a new chapter for all of us. Let's continue this dialogue, keep the lines of communication open, and work together towards common goals."

The leaders agreed, their expressions a mix of determination and optimism. They expressed their gratitude for the hospitality and the insights gained from the festival and the discussions.

As the delegates departed, Serena felt a sense of accomplishment. The festival had not only celebrated Eirene's cultural revival but had also laid the groundwork for lasting regional cooperation. The challenges ahead were numerous, but the foundations laid today promised a network of support and shared endeavor.

Serena walked back to the palace, the echoes of the day's discussions mingling with the festive music still filling the air. Each step was a reminder of the progress made and the potential that lay ahead, weaving a future of renewed hope and collective strength.

As the Festival of Tapestries drew to a close, the village of Myrtlewood began to quiet down, the vibrant bustle of the last few days giving way to a more contemplative atmosphere. Serena, feeling the weight of her recent commitments and the discussions with the northern leaders, took a moment to stroll through the now-emptying market square, reflecting on the potential impacts of the new alliances.

The stalls were being dismantled, and the tapestries carefully rolled and packed away, each movement by the villagers meticulous and filled with a sense of pride and accomplishment. Serena watched them, her heart swelling with pride at their resilience and creativity, which had turned a simple festival into a beacon of cultural and economic revival.

"Your Majesty," called a familiar voice. It was Eldric, the lorekeeper, approaching with a gentle smile. "The festival has been a resounding success. It's been many years since we've seen such life in Myrtlewood."

Serena returned his smile. "It has, Eldric. And it's more than just a celebration. It's a promise for the future—a future we are ready to build upon."

Eldric nodded, his eyes twinkling with wisdom. "Indeed, Your Majesty. And as we look forward, let us also remember the lessons of the past. The stories we've shared here are not just entertainment but guides."

"True," Serena agreed, pausing to watch a young girl carefully fold a tapestry depicting the legendary Eirene phoenix—a symbol of rebirth. "These legends remind us of who we were and who we aspire to be. They are a vital part of our identity."

The queen and the lorekeeper walked together toward the edge of the square, where the landscape opened up to reveal the lush greenery that surrounded Myrtlewood. The area, once overgrown and neglected, now thrived with new growth, a testament to the rejuvenation not only of the land but of the people themselves.

"As we forge new alliances and rebuild our roads and schools, we must keep our culture alive, as vibrant and enduring as these woods," Serena said, her gaze sweeping over the horizon. "Our recovery is not just about economics or safety but about restoring the soul of Eirene."

Eldric agreed, "The soul of the land is reflected in its people, Your Majesty. And you have rekindled hope in their hearts. That is the truest power of a ruler."

The conversation lulled as they reached the outskirts of the festival grounds. The air was cooler here, the sounds of the village faint behind them. In this quiet space, Serena felt the enormity of her task yet found comfort in the tangible signs of progress.

"This festival will be an annual event, Eldric," Serena decided, more to herself than to her companion. "A reminder of our resilience and a celebration of our culture. It will continue to draw us together, to weave our stories into the fabric of this kingdom."

"A wise decision, Your Majesty," Eldric responded, his voice filled with respect. "With each year, it will grow, just as we will."

As they turned to head back to the village, the setting sun cast long shadows over Myrtlewood, painting the scene with hues of orange and gold. Serena felt a quiet confidence settle in her heart. The challenges ahead were many, but the path forward was clear, lit by the lessons of the past and the renewed spirit of her people.

Tonight, the village would rest, but tomorrow would come with its demands, ready to be met by a queen who was not just a ruler but a restorer—a weaver of the past and the future. And as the stars began to appear in the twilight sky, Serena knew that the journey she was on was about much more than rebuilding a kingdom; it was about redefining what it meant to be a nation.

In the cool serenity of the early morning, before the village of Myrtlewood awoke, Serena convened a final meeting with her closest advisors and the visiting dignitaries in the Great Hall. The heavy wooden doors were thrown open, allowing the fresh, crisp air to invigorate the gathering, a symbolic gesture to reflect the transparency and fresh approach Serena was championing.

"Thank you all for gathering at this early hour," Serena began, standing at the head of the long oak table that had been set up in the middle of the hall. "The Festival of Tapestries has not only been a celebration but also a catalyst for forging our path forward."

Lord Teryn, rubbing his hands together for warmth, nodded. "Your Majesty, the festival was a brilliant showcase of what Eirene can become again under your leadership. It's clear you are building something lasting here."

Lady Arila leaned in, her expression earnest. "Indeed, Queen Serena. The discussions we've had these past days have been most fruitful. I am particularly interested in how we can continue to support each other through trade and knowledge exchange."

Serena smiled, pleased by their engagement. "I propose we establish a quarterly council where leaders from our regions can come together to discuss progress, challenges, and strategies. Eirene's revival should be a shared endeavor, benefiting from our collective insights."

"That's a commendable idea," responded Lord Teryn. "Regular communication will ensure that no one feels isolated and that our strategies are aligned and effective."

"I agree," said Lady Arila. "And perhaps these councils could rotate among our territories. It would give each of us a chance to host and show firsthand the improvements and innovations being implemented."

"An excellent suggestion," Serena acknowledged. "It will strengthen our bonds and foster a sense of unity and shared purpose."

The conversation shifted as they discussed logistics, potential dates, and the framework of these councils. Each leader expressed specific interests—trade, security, education, and cultural exchange—which were noted and integrated into the planning.

"As for the immediate future," Serena continued, "I believe we should focus on establishing secure, reliable trade routes. This is foundational to ensuring the prosperity we all strive for."

Lord Teryn, looking thoughtful, added, "Security is paramount. Perhaps we could also consider a joint task force to patrol these routes? It would serve as a deterrent to any who might wish to disrupt our progress."

"A joint task force is indeed wise," Serena agreed. "It symbolizes our mutual commitment to safeguarding our future."

Lady Arila, who had been making notes, looked up. "What about cultural exchanges? Festivals like the one we've just enjoyed are perfect for promoting understanding and unity. Maybe we could have a traveling cultural caravan that visits each of our territories throughout the year?"

Serena was quick to see the value in the proposal. "A traveling caravan would be a beautiful way to celebrate our diverse cultures and histories. It would also be a vibrant, living reminder of our interdependence and shared goals."

As dawn broke, casting a golden light into the hall, the meeting concluded with a sense of accomplishment and anticipation. Handshakes were exchanged, and commitments reaffirmed, each leader departing with a clear sense of direction and purpose.

Serena remained behind, gazing out of the open doors at the waking village. The discussions had sown seeds of cooperation that would, in time, blossom into prosperity and peace for Eirene and its allies.

Whisper, materializing beside her, reflected, "Today, you have laid the groundwork for a future not just rebuilt, but reimagined."

"Yes," Serena agreed, her eyes alight with resolve. "And together, we will see it flourish."

As the village of Myrtlewood stirred to life, its people unknowing but beneficiaries of the decisions made that morning, Serena felt a deep connection to the rhythm of their daily lives. It was here, in the intertwining of high strategy and everyday existence, that the future of Eirene was being woven, thread by vibrant thread.

Chapter 6
The Elders of the Mist

As the new day dawned over Eirene, the air crisp and the sky a clear blue, Serena prepared for her journey to the eastern provinces, a region that had long felt the sting of isolation. Her mission was to reinforce the newly forged alliances and ensure the implementation of the plans laid out during the recent council.

Accompanied by a small entourage and Whisper, Serena rode towards the first of the eastern villages, known for its struggling crafts and markets. Upon arrival, she was greeted by Mayor Alton, a man of middle age with a serious demeanor and a keen intellect.

"Your Majesty, it is an honor to welcome you to our village," Mayor Alton said, bowing slightly. "We are grateful for your efforts to reconnect us with the heart of Eirene."

Serena dismounted, offering him a warm smile. "Thank you, Mayor Alton. I am here to ensure that no part of our kingdom feels abandoned. Tell me, what are the immediate challenges your village is facing?"

Mayor Alton gestured towards the central market area, which was sparsely populated with vendors whose stalls displayed meager offerings. "As you can see, our market is barely surviving. The lack of secure trade routes has severely limited our ability to sell our goods and receive necessary supplies."

"Security for these routes is already being organized," Serena assured him as they walked through the market. "We will have patrols starting by the month's end, and I am here to see how else we can assist in revitalizing your economy."

"That is welcome news indeed," the mayor replied with a relieved sigh. "Another major concern is education. Our school has been without a qualified teacher for over a year now. Our children's education is suffering."

"Then we will address this immediately," Serena responded decisively. "I will send two of our finest teachers from the capital by week's end. Education is the cornerstone of a thriving community."

The mayor nodded appreciatively. "We are deeply thankful, Your Majesty. With education and trade restored, I believe we will see a significant turnaround in our fortunes."

As they continued their tour, a local craftsman approached Serena. "Your Majesty, if I may," he began, holding out a beautifully crafted leather satchel. "This is what we are capable of producing. If we had a more consistent supply of materials and better access to markets, we could contribute greatly to the economy."

Serena examined the satchel, impressed with the craftsmanship. "This is excellent work. With the roads secured, we will make sure you have access to both markets and materials. Additionally, I plan to host a kingdom-wide crafts fair in the capital. You will have a booth to showcase your work."

The craftsman's face lit up with hope. "Thank you, Your Majesty. That would mean the world to us."

Their conversation was a catalyst for more villagers to come forward, each discussing their trade and their needs. Serena listened attentively, committing to specific actions for each issue raised.

As the sun reached its zenith, Serena stood before the gathered villagers in the market square. "Today marks the beginning of a renewed commitment to the eastern provinces. Together, we will rebuild and restore. Let us bridge the divide that has grown over the years. Let us weave a future where no one in Eirene feels forgotten."

The villagers responded with enthusiastic applause, their spirits lifted by the queen's promises and presence.

As Serena prepared to leave for the next village, Mayor Alton approached her once more. "Your Majesty, your visit has rekindled hope here. We are ready to work hard and help implement every plan you have laid out."

Serena nodded, her heart full. "Together, we will see it done, Mayor Alton. Thank you for your hospitality and your candor."

Mounting her horse, Serena left the village with a renewed sense of purpose, the echoes of her promises mingling with the tangible plans set into motion. Her journey through the eastern provinces was just beginning, but the path forward was clear, each step underpinned by the commitment to unify and strengthen every corner of her kingdom.

The journey through the eastern provinces continued as Serena, accompanied by Whisper and her small entourage, traversed the rugged landscapes that had once thrived under the reign of ancient Eirenean kings. Now, these lands bore the scars of neglect, but beneath the surface, Serena could feel the potential stirring, ready to bloom with the right care.

Upon reaching the village of Easthaven, a place known historically for its lush orchards but now suffering from years of poor harvests, Serena was met by a gathering of farmers near the community's well, the center of village life. Their faces were lined with the hardships of their toil, yet their eyes sparkled with cautious optimism at her arrival.

"Good day," Serena greeted them warmly, dismounting with ease and approaching the group. "I've come to see how we might help rejuvenate these once-famous orchards."

An elder farmer, his hands gnarled like the branches of the fruit trees he tended, stepped forward. "Your Majesty, we're grateful for your attention. Our trees have suffered without proper irrigation and care. The water sources are not what they used to be, and without water, there's little hope for revival."

Serena nodded, her expression solemn. "Water is life, especially for your orchards. I will ensure that engineers from the capital assess and repair your irrigation systems. We must bring water back to your lands."

"Thank you, Your Majesty," the farmer replied, a trace of relief in his voice. "With water, we can do much. The soil is still rich; it only needs moisture to give life again."

As they walked through the withering orchards, another issue was brought to Serena's attention by a younger farmer, a woman whose energy and determination shone through her concern. "It's not just the orchards, Your Majesty. Our young people are leaving, moving to cities in search of better opportunities. We're losing our next generation of farmers."

Serena stopped among the trees, considering her words carefully. "To make farming appealing to them, we need to innovate. We will introduce new farming techniques and offer training sessions here. We also need to create opportunities for growth and entrepreneurship in agriculture. What if Easthaven could become a hub for agricultural innovation?"

The idea sparked interest and a lively discussion among the farmers. Ideas were exchanged, from introducing crop rotation and organic farming to setting up a small cooperative that could market their produce effectively.

"Let's establish a pilot project here," Serena decided. "We'll bring in experts to train anyone willing to learn, not just in traditional farming, but in new, sustainable methods that could set Easthaven apart."

The farmers, invigorated by the support and vision for the future, agreed enthusiastically. They began to outline potential plans, their voices overlapping with excitement.

Before departing, Serena spoke to the assembled villagers. "Change is a seed; with time and care, it will grow. I promise you that the crown will provide the support needed, but the heart of this change lies with you, the people of Easthaven. Let's nurture this seed together."

With plans set in motion and commitments made, Serena felt a profound connection to these people and their land. As she rode away from Easthaven, the fading sun cast long shadows over the fields, hinting at the end of a challenging day but also at the promise of a new dawn.

Back on the road, Whisper, ever present, floated beside her. "You are planting more than just crops, Serena. You are planting the seeds of a renewed kingdom."

"Yes," Serena replied, her gaze fixed on the horizon. "And together, we will watch them grow."

Each village visit added layers to her understanding of the kingdom's needs and her strategy for addressing them. The journey was far from over, but with each step, Serena's resolve deepened, spurred on by the tangible changes already beginning to take root.

As Serena continued her journey through the eastern provinces, the landscape slowly shifted from the arid, neglected fields of the outer villages to the slightly more prosperous central regions where rivers nourished the land and the people had managed a meager subsistence despite years of isolation. Here, the impact of her efforts began to show subtle signs of taking root, a testament to the resilience of the people and the land they cultivated.

Arriving in the village of Riverton, known for its weaving mills that stood silent more often than not in recent years, Serena was greeted with a cautious optimism by the village elders. They led her through the village, pointing out the old mills along the river, their waterwheels still, waiting for a chance to turn once again.

Serena, walking along the cobblestone paths that wound through Riverton, observed the shuttered windows and overgrown pathways, symbols of the stagnation that had taken hold. Yet, there was a stir in the air, a sense of anticipation as the villagers whispered about the queen's visit and what it might herald for their future.

At the heart of the village, by the main square that hosted a now-dormant market, Serena paused to address the small crowd that had gathered. "The strength of Eirene lies in each of its parts, in every village and every heart," she proclaimed softly yet firmly. "Here in Riverton, your mills can run once more, weaving not just fabrics but the very tapestry of our kingdom's resurgence."

The response was a murmur of agreement, the spark of hope fanning slowly into a flame as discussions began among the people about reopening the mills, about the crops that could support the weavers, about the children who could learn the trade.

Serena spent the remainder of the day meeting with the village leaders, discussing plans to repair the waterwheels and restore the mills. Agreements were struck for engineers from the capital to come and assess the necessary repairs, for teachers to educate the young on the art of weaving, and for traders to once again visit Riverton, ensuring that the products of their looms reached markets far and wide.

As evening fell, Serena stood by the river, watching the water flow past, a relentless force that shaped its path through the landscape. Whisper floated beside her, its presence a comforting reminder of the continuity between past and future.

"The river, like our people, follows a path laid down through the ages," Whisper observed, its voice blending with the rush of the water. "It carves its way, sometimes gently, sometimes with force, but always moving forward."

"Yes," Serena replied, her gaze reflective. "And like the river, our kingdom is finding its new course. With each village revitalized, with every heart rekindled, we carve a path toward a future forged from the best of what was and the brightest of what can be."

That night, as Serena left Riverton, the glow from the village windows cast warm patches of light onto the cobblestone paths. The air was cooler now, the sky a tapestry of twilight hues, and as she rode away, the sounds of the village—of laughter, of machinery beginning to churn, of life resuming—followed her.

The journey through the eastern provinces was nearing its end, but the work was just beginning. Serena knew that the challenges ahead were many, but with each step, the fabric of the kingdom grew stronger, woven from threads of perseverance, unity, and a shared vision of a prosperous future. Each village, each heart won over, added to the strength of that fabric, making it unbreakable, resilient, and everlasting.

The final leg of Serena's tour through the eastern provinces brought her to Glenfall, a village nestled in the foothills of the Misty Peaks and known for its herbalists and healers. The village, shrouded in the early morning fog, appeared as if it were a part of the very mist it lay beneath. As she entered the village square, Serena was met by Elder Mirene, the village's respected healer.

"Welcome, Your Majesty," Elder Mirene greeted her, her voice as calming as the herbal concoctions she was famous for. "Glenfall is honored by your visit. We have long awaited a leader who would see the value in our ancient practices."

"Thank you, Elder Mirene," Serena responded, dismounting with grace. "I am here to learn from you and to see how the crown can support your valuable work."

Elder Mirene led Serena through the village, passing small cottages where other healers displayed their herbs and remedies. "As you can see, our knowledge is vast, but our reach has been limited. We struggle to acquire certain herbs that are vital for our medicines, and our methods remain isolated from the wider medical community of Eirene."

"Let us address that isolation," Serena suggested. "I propose establishing a network that not only supplies you with necessary materials but also integrates your knowledge with the medical institutions of the capital. Your wisdom is a resource that should be shared across Eirene."

"That would be a blessing, Your Majesty," Elder Mirene replied, her eyes reflecting a mix of relief and hope. "Many here can benefit from such integration, especially our young apprentices."

As they continued their walk, a young apprentice approached, a bundle of dried herbs in his hands. "Your Majesty, if I may," he said, offering the bundle to her. "These are some of our most effective remedies. With proper support, we could develop these further and aid many across your kingdom."

Serena accepted the bundle, inhaling the deep, earthy scent. "Your work is essential, and it shall not go unnoticed. I will send experts from the Royal College of Medicine to collaborate with you. Together, we can enhance the efficacy of your remedies and ensure they are available to all who need them."

The apprentice bowed deeply, gratitude evident in his demeanor. "Thank you, Your Majesty. This is a dream we scarcely dared to hope for."

Her conversation with the villagers continued as they discussed specifics: supply routes for herbs, training seminars for both traditional and modern medical practitioners, and the establishment of an annual conference in Glenfall where knowledge could be exchanged freely.

"Your Majesty," Elder Mirene said as they concluded their walk, "your visit marks a new dawn for Glenfall. We are ready to emerge from the mist, to share our healing touch with the world."

"I am committed to making that a reality," Serena affirmed, her voice firm yet warm. "Glenfall's light will no longer be hidden."

As Serena prepared to leave, the villagers gathered, offering her small tokens of their craft—vials of essential oils, sachets of dried herbs, and small charms made from local stones. Each gift was a symbol of their trade and their thanks.

Mounting her horse, Serena looked back at the gathering crowd, their faces bright with newfound purpose. "Glenfall will not be forgotten," she called out. "Together, we heal, we grow, and we prosper."

Riding out of Glenfall, Serena felt the weight of her responsibilities and the joy of her achievements intertwine. Each village's revival added to the mosaic of her reign, each promise kept wove tighter the bonds of trust and loyalty that would define her legacy. The path ahead was long, and the work unending, but Serena rode on, fueled by the successes of her journey and the certainty that the eastern provinces—and with them, all of Eirene—were awakening to a new era of prosperity and unity.

Chapter 7
Morana's Shadows

As autumn's first leaves began to change, heralding the season's shift, Serena returned to the capital, her mind rich with the experiences and insights gathered from her travels through the eastern provinces. The capital, bustling and vibrant, welcomed her back with the familiar sights and sounds of a city poised on the brink of revitalization.

Upon her return, Serena convened a meeting with her chief advisors and the ministers responsible for the kingdom's infrastructure and economic development. The grand council room, with its high ceilings and long, polished oak table, served as the setting for these crucial discussions, the walls echoing with the gravity of their purpose.

"Welcome, everyone," Serena began, her tone both commanding and inclusive. "Our travels have shed light on the immediate needs of our provinces. It's imperative that we integrate these needs into our national strategy to ensure a balanced development across Eirene."

Minister Darion, an older man with a keen strategic mind, nodded in agreement. "Your Majesty, your insights from the provinces are invaluable. Could you share the key areas where you believe we should focus our immediate efforts?"

"Firstly, our agricultural sector requires significant investment," Serena responded, laying out the documents she had prepared. "We need to modernize our farming techniques and ensure that all communities have access to water and quality seeds. This is fundamental to food security and the stability of our kingdom."

"Indeed," replied Minister Lorne, who oversaw agricultural development. "I propose we set up a task force to implement modern irrigation systems and introduce crop rotation and sustainable farming practices as demonstrated in the pilot projects in Easthaven."

"Excellent," Serena approved, making a note. "Secondly, education must be a priority. We need a kingdom-wide curriculum that not only focuses on academic skills but also vocational training tailored to local industries."

Minister Tala, a younger woman with a passion for educational reform, chimed in, "I suggest establishing regional training centers, especially in isolated areas. These centers can double as community hubs, where people can gather to learn and share knowledge."

"I support that," Serena said. "It aligns perfectly with our vision for community-driven growth. Additionally, the revival of local industries and crafts must be linked to these educational initiatives."

The discussion then shifted to the topic of health and wellness, a concern that had emerged strongly during Serena's visit to Glenfall. "Healthcare is not just a matter of treatment but of prevention and well-being," Serena stated. "We should expand our network of local healers and integrate them more closely with our national health services."

Minister Halen, responsible for health services, responded, "An integration project could indeed harness the traditional knowledge of healers like those in Glenfall. It would be a step forward in creating a holistic healthcare system."

As the meeting progressed, the strategies became more defined, each minister tasked with developing actionable plans for their respective areas. The atmosphere was collaborative, the shared goal of a thriving Eirene driving the discourse.

"Finally," Serena concluded, "we must ensure that our policies are not just top-down but embrace feedback from the communities they are designed to help. Regular town hall meetings and community feedback sessions will be crucial."

The advisors and ministers nodded, the weight of their responsibilities clear but their determination evident. They were united in their mission, inspired by Serena's leadership and her hands-on approach during her travels.

As the meeting adjourned, Serena stayed back to look over the city from the balcony of the council room. The capital, alive with the activities of its citizens, reflected the dynamic changes underway. Serena felt a deep sense of commitment to these people and the land they shared.

With the plans set into motion, the groundwork for a renewed and unified Eirene was being laid, each policy and project a brick in the foundation of the future she envisioned. As she turned from the balcony to return to her duties, Serena carried with her a resolve to see these plans to fruition, to build an Eirene that would stand as a testament to the resilience and unity of its people.

In the weeks following her return to the capital, Serena watched as her initiatives began to take root. The palace grounds, once purely ornamental, were transformed under her direction into demonstration gardens for sustainable agriculture practices. Here, Serena often walked with Minister Lorne, discussing the progress and the propagation of these practices across the kingdom.

"This new section of root vegetables and legumes will be crucial for understanding crop rotation," Minister Lorne pointed out as they strolled past rows of budding plants. "Once proven here, we can replicate it in the provinces where soil depletion is a concern."

Serena nodded, brushing her hand against the green leaves. "Education is key. We need to ensure that our farmers understand the benefits not only for their yields but for the land itself. Perhaps we should consider seasonal workshops?"

"An excellent idea," Lorne agreed. "If we pair that with the local schools, we can integrate agricultural education early, instilling an appreciation for the land and its care from a young age."

Their walk took them past a group of students and teachers from the city's school, who were taking notes and asking questions. It was a living classroom, and the excitement was palpable.

"We are also seeing great interest from the urban population," Lorne added. "Urban gardening initiatives have sprouted, no pun intended, across the city. It's heartening to see the community so engaged."

As autumn deepened, bringing with it the rich hues of the season, Serena shifted her focus to the health of her people. Accompanied by Minister Halen, she visited several newly integrated health centers where traditional healers and medically trained doctors worked side by side.

During one visit, Halen remarked, "The integration has been smoother than anticipated. Both sides have shown a willingness to learn from each other, which has been key."

"I'm glad to hear that," Serena responded, watching a traditional healer prepare a herbal concoction. "How are the communities responding to the new services?"

"Very positively, Your Majesty," Halen replied. "There's been an increase in preventative care visits. People feel more comfortable seeking help when they see familiar faces and practices alongside new medical techniques."

The education sector was not left behind in Serena's sweeping reforms. With Minister Tala, Serena visited the new community hub, which doubled as a vocational training center in one of the eastern provinces. Here, locals of all ages engaged in learning trades that were both traditional and innovative, bridging the gap between old and new.

"The response has been overwhelming," Tala shared as they observed a class in session. "Not only are the youth engaged, but many adults are taking the opportunity to learn new skills that could lead to better employment."

Serena smiled as she watched a young woman expertly maneuver through a lesson on solar panel installation, a skill recently introduced to the curriculum. "Empowering our people not just to find jobs but to create them, to innovate within their communities—that's the future of Eirene."

"Yes, Your Majesty," Tala replied. "And with the added focus on literacy and numeracy, we're laying a foundation that will benefit generations to come."

Each visit, each report received, showed Serena the tangible outcomes of her policies. The kingdom was knitting together, much like the tapestries for which Myrtlewood was famous, each thread strengthening the whole.

Yet, as she returned to the palace one chilly evening, Serena knew that the work was far from complete. The initial successes were promising, but the true test would be in sustaining the momentum and ensuring that the roots of change grew deep and unshakeable. Her resolve was firm, and her vision clear—Eirene would rise, rejuvenated and resilient, a testament to the spirit of its people and the will of their queen.

In the heart of the capital, as autumn leaves painted the city in shades of gold and crimson, Serena presided over a large gathering in the newly established community center, which had become a hub of learning and innovation. The meeting was crucial, designed to foster communication between the citizens and their queen, to discuss the ongoing projects, and to solicit feedback directly from those most affected by the changes.

As Serena entered the hall, filled with citizens from various sectors— farmers, educators, healthcare workers, and small business owners—the room buzzed with anticipation and a few nerves. Serena addressed the crowd with a warm, confident smile.

"Thank you all for joining this discussion today," Serena began, standing before the assembly. "This is your time as much as mine. I am here to listen, to learn from your experiences, and to understand how we can continue to improve our great kingdom together."

A middle-aged woman, a teacher from the northern district, stood first. "Your Majesty, the new curriculum you've introduced has significantly impacted our students. They're more engaged than ever. However, we lack enough teaching resources. We need more books and materials to handle the increased interest."

Serena nodded, acknowledging the issue. "Thank you for raising this. We'll prioritize the distribution of additional resources to your district immediately. Education is the cornerstone of our future, and no student should go without necessary materials."

A young man, representing the agricultural sector, then spoke up. "Your Majesty, the irrigation projects have transformed our farming practices, but we're facing a new challenge with pest control. We need guidance on sustainable methods that align with our new practices."

"Absolutely," Serena responded. "I will arrange for a team of agricultural specialists to conduct workshops on integrated pest management. Sustainable farming is not only about irrigation but also about maintaining the health of the soil and crops without harmful chemicals."

The dialogue continued, with a healthcare worker highlighting the successes and challenges of integrating traditional and modern medicine. "The integration has brought many positive changes, Your Majesty, but some traditional practitioners feel overshadowed by medical doctors. We need to ensure that both are seen as equal contributors to our health system."

Serena considered this carefully. "Thank you for sharing this perspective. Perhaps we could organize joint conferences and workshops where knowledge is shared equally between traditional healers and medical doctors. It's essential that all health practitioners feel valued and respected."

As the meeting drew on, each comment and concern was met with Serena's earnest attention and immediate action plans. The atmosphere in the room shifted from tentative to collaborative, a sense of collective purpose taking root among the attendees.

An elderly man, a local craftsman, stood to speak, his voice steady despite his age. "Your Majesty, it's heartening to see you among your people, seeking our counsel. This center, these meetings, they've brought a new sense of community to the capital. We see ourselves in your vision for Eirene, and it gives us great hope."

Serena's response was heartfelt. "Thank you. These meetings are fundamental to our progress. They ensure that the path we walk, we walk together. Your insights, your challenges, and your successes guide our journey forward."

As the meeting concluded, the crowd dispersed with a feeling of accomplishment and inclusion. Conversations continued in smaller groups outside the hall, a community invigorated by involvement and recognition.

Serena lingered to speak with several individuals, offering personal assurances and noting down particular issues to be addressed. As she finally stepped out of the community center, the late afternoon sun casting long shadows over the bustling streets, her commitment to her people was stronger than ever. Each voice that had risen in that hall, every story shared, wove deeper into the fabric of Eirene's renewal, strengthening the bonds of community and leadership.

This tapestry of progress was not just made of policies and plans, but of people and their passion for a better Eirene. As Serena walked back to the palace, the echoes of the day's dialogue filled her with a resolve to keep this momentum, to continue building a kingdom as vibrant and enduring as the autumnal hues that framed the capital.

As winter approached, bringing a crisp chill to the air, Serena found herself within the stately confines of the palace library, surrounded by scrolls and books that spoke of Eirene's long history. Today, however, she was not alone in her scholarly retreat. She was joined by her council of advisors and two guest experts in urban planning and public welfare, convened to draft the final plans for the winter initiatives.

"Thank you all for coming," Serena began, her voice echoing softly among the high shelves. "Today, we finalize our strategies for the colder months, focusing on infrastructure and welfare that will not only see us through the winter but set the stage for the coming year."

Dr. Fenley, one of the guest experts, adjusted his glasses before speaking. "Your Majesty, considering the forthcoming winter, our first priority should be ensuring that every home has adequate heating. There have been reports of shortages in the northern provinces."

Serena nodded, acknowledging the concern. "Indeed, Dr. Fenley. We must address this immediately. Minister Darion, how are our stockpiles of wood and coal?"

Minister Darion, responsible for natural resources, replied promptly, "We're currently below desired levels, Your Majesty. However, we can redirect some of our emergency reserves and expedite logging and mining operations, with the proper environmental safeguards, of course."

"That will be necessary," Serena agreed. "Let's also explore alternative heating solutions. We've been too reliant on traditional methods. Perhaps it's time we considered more sustainable, long-term options."

Dr. Niles, the other expert specializing in sustainable development, chimed in, "There are several models of geothermal heating that could be viable for the colder regions. It's more of an investment initially but far more efficient and sustainable in the long run."

"I like that idea," Serena responded enthusiastically. "Let's pilot a project in one of the northern villages. If successful, it could be a model for the whole kingdom."

The conversation shifted towards public welfare. "With the cold, food scarcity becomes a pressing issue," Serena continued. "We need to ensure that our food distribution networks are robust and that no one goes hungry this winter."

Minister Tala, overseeing social services, added, "We're coordinating with local leaders to identify the most vulnerable communities. Our aim is to set up additional distribution centers and possibly initiate a mobile service for those in remote areas."

"That's good," Serena said. "But let's also make sure we're not just handing out food but supporting local farmers and producers. Buy from them first. This supports our economy and ensures freshness and nutritional value."

The meeting moved into deeper logistical discussions, each member contributing from their expertise, weaving a comprehensive plan that covered not only immediate needs but also sustainable practices that would benefit the kingdom in the long term.

As the meeting drew to a close, Serena summarized the session with firm directives. "We have a clear plan now. Let's move forward with urgency and precision. Winter will not wait, and neither will we."

Everyone in the room nodded in agreement, energized by the clarity and scope of the plan. They began to file out, each to their respective tasks, leaving Serena with a moment of quiet reflection in the now-silent library.

Looking out the window at the first signs of frost creeping across the palace gardens, Serena felt a resolve as sharp as the air outside. The plans laid today would not only protect her people through the winter but strengthen the foundations of her kingdom. With each decision, each action taken, the future of Eirene was being built—a future envisioned not just by a queen, but by her entire people, working together to weave a tapestry of resilience and renewal.

Chapter 8
Allies in the Shadows

As winter's embrace tightened around the kingdom of Eirene, the capital city buzzed with activity, its citizens bolstered by the initiatives set in motion by their queen. The cold was biting, yet the warmth of progress and shared purpose kept the chill at bay. Serena, wrapped in a cloak trimmed with fur, surveyed the ongoing construction of a new civic center, designed to be a beacon of community and government.

Accompanied by Minister Lorne, she walked through the bustling construction site where workers laid the foundation stones. The sound of hammers and chisels rang clear in the frosty air, a symphony of industry.

"This civic center," Serena remarked, observing a craftsman carefully position a block of stone, "will stand as a testament to what we can achieve when we unite in purpose. It's not just a building; it's a statement."

Minister Lorne nodded, his breath visible in the cold air. "Indeed, Your Majesty. It will house not only government offices but also community spaces where people can meet, learn, and celebrate together. It's about transparency and accessibility."

Serena smiled, pleased. "Exactly what I envisioned. How are the other projects coming along?"

"Quite well, Your Majesty," Lorne replied. "The new schools in the eastern provinces are nearly complete, and the geothermal heating pilot project has begun. There's a tangible sense of renewal throughout the kingdom."

They continued their inspection, Serena stopping occasionally to speak with the workers, thanking them for their hard work and dedication. Her interactions were genuine, bridging the gap between royalty and commoner, making her a beloved figure among her people.

"Seeing this," she said as they paused to look at the layout plans a foreman displayed, "reminds me of the importance of our journey. We're not just rebuilding; we're reimagining what our society can be."

"The people feel it, Your Majesty," Lorne assured her. "There's a newfound optimism in the air. Even with the cold, the energy is palpable."

As the tour concluded, Serena and Lorne warmed themselves with cups of hot tea in a nearby tent set up for the workers to take breaks. "We must ensure that the momentum we have is not lost," Serena mused, holding the steaming cup close. "The winter may slow some of our physical progress, but we must continue to plan and prepare for the spring."

"Agreed," said Lorne. "I'll oversee the ongoing projects personally and ensure that our plans for the spring are ready to be implemented as soon as the weather permits."

"Good," Serena responded. "Let's keep pushing forward. Every stone laid, every beam erected, brings us closer to the Eirene we dream of."

As they stepped back out into the cold, the clear winter sky stretched wide above them, the sun a bright jewel against the pale blue. Serena felt a surge of hope and determination. This was her legacy—not just the stones and mortar, but the spirit and unity they represented.

Walking back towards the palace, her path took her past the city's main square, where citizens bustled about, wrapped in their winter garb. Their faces, some flushed from the cold, others bright with laughter, reminded her why she embarked on this path. For them, for their future, she would build an Eirene that would endure through the ages, a realm rekindled with hope and striving toward prosperity.

The day faded into evening, and as the first stars appeared in the twilight sky, the lights from the construction site cast a warm glow against the snow. Serena knew there was much to be done, but as each day passed, her vision for a revitalized Eirene became ever more a reality.

With the civic center's foundation set, Serena shifted her focus to strengthening Eirene's economic sinews. Her next strategic move involved revitalizing the central marketplace, an ancient hub that once pulsed with the vibrant trade of goods and ideas but had dwindled into quiet disuse.

Accompanied by Minister Darion, responsible for commerce and trade, Serena walked through the marketplace, its stalls sparse and some completely abandoned. The cold wind whipped through empty spaces, stirring up leaves and debris.

"Look at this place, Darion," Serena said, gesturing broadly at the expanse of the marketplace. "It was once the heart of our economy, bustling with traders from across the realm. We need to bring it back to life, make it a center of commerce again."

"Absolutely, Your Majesty," Darion replied, following her gaze. "Revitalizing the marketplace is essential. We should consider incentives for merchants to return, perhaps a temporary waiver of stall fees and a campaign to draw in traders from outside the city."

Serena nodded thoughtfully. "That's a good start. What about the infrastructure? Many of these stalls and pavilions are in disrepair."

"We can allocate funds from the city's development budget to renovate this area," Darion suggested. "New pavilions, better security, and even some aesthetic enhancements to make it more inviting."

"I like that," Serena agreed. "And let's not just focus on commerce. The marketplace should be a place for the community, too. Perhaps we could integrate spaces for public performances and art displays."

Darion wrote down notes, his mind already turning over the logistics. "Integrating culture into commerce. I think it's a brilliant way to attract a diverse crowd. It could become a place where business and pleasure mix seamlessly."

"Exactly," Serena said, pleased. "I want it vibrant, day and night. A place where families come to shop, where artists gather to perform, where ideas and goods are exchanged freely."

As they continued their tour, they discussed potential challenges, such as logistics, security, and how to maintain the character of the old marketplace while introducing modern conveniences.

"How soon can we start the renovations?" Serena asked, looking at a rundown pavilion fondly remembered from her childhood.

"With your approval, we could start as early as next month," Darion answered. "I'll organize a team to begin the design and planning phase immediately."

"Proceed," Serena directed with a decisive nod. "And keep me updated. I want to be closely involved in this project."

"Understood, Your Majesty," Darion said, his respect for her dedication evident.

As they wrapped up their visit, a local fruit vendor approached Serena, offering her a sample of winter berries. "Your Majesty, it's an honor. We've heard about the plans, and we're all hopeful. This marketplace is more than just a place of trade; it's where community is forged."

Serena accepted the berries, tasting the tart sweetness. "Thank you. And yes, that's precisely why we're investing in its future. The marketplace isn't just about buying and selling—it's about building relationships and a community."

Leaving the marketplace with a renewed sense of purpose, Serena felt energized by the project's potential to not only revive the economy but also to rekindle the community spirit that had always been the true wealth of Eirene.

Back at the palace, as she shared the fruits with her advisors, her thoughts were already racing ahead to the next phases of the kingdom's renewal.

Each step forward was a step toward the Eirene she dreamed of—an Eirene reborn, thriving, and united.

As the winter months began to wane, giving way to the crisp beginnings of spring, the plans for the revitalized marketplace moved from concept to reality. Construction crews worked diligently under the emerging sun, laying down new cobblestones and erecting sturdy, inviting stalls. Meanwhile, Serena, ever mindful of the broader implications of these renovations, convened a meeting with local artisans, merchants, and cultural leaders in a temporary pavilion at the heart of the construction site.

"Thank you for joining me today," Serena began, her voice carrying over the sounds of ongoing construction. "This marketplace is not merely a center of commerce but a symbol of our collective recovery and future prosperity."

A seasoned potter, whose hands were as much a part of his tools as the clay he molded, nodded appreciatively. "Your Majesty, we are grateful for the investment. For many of us, this place is more than a market; it's a second home, a community."

Serena smiled at his words. "I hope to see it bustling with activity soon. What can we do to ensure that once the construction is complete, it doesn't just serve our current needs but attracts new vendors and customers?"

An experienced merchant, known for her vibrant textiles, chimed in. "Perhaps we could host a grand reopening festival. It could feature not only our traditional goods but also spotlight emerging artisans and culinary talents from across Eirene."

"That's a wonderful idea," Serena responded enthusiastically. "A festival could indeed showcase the diversity and richness of our kingdom. It would also draw visitors from outside the city, helping to reestablish our marketplace as a premier trading hub."

A young musician, whose innovative compositions had begun to gain popularity, added, "And if I might suggest, Your Majesty, incorporating music and performances could turn it into a cultural celebration as well, bridging commerce with the arts."

"I agree," said Serena. "Culture breathes life into commerce. Let's ensure that our plans for the festival include a strong cultural component."

As they discussed, an architect unrolled plans for the new marketplace layout, pointing to areas designated for performances and communal gatherings. "We've designed these spaces to be flexible, accommodating everything from concerts to public meetings."

"Flexibility will be key," Serena affirmed, examining the plans. "We must adapt to the needs of the community as they evolve."

The meeting continued with discussions on logistics, such as traffic flow, security, and amenities that would make the marketplace welcoming and accessible to all ages. Each participant contributed, their expertise and local knowledge shaping the final preparations.

As the meeting drew to a close, Serena addressed the group once more. "Your input has been invaluable. Together, we are not just rebuilding a marketplace; we are laying the foundation for a vibrant community hub that will serve generations to come."

The artisans and merchants left the meeting with a sense of ownership and excitement about the future. Serena remained behind for a moment, gazing at the workers who laid each stone with care and precision.

Whisper, ever present, hovered beside her. "The seeds you've planted here will grow, Serena. This marketplace will be a testament to Eirene's resilience and your vision."

Serena looked around at the half-completed stalls and imagined them filled with goods, the air ringing with the voices of traders and families. "This is just the beginning," she said, her voice tinged with determination and a hint of reflection. "Our work continues, and with each project, we weave tighter the fabric of our community."

With a final look at the bustling construction site, Serena returned to the palace, her mind already turning to the next challenges and opportunities that awaited her leadership. The path was long, but the progress was palpable, each step forward marking a new chapter in the story of Eirene.

The morning of the marketplace's grand reopening was bright and clear, a perfect backdrop for what was anticipated to be a landmark event in the history of Eirene's capital. Stalls were adorned with vibrant banners, and the air was filled with the enticing aromas of local delicacies and the sounds of musicians tuning their instruments. Serena, dressed in the traditional garb of Eirene, walked among the stalls with Minister Darion, her presence a reassuring sign of the crown's commitment to this revitalized heart of commerce and culture.

"Everything looks wonderful," Serena remarked, her eyes taking in the colorful displays of crafts and the lively expressions of the vendors. "This festival not only marks the reopening of the marketplace but also symbolizes our progress and unity."

"It truly does, Your Majesty," Darion agreed, adjusting his ceremonial sash. "The turnout is impressive. Merchants from every corner of the kingdom have come. It's a strong indicator of the economic revival we've hoped for."

As they continued their walk, a vendor approached, offering them samples of honeyed nuts, a regional delicacy. "Your Majesty, try these. They're from the southern orchards, rejuvenated under your initiatives."

Serena accepted graciously, savoring the sweet treat. "Delicious! Your efforts and those of your fellow orchard keepers are commendable. It's goods like these that will draw people from far and wide."

"Thank you, Your Majesty," the vendor replied, beaming. "We are hopeful and grateful."

Their path took them to a stage where a group of dancers was preparing for a performance. The choreographer, a renowned artist in Eirene, greeted Serena with a deep bow. "Your Majesty, we're about to start. These dances tell the story of Eirene's renewal. It would be an honor to have you watch."

"We would love to," Serena responded, taking her seat beside Minister Darion as the music began. The dancers moved with grace and precision, their motions telling a poignant story of struggle, resilience, and hope.

After the performance, Serena clapped heartily. "That was beautiful. Thank you for sharing such a moving piece of our history and our ongoing journey."

"Your support makes all the difference, Your Majesty," the choreographer replied, joining them briefly. "The arts flourish when they are nurtured, much like the people of this kingdom."

The festival continued with Serena meeting various artisans and entrepreneurs, each conversation reinforcing her understanding of the direct impact of her policies on the lives of her people. At one stall, a young inventor showcased a new type of water filtration device.

"This device could change the way villages access clean water," the inventor explained, demonstrating the simple yet effective mechanism.

"Remarkable," Serena remarked, examining the device. "Let's ensure your invention reaches all corners of Eirene. Innovations like yours are key to our sustainable development."

"Thank you, Your Majesty. With your support, I believe we can make a significant difference," the inventor said, his eyes bright with the prospect of contributing to the kingdom's welfare.

As afternoon turned into evening, the festival showed no signs of winding down. The energy was infectious, the community's spirit lifted by the joy and pride of what they had accomplished together.

Standing beside Minister Darion, watching children chase each other through the crowd, Serena felt a profound sense of accomplishment. "Today has been a testament to what we can achieve as a unified kingdom.

Let's continue to build on this foundation, fostering growth and innovation at every turn."

"Indeed, Your Majesty," Darion replied. "Days like today remind us of the potential within our reach when we come together."

As the sun set over the newly opened marketplace, casting long shadows and bathing the square in golden light, the festival continued into the night. Serena's vision for a revitalized Eirene was coming to life, each moment of celebration a stitch in the fabric of the kingdom's renewed tapestry. The challenges ahead remained, but for now, the joy and unity of the festival echoed through the streets, promising a bright future for all.

Chapter 9
Labyrinthine Caves

The resurgence of the marketplace had sparked a wider revival across the kingdom of Eirene, a renewal that brought not only economic prosperity but a rebirth of cultural and historical appreciation. As spring unfurled its vibrant colors across the land, Queen Serena turned her attention to the restoration of the Royal Library, a repository of knowledge that had suffered from neglect during the years of turmoil.

Nestled within the heart of the capital, the Royal Library was a grand structure of stone and wood, its spires reaching towards the sky as if in silent plea for restoration. Serena walked its ancient halls, her steps echoing off the marble floors, surrounded by the musty scent of old books and the weight of history. The walls were lined with shelves that reached the ceiling, but many stood empty or held volumes that were faded and worn by time.

Accompanied by her chief librarian, Master Pellen, a man of quiet demeanor and deep knowledge, Serena surveyed the extent of the decay. "It is a great undertaking, but we must preserve our heritage," she stated, her voice resolute amidst the quiet of the vast room.

Master Pellen, adjusting his spectacles, nodded in agreement. "Indeed, Your Majesty. Many of these tomes are irreplaceable. The knowledge contained here is vast. It chronicles Eirene's entire history, its culture, its sciences, and arts. We can restore not just the physical structure but the soul of this place."

Plans were drawn up, and experts in preservation were consulted. As the work began, Serena often visited, overseeing the progress. Under her direction, the library was not merely repaired but reimagined. Modern systems for cataloging and preservation were introduced, blending seamlessly with the traditional aesthetics of the library's architecture.

Workers delicately handled each book, manuscript, and scroll, treating each page as a treasure. Conservators worked meticulously to restore damaged bindings and faded writings, their skills ensuring that future generations would have access to the collective wisdom of the past.

As the restoration neared completion, new life was breathed into the Royal Library. The once-dim interior was now illuminated by restored glass-paneled ceilings that cast patterns of light across the polished floors. Computers and digital archives found their places alongside ancient texts, providing a bridge between the old and the new.

Serena, during one of her visits, paused by a newly restored window, looking out over the bustling city. The library was a symbol of the kingdom's resurgence, a beacon of knowledge that would enlighten future leaders, scholars, and citizens. She felt a deep connection to those who had walked these halls before her, rulers and scholars who had also sought to nurture the spirit of Eirene through knowledge and learning.

The library's grand reopening was marked by a ceremony that drew scholars from across the realm and beyond. Serena spoke briefly, her words echoing in the hallowed hall, "Let this library be a center of learning and a source of inspiration for all who seek knowledge. May it stand as a testament to our respect for the past and our commitment to the future."

As the guests explored the revitalized library, marveling at the harmonious blend of ancient and modern, Serena stood quietly for a moment, her gaze sweeping over the room. Here, in the quietude of this temple of knowledge, the past met the present, promising a future where the wisdom of the ages would continue to guide and enrich the kingdom of Eirene.

Her work here was a vital part of the broader tapestry of renewal she was weaving across her realm, each thread intertwined with the legacy of those who had come before and the dreams of those yet to come. As she left the library, the weight of her responsibilities felt lighter, buoyed by the knowledge that this sacred place was once again alive with the pursuit of understanding.

With the Royal Library now a bastion of knowledge and a beacon of the cultural renaissance sweeping through Eirene, Serena's focus shifted to another cornerstone of her kingdom's heritage: the Royal Archives. Nestled within the quieter, more secluded section of the capital, the archives were home to documents and records dating back centuries, many of which remained unexamined in recent years due to their fragile state.

Serena, accompanied by the Royal Archivist, Master Toren, embarked on a project to digitize these precious records, ensuring their preservation and accessibility for future generations. As they walked through the dimly lit corridors lined with towering shelves filled with aging scrolls and manuscripts, the importance of the task at hand was palpable.

"Master Toren, how extensive is the collection that still needs digitizing?" Serena inquired, her voice echoing softly amid the quiet rustle of parchment.

"We have thousands of documents, Your Majesty, spanning several hundred years. Each piece is a fragment of our history, waiting to be preserved," Master Toren explained, leading her towards a large table where some of the documents were laid out for review.

"Let us begin then. What support do you need from me to expedite this project?" Serena asked, her eyes scanning the delicate writing on a scroll depicting the lineage of Eirenean monarchs.

"Additional resources would certainly help, Your Majesty. More hands, more scanners, and perhaps enhanced technology to handle particularly delicate items without causing damage," Master Toren suggested, pointing to a particularly worn manuscript that seemed to crumble at the edges.

"Consider it done," Serena affirmed decisively. "I will allocate additional funds from the treasury for this project. The preservation of our history is paramount."

As they continued their inspection, Serena stopped by a set of maps depicting ancient Eirene. "These maps—are there records of the places that no longer exist or have changed over the centuries?"

"Yes, indeed," Master Toren replied, unrolling another map. "These documents are invaluable for historians and scholars, providing insight into the geographical and political shifts over the ages. They also serve as guides for any restoration projects we might undertake in the future."

Serena nodded thoughtfully. "Let's ensure these are among the first to be digitized. I would like our citizens, especially our students, to have access to these maps. Understanding our past geography can enlighten our present and future decisions."

"Absolutely, Your Majesty," Master Toren agreed, making a note. "I'll prioritize these maps. The educational value is immense, and they could also be featured in our schools' curriculum."

As they wrapped up their tour, Serena reiterated her commitment to the archives. "Master Toren, this is more than just preservation; it's an act of reclamation. We're reclaiming our past to inform our future. Keep me updated on the progress, and do not hesitate to request anything that could aid in the success of this project."

"I will, Your Majesty, and thank you," Master Toren responded, his voice filled with genuine gratitude. "Your support not only revitalizes these archives but also breathes new life into our history."

As Serena left the archives, the weight of the centuries seemed to lift slightly, the knowledge that they were safeguarding their past providing a deep sense of satisfaction. Each document, each map, each record was a pulse in the heart of Eirene, and as they moved forward, those pulses grew stronger, echoing through the corridors of time into the vibrant, thriving present.

As the digitization of the Royal Archives progressed, the layers of Eirene's past were carefully unraveled and preserved, illuminating aspects of the kingdom's history that had long been obscured or forgotten. Amidst these revelations, Serena found a particular interest in the restoration of historical sites throughout the capital, which had suffered from neglect or had been repurposed over the centuries without consideration for their historical significance.

One crisp morning, Serena visited the site of an ancient fortress on the outskirts of the city, which was believed to have been a pivotal location during the reign of the early Eirenean kings. Accompanied by Lord Kael, the Minister of Cultural Affairs, they walked among the ruins, which offered scant hints of their former grandeur.

"This fortress, according to the archives, was once a stronghold against invasions from the north," Serena noted, examining a partially collapsed wall that bore the faint remnants of old frescoes. "It's a shame to see it in such a state."

"Indeed, Your Majesty," Lord Kael agreed, his voice tinged with reverence for the site. "Its strategic and historical importance is immense. With proper restoration, it could serve as a monument to our resilience and history."

Serena nodded, her gaze lingering on the patterns of the frescoes. "Let's prioritize this fortress for restoration. It's not only about preserving a building but about reclaiming a piece of our identity. What do we know of the original structure?"

"From the archives, we have detailed accounts of its construction and even some artistic depictions," Lord Kael responded, pulling a folded document from his satchel. "Our challenge will be to restore it in a way that honors its historical authenticity while ensuring it remains preserved for future generations."

"Proceed with the utmost care," Serena instructed, her decision clear. "Consult with historians and use materials that are as close as possible to the original. This fortress can be a learning center, a place where our people can touch the tangible legacy of their forebears."

As they continued their inspection, they discussed potential uses for the site once restored. Ideas ranged from a museum housing artifacts from various periods of Eirenean history to a venue for cultural events that could draw visitors and scholars alike.

"Additionally," Serena added, "let's ensure there are educational programs designed for schools. Children should grow up knowing the stories of those who walked these lands before them."

"An excellent idea, Your Majesty," Lord Kael said, making a note. "Education will breathe life into these stones."

Returning to the city, Serena felt a profound connection to her role not just as a ruler but as a steward of her kingdom's history. Each project, from the archives to the fortress, was a thread in the rich tapestry of Eirene's past, now being woven into the present.

Back at the palace, Serena received a report from Master Toren, indicating that several other sites had been identified for similar restoration efforts. Each site was a chapter of their collective history, waiting to be told.

As the day drew to a close, Serena stood at her window overlooking the capital, her thoughts on the days ahead. The work was ongoing, the challenges were many, but the rewards of preserving their heritage were immeasurable. With each step taken to restore and honor their past, the people of Eirene were reminded of their shared journey through time—a journey that Serena was dedicated to illuminating and celebrating.

As the restoration of the ancient fortress neared completion, Serena organized a visit to assess the progress and to plan for its upcoming unveiling as a historical museum and educational center. Accompanied by Lord Kael and a group of historians and architects, Serena walked through the newly stabilized gates, her eyes capturing every detail of the meticulously restored stonework.

"This restoration has exceeded my expectations," Serena commented as they entered the main courtyard, where workers were busy with the final touches. "It's as if we've stepped back in time."

Lord Kael, sharing her enthusiasm, replied, "Indeed, Your Majesty. The historians and architects have worked diligently to ensure authenticity in every aspect of the restoration. From the frescoes to the battlements, every element has been based on extensive research and archaeological findings."

As they proceeded towards the central hall, now transformed into an exhibition space, an architect named Maris approached them, holding a set of old blueprints. "Your Majesty, these are the plans we discovered in the archives, which guided our restoration. Comparing the fortress now to these plans, it's as if we've brought the architect's vision back to life."

Serena examined the blueprints, noting the detail and care in the drawings. "Marvelous work, Maris. This fortress will serve as a cornerstone of our cultural heritage, educating our people about the rich history that shaped Eirene."

They walked through a series of exhibits that depicted various eras of Eirene's history, each accompanied by artifacts that had been recovered during the restoration. "These exhibits," Serena said, "not only tell our history but also highlight the continuity of our culture. They remind us of where we came from and guide us where we are going."

One of the historians, an elderly man named Professor Thorel, nodded in agreement. "Absolutely, Your Majesty. It's crucial that we remember our past—it informs our present and shapes our future. This fortress, once a symbol of our military strength, is now a beacon of our commitment to preserving and understanding our heritage."

Serena paused by a display of medieval weaponry, her thoughts on the generations of Eireneans who had defended their kingdom from these walls. "Let's ensure that the educational programs here are robust. We should have regular tours for schools, interactive workshops, and even reenactments to bring our history to life for all ages."

Lord Kael made a note of her suggestions. "I will coordinate with the education ministry to integrate visits to this fortress into the school curriculum. And perhaps we can host annual festivals here, celebrating the eras depicted in these exhibits."

"That would be splendid," Serena smiled. "Festivals would bring people together, not just to learn but to celebrate our shared heritage."

As they concluded their tour, standing atop the fortress walls overlooking the capital, Serena felt a deep satisfaction. "This project," she said, turning to her companions, "is a testament to what we can achieve when we honor our past while building our future. Let us continue to uncover and cherish our history."

Lord Kael, looking out over the landscape, added, "This fortress will stand for generations to come as a symbol of our resilience and our dedication to our culture. It's a project that has truly unified our efforts across multiple disciplines."

With the fortress restoration complete, Serena was eager for its official opening, planned to coincide with the upcoming national heritage celebration. It would be a day of reflection, education, and unity, marking another milestone in her reign—a reign defined by a reverence for history and a vision for the future.

As they descended the ancient stone steps back towards the exit, the late afternoon sun cast long shadows across the courtyard, the light playing off the old stones, each one a silent witness to the ages of Eirene. Serena knew that the stories these stones held were now safe, ready to be shared with all who walked these grounds.

Chapter 10
Festival of Reminiscence

Spring was in full bloom across Eirene, its warmth not just reviving the natural landscape but also the spirits of its people. With the successful restoration and reopening of historical sites across the kingdom, Serena now turned her attention to addressing more immediate societal needs, focusing particularly on health and education. She organized a meeting with Minister Halen, who was responsible for health services, and Minister Tala, overseeing education, to discuss the integration and expansion of these critical sectors.

Gathered in the sunlit garden of the palace, the trio sat around a wrought-iron table, the air filled with the scent of blooming flowers. Serena opened the discussion with a sense of purpose. "Minister Halen, Minister Tala, our efforts in preserving our heritage are well underway. However, we must also ensure that our advancements in health and education are not just continuing but accelerating. What is the current status of our initiatives?"

Minister Halen was the first to respond. "Your Majesty, our new health initiatives have been met with positive feedback. The integration of traditional healers into our public health system has been particularly successful. However, we are experiencing a shortage of trained healthcare professionals in rural areas."

Serena nodded thoughtfully. "What steps can we take to address this shortage?"

"We could expand our scholarship programs to encourage more students to enter the health sciences," Minister Halen suggested. "Additionally, offering incentives for professionals to work in these underserved areas could help alleviate the gap."

"That sounds like a practical approach," Serena agreed. "Minister Tala, could these scholarships also be integrated into our educational outreach programs?"

"Certainly, Your Majesty," Minister Tala replied. "By targeting high school students in rural areas, we can begin to cultivate interest in the health sciences early. We can also incorporate more health education into the curriculum to raise awareness and interest."

Serena smiled, pleased with the collaboration. "Let's ensure these programs are well-publicized and accessible. I want every potential student to know that these opportunities are available."

Turning her attention back to Minister Halen, Serena inquired, "What about the infrastructure for healthcare? Are our facilities in these rural areas adequate?"

"That's a challenge, Your Majesty," Minister Halen admitted. "Many of our rural clinics need modernization. We're also looking at expanding telemedicine capabilities, which would allow for greater reach with fewer resources."

"Excellent idea," Serena said. "Let's prioritize the modernization of these facilities. Access to healthcare is a right, not a privilege. We must make it possible for every citizen to receive the care they need, regardless of where they live."

The conversation shifted towards education. "Minister Tala, beyond health sciences, how are we advancing our educational initiatives overall?"

"We are making great strides, Your Majesty," Minister Tala responded. "The new digital classrooms have been a success, and we're seeing improved literacy rates as a result. However, we still face challenges with teacher retention and training, especially in specialty subjects."

"What support can we provide to improve this?" Serena asked, her gaze steady.

"Further investment in teacher training programs, particularly in STEM fields, would be beneficial," Minister Tala suggested. "We could also look into partnerships with international education bodies to provide ongoing training and development."

"Proceed with those plans," Serena instructed, her decision clear. "Education and health are the pillars upon which a prosperous society is built. We must invest in them accordingly."

As the meeting concluded, the trio stood, each fortified by the clear direction and mutual goals outlined. Serena, looking over the blooming garden, felt a renewed sense of commitment to these causes.

"Thank you both," she said warmly. "Your dedication not only strengthens these initiatives but ensures that our future will be as vibrant and healthy as this garden in spring."

As they parted ways, each to their respective duties, the promises made that day were set into motion, weaving together the threads of health and education to form a strong and inclusive tapestry for the future of Eirene.

With the initial plans for enhancing the health and education sectors set into motion, Serena turned her focus to agricultural innovations that could sustain Eirene's growing population and rejuvenate its rural economies. An upcoming summit, dedicated to sustainable agriculture and food security, provided the perfect opportunity to drive these initiatives forward. Serena planned to meet with leading agricultural experts, environmental scientists, and representatives from various farming communities.

The summit took place in the verdant outskirts of the capital, where the test fields for new agricultural techniques were located. Here, amid rows of experimental crops, Serena walked with Minister Lorne and Dr. Elara, a leading agricultural scientist, discussing the integration of traditional farming practices with modern technology.

"Dr. Elara, I'm impressed with the progress I've seen today," Serena began, examining a plot where permaculture techniques were being applied. "How scalable are these methods for broader use across Eirene?"

Dr. Elara, her face shaded by a wide-brimmed hat, replied enthusiastically, "Very scalable, Your Majesty. With proper training and resources, these methods can significantly increase yield and sustainability. They're designed to be adaptable to various climatic and soil conditions throughout the kingdom."

"That's promising," Serena noted. "Minister Lorne, how can we ensure that these innovations reach all our farmers, especially those in remote areas?"

Minister Lorne, clipboard in hand, responded, "We are planning a series of workshops and pilot programs in different regions. Each program will be tailored to the specific needs and conditions of the area. Additionally, we're developing a grant system to help small-scale farmers adopt these techniques."

"Accessibility is key," Serena affirmed. "Dr. Elara, are there particular challenges you foresee in implementing these methods on a larger scale?"

"One major challenge is resistance to change," Dr. Elara explained as they continued their walk. "Many farmers are accustomed to traditional methods and may be hesitant to adopt new techniques. Education and demonstration of benefits will be crucial."

"We'll need to address this carefully," Serena said thoughtfully. "Perhaps success stories from early adopters could be showcased at community meetings. Seeing is believing, after all."

"An excellent idea," Dr. Elara agreed. "We could also offer incentives for communities that achieve significant improvements in sustainability and yield."

As the discussion shifted toward environmental impact, Serena was keen to understand the balance between agricultural expansion and conservation. "It's important that our efforts to increase production do not come at the expense of our natural heritage. What measures are we putting in place to protect our ecosystems?"

Dr. Elara nodded, clearly passionate about the topic. "We're integrating eco-friendly practices at every level, from water conservation systems to natural pest control. These practices not only protect the environment but often result in better crop health and yield."

"I am reassured to hear that," Serena responded, her commitment to a balanced approach evident. "Let's ensure these practices are not just recommended but enforced where necessary. Our environmental health is just as important as our economic prosperity."

As the summit drew to a close, the group gathered for a final review of their action plan. Commitments were made, responsibilities assigned, and Serena, satisfied with the outcomes, expressed her gratitude and expectations to the assembly.

"Today, we've laid down the groundwork for a sustainable agricultural future," Serena concluded. "Let us move forward with determination and vigilance, for the health of our land and our people depends on the choices we make today."

With the summit's successful conclusion, Serena left the fields feeling hopeful. The strategies discussed and developed here would soon take root across Eirene, promising not only to enhance the kingdom's food security but also to ensure that its agricultural practices could sustain and enrich future generations. Each step forward in this fertile landscape was a step toward a thriving, resilient Eirene.

As the initiatives from the agricultural summit began to take root, Serena's attention shifted towards fostering innovation and entrepreneurship within Eirene. Recognizing that the kingdom's future depended as much on new ideas as on preserving traditions, she launched an innovation fund designed to support startups and small businesses that were pioneering new technologies and services.

On a mild, sunny day, Serena visited a new technology incubator in the capital, a modern facility nestled in the heart of the city's revitalized industrial sector. The incubator, a sleek building of glass and steel, buzzed with the energy of creative minds at work. Here, young entrepreneurs and seasoned mentors collaborated on a range of projects, from renewable energy solutions to advanced agricultural tools.

Serena was met by the director of the incubator, a sharp-minded woman named Dr. Caris, who guided her through the open-plan workspace where teams of innovators worked intently. "Your Majesty, this space is a testament to Eirene's commitment to the future. Each project here benefits from the innovation fund, allowing these bright minds to focus fully on developing their ideas," Dr. Caris explained.

"That's exactly what I hoped for," Serena responded, pausing to watch a demonstration of a new water purification device. "Innovation drives progress. How do we ensure that the projects developed here reach their full potential?"

Dr. Caris led Serena to a meeting area where they could talk more quietly. "We provide not just funding but comprehensive support, including mentorship, market analysis, and even assistance with scaling up successful projects. Our aim is not just to incubate these ideas but to integrate them into the broader economy."

Serena listened intently, nodding. "Integration is crucial. It's not enough to invent; we must ensure these innovations make a tangible difference in people's lives. Are there success stories we can highlight to encourage more participation?"

"Indeed, there are several," Dr. Caris replied. "One of our early beneficiaries developed a solar-powered crop monitoring system that's now being used in several regions across Eirene. It's significantly increased crop yields while reducing water and pesticide use."

"Wonderful," Serena said, visibly pleased. "Stories like these not only inspire new entrepreneurs but also show the practical benefits of embracing innovation. We should feature these successes in a public campaign to inspire more people to bring their ideas forward."

As they continued their tour, Serena engaged with several entrepreneurs, each eager to share their projects. Their enthusiasm reaffirmed her belief in the vital role that innovation must play in shaping the future of Eirene. Before leaving, she addressed a gathering of the incubator's participants, emphasizing her commitment to supporting their efforts.

"Your creativity and dedication are key to our kingdom's prosperity and sustainability," Serena declared. "The royal family and the government are proud to support you. We are committed to creating an environment where innovation can flourish and where every good idea receives the attention it deserves."

Back at the palace, Serena reflected on her visit. She felt reassured that the investment in innovation was not just about economic development but about building a resilient society capable of meeting future challenges. The young entrepreneurs at the incubator were not just building businesses; they were constructing the very future of Eirene, brick by brick.

This initiative, like the seeds sown in the fields and the manuscripts preserved in the archives, was part of a broader vision to weave resilience and vitality into the fabric of the kingdom. As she reviewed reports and plans for expanding the innovation fund, Serena was more convinced than ever of the transformative power of creative thinking and entrepreneurial spirit in securing a prosperous future for all Eireneans.

Late spring brought with it a verdant flush to the kingdom of Eirene, a visual testament to the fertility and richness that Serena's policies aimed to enhance and protect. The kingdom was not merely surviving; it was thriving, with innovations blooming as robustly as the gardens of the palace. Amidst this backdrop of renewal, Serena organized a review session with her key ministers to assess the impact of the initiatives implemented throughout the spring and to plan for the summer.

In the stately conference room overlooking the palace gardens, Serena convened with Minister Halen, Minister Tala, and Minister Lorne. The large windows were thrown open to let in the fresh air, which mingled pleasantly with the scent of blossoming flowers.

"Let us begin with the updates," Serena said, her tone both commanding and encouraging. "Minister Halen, how are the health initiatives progressing in the rural areas?"

"Very well, Your Majesty," Minister Halen began, shuffling through his notes. "The new clinics are operational, and there's been a significant increase in community health outreach. However, we are still facing challenges with staffing these facilities."

"What solutions do we have in place for these staffing issues?" Serena inquired, her brow furrowed in concern.

"We are expanding our training programs to include more local residents in healthcare roles," replied Halen. "Additionally, we're exploring incentives for medical professionals to relocate to these areas."

"Excellent. Ensuring that our citizens have access to healthcare is paramount," Serena affirmed. "Minister Tala, what about our educational initiatives?"

Minister Tala adjusted her glasses before responding. "The digital classrooms have been a success, Your Majesty. Attendance rates have risen, and test scores are improving. The challenge now is to ensure that the technology is maintained and that the teachers receive ongoing training to best utilize these tools."

"Let's allocate more funds for training and maintenance then," Serena decided. "It's crucial that these tools are used effectively to continue improving our educational standards."

As the meeting progressed, Minister Lorne updated Serena on the agricultural projects. "The sustainable farming techniques have been well received, and we are seeing improvements in crop yields already. The next step is to expand these techniques to more farms and to integrate more advanced technology to monitor crop health."

"I am pleased to hear this," Serena responded. "Let us also focus on improving the infrastructure for food distribution to ensure that the increase in production is matched by an increase in market reach."

The ministers noted her directives, their expressions reflecting a mixture of determination and optimism.

As the session drew to a close, Serena stood and walked toward the window, looking out over the lush palace gardens. "Our efforts are bearing fruit, but we must not become complacent. We need to sustain the momentum and continue to address any new challenges that arise."

The ministers gathered their papers, their nods indicating agreement and respect. "We will continue to work diligently, Your Majesty," Minister Halen assured her.

"And I will continue to support your efforts," Serena added, turning from the window. "Together, we are building a stronger, healthier, and more educated Eirene."

The ministers departed, leaving Serena to her thoughts in the quiet of the conference room. As she pondered the future, her resolve to guide her kingdom toward prosperity and enlightenment remained unshaken. Each project, each policy, each initiative was a step toward a vision of Eirene that would stand as a beacon of success and sustainability in a changing world.

With the setting sun casting a golden glow across the gardens, Serena felt a deep connection to the land and its people—a connection that fueled her dedication to serve and protect. The work was ongoing, the path sometimes arduous, but the journey was hers to lead, and she would do so with unwavering commitment and hope.

Chapter 11
Betrayal

Summer's warmth had settled over the kingdom of Eirene, bringing with it the promise of fruitful harvests and vibrant festivals. But for Queen Serena, it was also a time to touch base with the rural communities, whose voices were crucial in shaping policies that affected their daily lives and livelihoods. Determined to ensure that the rural sectors felt supported and heard, Serena organized a series of town hall meetings across various villages.

The first of these meetings was held in the village of Greendale, a community primarily sustained by its agriculture, particularly its expansive wheat fields. As Serena arrived at the village square, she was greeted by a crowd of local farmers and their families, all eager to share their experiences and concerns.

"Good day to you all," Serena began, standing on a small wooden platform set up for the occasion. "I am here to listen, to understand your needs, and to discuss how we can work together to address them."

An older farmer, his face lined with the years of toil under the sun, stepped forward. "Your Majesty, we are grateful for your visit. The new irrigation techniques have helped, but we are struggling with the market fluctuations in wheat prices. It's becoming difficult to plan for the future."

Serena nodded sympathetically. "I understand your concerns. Minister Lorne, could you share how we might stabilize these fluctuations?"

Minister Lorne, who had accompanied Serena, addressed the crowd. "Certainly, Your Majesty. We are exploring the establishment of a minimum guarantee price for wheat and other staple crops. This should provide you with a stable income base and protect you from unexpected market drops."

"That sounds promising," a young farmer added, adjusting his hat. "What about transportation? Getting our produce to the markets is still a challenge due to the poor condition of rural roads."

"Improving our infrastructure is a priority," Serena affirmed. "We have allocated funds for the maintenance and construction of rural roads. The first phase of this project will commence this autumn, starting with the most critical routes."

Another voice came from the crowd, a middle-aged woman who ran a small dairy farm. "Your Majesty, our dairy products have a demand in the city, but we lack the cooling facilities to store them until they can be transported. Many times, we face spoilage."

Serena turned to another of her aides, who took notes diligently. "Let's look into expanding our agricultural support services to include storage and cooling facilities in key locations. It's essential that your hard work doesn't go to waste."

The discussion continued, with Serena and her ministers responding to a variety of questions and concerns. Each answer was met with nods and murmurs of approval, the community visibly heartened by the direct dialogue with their queen.

As the meeting drew to a close, Serena addressed the crowd once more. "Your feedback today is invaluable. It will directly influence our policies and ensure that they truly benefit those for whom they are intended. Let's continue this conversation, and together, we will ensure that Greendale, and villages like it across Eirene, thrive."

The villagers applauded, their expressions one of renewed hope and confidence in their leadership. Serena stayed a while longer, speaking more personally with several attendees, reaffirming her commitment to their wellbeing.

As she departed Greendale, the weight of responsibility felt lighter, buoyed by the honest exchanges and the tangible solutions they had outlined. The journey back to the capital was a time for reflection, a reminder of the vital connections between ruler and ruled, and the shared goal of prosperity for all within the kingdom. These conversations, held in village squares under the open sky, were the threads that strengthened the fabric of Eirene, weaving together the diverse experiences and hopes of its people.

Continuing her tour, Serena arrived at the village of Hilltop, nestled in the gentle slopes of Eirene's northeastern hills. The village was known for its fruit orchards and vineyards, but recent shifts in climate had posed new challenges for its farmers. In the town hall, a rustic building with a thatched roof and wooden beams, Serena convened a meeting with the local agricultural community to address these challenges.

As the villagers gathered, a buzz of conversation filled the air, a mixture of anticipation and concern. Serena, alongside her advisor on environmental affairs, began the meeting with a warm greeting. "Thank you for welcoming us to your beautiful village. Today, I am here to listen and learn from you, to understand how we can better support your efforts in these changing times."

An elderly orchard owner, Mr. Alden, stood first. "Your Majesty, we appreciate your visit. The problem we're facing is with the unpredictable weather patterns. Last spring's frost came late and damaged much of the bloom. We weren't prepared."

Serena nodded, turning to her environmental advisor. "What can be done to help our farmers anticipate and mitigate these issues?"

The advisor, a middle-aged woman with expertise in climatology, responded, "We are developing a regional weather alert system that can provide more accurate forecasts. Additionally, we can explore frost protection techniques, such as wind machines and water sprinklers, which have been effective in other regions."

"That sounds very helpful," Mr. Alden replied, visibly relieved. "Knowing when the frost might hit and having a way to fight it could save our crops."

A younger farmer, whose energetic approach to viticulture had revitalized several local vineyards, then spoke up. "Your Majesty, my concern is about water. With the dry spells becoming more frequent, our traditional irrigation methods aren't sufficient."

"Water management is indeed crucial," Serena acknowledged. "We are initiating a program to construct new water reservoirs and introduce drip irrigation systems that are more efficient. Would Hilltop be interested in participating in the pilot phase?"

"That would be marvelous," the young farmer exclaimed, his face brightening. "More efficient water use could make a huge difference for us."

A woman from the back, known for her robust vegetable garden that supplied much of the village, added, "And what about support for smaller gardens like mine? We contribute to the village's food supply too."

"Absolutely," Serena assured her. "Our agricultural support extends to gardens as well. We will provide training on sustainable gardening practices and small-scale irrigation solutions."

The dialogue continued, with Serena and her team taking notes and providing responses that reassured the community of Hilltop that their concerns were not only heard but were being actively addressed.

As the meeting drew to a close, Serena stood and addressed the room once more. "Your input today has been invaluable. By working together, we can overcome the challenges posed by nature and continue to thrive. Please keep the lines of communication open. Your feedback is crucial as we roll out these initiatives."

The villagers nodded, their earlier apprehension replaced by a sense of partnership and hope. Conversations lingered even after the formal discussion had ended, with many approaching Serena to express their gratitude or to share a bit more about their personal experiences.

As she left Hilltop, the late afternoon sun cast long shadows over the lush landscapes that the village's farmers had tended for generations. The meeting had reinforced Serena's belief in the power of direct dialogue to foster trust and collaboration. Each visit, each conversation, strengthened the bonds between the crown and the countryside, ensuring that the policies enacted were not only informed but embraced by those they meant to benefit.

Driving away from Hilltop, Serena felt a renewed commitment to these engagements. The challenges were many, but so were the opportunities. By continuing to engage directly with her people, Serena was not just ruling a kingdom; she was nurturing a community, ready to face the future together.

The summer's warmth permeated even the most remote villages of Eirene, carrying with it the queen's steadfast commitment to dialogue and development. The next stop on Serena's journey was the coastal village of Mariner's Cliff, known for its fishing industry and picturesque seascapes. Here, the community faced unique challenges related to the sea: overfishing, erosion, and the preservation of marine life.

Gathered in the village hall, a building adorned with nets and seashells, Serena met with local fishermen, environmental experts, and representatives from the tourism sector. The air was filled with the salty scent of the ocean, a constant reminder of the community's lifeblood.

"Thank you for gathering here today," Serena began, addressing the room filled with concerned yet hopeful faces. "The sea is a vital part of Mariner's Cliff, not just economically but culturally. Let's discuss how we can sustainably manage its resources."

An old fisherman, his face weathered like the wooden boats he sailed, was the first to speak. "Your Majesty, we've fished these waters for generations. But the fish are fewer each year. We're struggling to maintain our catches without depleting what's left."

Serena turned to her environmental advisor, who accompanied her. "What measures can we implement to help balance their need to fish with the need to conserve?"

The advisor, a middle-aged woman with a background in marine biology, suggested, "We could introduce a quota system to limit the amount of catch per season, allowing fish populations to recover. Additionally, setting up protected marine areas could help rejuvenate marine life."

"That's a start," the fisherman replied thoughtfully. "But we need assurance that these changes won't just push us out of our own waters."

"Fair enough," Serena acknowledged. "Let's explore financial aids and training programs for sustainable fishing practices. We want to ensure that while we protect the marine environment, we also protect your livelihoods."

A younger woman, involved in the local tourism industry, added, "And what about the erosion? The beaches are wearing away, affecting both our homes and our businesses."

Serena nodded, aware of the dual threat to property and profitable tourism. "Erosion control is critical. We are considering the construction of sea barriers and the restoration of mangroves, which can help reduce erosion naturally. Additionally, we'll assess the impact of tourism on erosion and adjust our policies accordingly."

The room buzzed with murmurs of approval and further questions, as community members expressed their concerns and suggestions. Serena listened, her advisors taking meticulous notes.

A local schoolteacher, who had brought some of her students to listen, asked, "How can we educate our young about these issues? They need to understand the balance between use and conservation."

"That's an excellent point," Serena responded. "Education is key. We'll develop educational programs in schools here about marine biology and environmental stewardship. Perhaps even sponsor field trips to marine research centers."

The meeting continued with vibrant discussions, each participant contributing to a holistic plan that encompassed economic, environmental, and educational strategies. As the meeting drew to a close, Serena stood, her expression resolute yet optimistic.

"Today's discussions have been invaluable. Together, we are charting a course that respects both our heritage and our environment. Mariner's Cliff is not just a village; it's a vital part of Eirene's ecosystem. Let's proceed with these plans, united in our efforts to safeguard our future."

As the villagers dispersed, many stayed to speak personally with Serena, thanking her for her attention and dedication. Walking back to her carriage, Serena felt the weight of her responsibilities intertwined with the deep satisfaction of collaborative governance. Each step taken today at Mariner's Cliff was a step towards sustainability and mutual respect—a true reflection of governance that listened and responded to the needs of its people.

As the summer sun began to wane, casting longer shadows over the lush landscapes of Eirene, Queen Serena found herself reflecting on the extensive journey she had undertaken throughout her kingdom. From the bustling markets of the capital to the remote and rugged landscapes of Mariner's Cliff, each visit had not only solidified her understanding of her people's needs but also reaffirmed her commitment to address them effectively.

The final leg of her summer tour took her to the village of Windvale, nestled in the hills where the wind was said to carry whispers of the past and promises of the future. Here, the community was primarily composed of weavers and textile artisans, whose looms and fabrics were as much a part of their identity as the very air they breathed.

Upon her arrival, Serena was greeted with displays of intricate tapestries and vibrant textiles that told stories of Windvale's history and culture. The village square, usually quiet, today thrummed with the excitement of her visit. Serena, dressed in a gown that featured embroidery from the local artisans, addressed the gathered crowd with a warmth that matched the afternoon sun.

"Thank you for such a beautiful welcome," Serena began, her eyes reflecting the vivid colors that surrounded her. "It's clear that Windvale holds not just the talent of weaving textiles but also the skill of weaving community and tradition into every thread."

A master weaver, an elderly woman with hands as skilled as they were wrinkled, stepped forward to speak with Serena. "Your Majesty, we are thankful for your visit. But our craft needs more than just appreciation to survive. The young people are moving to the cities; the looms are quieting."

"I understand," Serena replied, her voice laden with both concern and determination. "Let us think about how we can revitalize your craft. Perhaps integrating modern designs and marketing them to broader markets could help. What support would you need from us to make this possible?"

The weaver suggested, "Training in new techniques and help in marketing our products would keep our traditions alive but also appealing to the younger generations and markets outside our village."

Serena nodded, making a mental note to discuss this further with her advisors. "We will work on creating workshops and partnerships that can help you achieve these goals. Your heritage is invaluable, and it should thrive, not just survive."

As the day progressed, Serena engaged with various artisans, discussing potential initiatives that could breathe new life into their crafts. She also met with young villagers, listening to their aspirations and concerns, which often strayed from tradition towards the lure of modern city life.

These conversations were crucial in shaping the royal initiatives aimed at rural revitalization, blending tradition with innovation to create sustainable models of living and working.

As the visit concluded, Serena stood once more at the center of the village square, surrounded by the very tapestries that had welcomed her. "Windvale, like many of our kingdom's treasures, is a vibrant testament to our past but also a beacon for our future. Let us work together to ensure this beacon continues to burn bright."

With a promise to return, Serena departed Windvale, her mind filled with the thoughts of the day's discussions. The drive back to the palace was contemplative, with the landscape rolling by like the very fabric the villagers wove—each thread a story, each color a dream.

Reaching the palace, Serena felt a profound connection to her role not just as a monarch but as a custodian of Eirene's diverse heritage. The summer's journey had woven a tapestry of insight and initiative, each thread pulled taut by the discussions and meetings that had taken place across the kingdom.

Now, as she prepared for the challenges ahead, Serena knew that the true strength of Eirene lay in its people—their hopes, their work, and their dreams. These were what she would continue to champion, ensuring that the kingdom, much like the tapestries of Windvale, would tell a story of beauty, resilience, and endless possibility.

Chapter 12
Regaining Strength

As autumn's crisp breath swept through the kingdom of Eirene, the leaves began their colorful dance to the ground, signaling a time of harvest and reflection. Queen Serena, having spent the summer months deeply engaged with her people across the land, chose this season of change to convene a meeting with the Council of Elders, a venerable group of advisors representing various aspects of Eirenean life.

In the grand council chamber, with its high ceilings and walls lined with portraits of past monarchs, the Elders gathered, their aged faces reflecting wisdom and the weight of responsibility. Serena entered the room, her presence commanding yet graceful, and took her place at the head of the ancient oak table.

"Thank you for joining me today," Serena began, her voice resonating with authority and warmth. "This meeting is convened to gather wisdom and guidance as we prepare to usher in not only the end of the year but also the future phases of our kingdom's development."

Elder Marnin, a scholar of Eirene's history, nodded sagely. "Your Majesty, it is we who are thankful. Your initiatives have breathed new life into our land. How may we assist you further in these endeavors?"

Serena smiled at him appreciatively. "I seek your counsel on sustaining the momentum we have built. We've seen significant advancements in agriculture, healthcare, and education. My concern now is how we maintain these improvements and ensure they benefit all Eireneans."

Elder Lysa, known for her expertise in economic matters, leaned forward. "Your Majesty, the key is in creating self-sustaining systems. For instance, in agriculture, could we not enhance our focus on local cooperatives that not only produce but also process and market their goods?"

"A fine point, Elder Lysa," Serena responded thoughtfully. "Such cooperatives could indeed foster economic independence and resilience.

Minister Lorne, let's explore this further and draft some preliminary plans."

Elder Bram, whose life's work lay in healthcare, chimed in. "And in health, while our new facilities are a boon, we must also invest in continuous training for our healthcare workers. Keeping our medical staff updated with the latest practices will be crucial for the longevity of our healthcare initiatives."

"Absolutely," Serena agreed, nodding to Minister Halen who was also present. "Continuous education and development for our healthcare professionals must be a priority. Let's allocate funds and perhaps look into partnerships with medical institutions abroad."

The dialogue turned to education, with Elder Nyra providing insight. "Your Majesty, while our digital classrooms have improved education access, there is a cultural component that we must not neglect. Our children need to be rooted in Eirenean culture even as they reach for global ideas."

"That balance is essential," Serena acknowledged, her expression contemplative. "Let's introduce more cultural studies into the curriculum. Perhaps even exchange programs with other nations to broaden our students' perspectives while grounding them in their heritage."

As the meeting progressed, each Elder contributed insights from their vast experience, weaving a tapestry of ideas that Serena absorbed and integrated into her vision for the future.

As the council meeting drew to a close, Serena stood and addressed the room once more. "Your wisdom today has been invaluable. With your guidance, I am confident in the path we are charting for Eirene. Together, we will continue to build on the foundation we have laid, ensuring prosperity and well-being for every citizen."

The Elders rose, bowing slightly to their queen, their faces etched with respect and a shared sense of purpose. They departed the chamber, leaving Serena to reflect on the discussions. The path forward was clearer now, enriched by the counsel of those who had served before her and those who would continue to serve under her reign.

Serena remained for a moment longer, looking out the large window at the autumn-colored landscape of her kingdom, feeling a profound connection to the land and its people. This connection, fortified by the advice of her Elders, would guide her as she navigated the challenges and opportunities that lay ahead. Each decision, each policy, each innovation was a step toward a thriving Eirene, a kingdom renewed under her leadership and continued in the spirit of unity and progress.

With the Council of Elders' insights still fresh in her mind, Queen Serena convened a strategic planning session aimed at implementing the enriched policies discussed. Gathered in the opulent strategy room of the palace, where maps and charts adorned the walls and a large round table dominated the center, were her key ministers and advisors. They were there to transform the council's wisdom into actionable plans.

"Thank you all for being here," Serena started, her voice clear and purposeful. "We have valuable guidance from the Council of Elders, and it is now our task to turn their wisdom into tangible outcomes for Eirene."

Minister Lorne, eager to begin, leaned forward. "Your Majesty, regarding the agricultural cooperatives Elder Lysa mentioned, I suggest we start by identifying potential pilot regions. These areas should represent different agricultural challenges across Eirene to test the cooperatives' adaptability."

"That's a prudent approach," Serena agreed, noting down his point. "Let's ensure we also include a robust support system for these pilots, including financial grants and expert advisement. How soon can we initiate this, Minister Lorne?"

"I believe we can start identifying suitable regions within the month and launch the first pilots by early spring," Lorne replied confidently.

Serena then turned to Minister Halen, concerning healthcare. "Minister Halen, Elder Bram emphasized the need for continuous training for our healthcare workers. What steps can we take to implement this?"

"We can establish ongoing training programs in partnership with medical schools and perhaps even international healthcare institutions," Halen proposed. "This could include both on-site and digital learning platforms to ensure broad and consistent reach."

"Excellent idea," Serena responded. "Let's also create a feedback loop where healthcare workers can report back on the efficacy of their training, ensuring it remains relevant and effective."

Attention then shifted to educational development. "Minister Tala, about integrating more cultural studies into our curriculum, how do you propose we proceed?"

Minister Tala, who had been taking notes, looked up. "We can develop a new curriculum module that focuses on Eirenean history, arts, and society. This module could be mandatory across all schools. Additionally, setting up student exchange programs with other countries would offer a practical experience of other cultures while valuing their own."

"I like that," Serena nodded. "Let's be sure those programs are accessible to students from all socio-economic backgrounds."

"Yes, Your Majesty," Tala affirmed, "I'll ensure inclusivity is at the heart of these programs."

The meeting continued with discussions on each topic, each minister presenting their sector's action plans, timelines, and expected challenges. Serena facilitated the session with a keen focus on detail and feasibility, ensuring each plan was robust and comprehensive.

As they wrapped up, Serena looked around the table, a sense of satisfaction evident on her face. "This session has laid down a strong pathway for the coming months. Each of you has brought insightful and innovative ideas to the table. It's imperative that we maintain this momentum and keep our lines of communication open as these plans roll out."

"Absolutely, Your Majesty," the ministers chorused, their dedication palpable in the room.

Serena concluded, "We are shaping the future of Eirene together, and it is our united efforts that will ensure our success. Thank you for your hard work and commitment. Let us meet again next quarter to review our progress."

As the advisors left the room, each with their directives and renewed vigor, Serena remained seated, gazing at the maps that depicted her beloved Eirene. Her heart was full of hope and determination, the challenges ahead not daunting but invigorating, as she led her kingdom into a future that promised prosperity and well-being for all her people.

As the leaves of Eirene turned from gold to the deep, russet tones of late autumn, Queen Serena's initiatives began to manifest across the kingdom. From the bustling capital to the smallest rural villages, each community started to feel the impact of her administration's dedicated efforts. Now, with the strategic foundations laid, it was time to oversee the progress of these projects, ensuring they not only started strong but also had the momentum to sustain themselves long into the future.

One crisp morning, Serena, wrapped in a cloak that swirled with the autumn winds, visited the newly established agricultural cooperative in the fertile valley of Elderglen. Here, the fields were alive with the first pilot implementations of the advanced farming techniques discussed during the summer councils. As she walked through the rows of burgeoning crops, flanked by Minister Lorne and local farmers, she observed the fruits of their labor.

Minister Lorne was quick to point out the successes. "Your Majesty, the new irrigation systems have doubled the water efficiency of these fields. And the crop yield forecasts are promising—nearly a thirty percent increase from last year."

"That is excellent news," Serena replied, inspecting a grain sample provided by a proud farmer. "It's tangible proof that our policies are on the right track. But let's not forget the importance of feedback. What are the farmers saying?"

"The response has been overwhelmingly positive," the farmer interjected, eager to share his experience. "We appreciate the support and training. It's made a real difference not just in our yields but in our community's spirit."

Encouraged by these reports, Serena's next stop was a rural healthcare facility in the village of Greenbrook. The facility had been one of the first to benefit from the upgraded healthcare infrastructure and training programs initiated earlier in the year. As she toured the facility, she saw new medical equipment in use and spoke to healthcare professionals about the improvements.

"The additional training has been invaluable," one nurse shared with Serena during the visit. "We feel more equipped to handle a range of health issues and provide better care to our patients."

Satisfied with the progress but always vigilant, Serena emphasized the need for ongoing assessment. "Let's ensure that we continue to monitor patient outcomes and staff satisfaction. It's the only way we'll know if we need to adjust our strategies."

Her final visit of the day took her back to the capital, where the educational reforms had introduced enhanced digital classrooms and cultural studies programs. At a local school, she observed a class where students engaged with interactive learning modules about Eirene's history.

Watching the children learn about their heritage with such enthusiasm, Serena felt a deep connection to her mission. These young minds were not just absorbing knowledge; they were being equipped to shape their kingdom's future.

Before leaving, Serena discussed the programs with the school principal. "The integration of cultural studies has enriched the curriculum," the principal noted. "It helps students understand their identity in the context of the wider world."

"I'm pleased to hear that," Serena acknowledged. "It's vital that our youth not only excel academically but also grow up with a strong sense of who they are and where they come from."

As the day drew to a close, Serena reflected on the progress made and the journey still ahead. Each project, each reform, each policy she had initiated was like a seed planted, now slowly but surely taking root. The real test would be in nurturing these seeds to maturity, ensuring that the benefits of today's efforts would be felt for generations to come.

With a sense of quiet optimism, Serena looked forward to the challenges and achievements that the coming winter would bring, knowing that the work done under her rule was crafting a legacy of prosperity and care for the kingdom of Eirene. Each step taken, each decision made, was weaving a stronger, more resilient future, a testament to the enduring spirit of her people and the land they called home.

As the year drew to a close and the first snows of winter dusted the rooftops of Eirene's capital, Queen Serena convened a significant meeting within the palace's ornate Winter Room, where the glow of the fireplace cast a warm light over the faces of her most trusted ministers and advisors. The meeting was crucial to evaluate the year's progress and to solidify plans for the upcoming year, ensuring that the initiatives set in motion continued to thrive and expand.

Serena, sitting at the head of the long mahogany table, opened the discussion with a clear and focused tone. "This year has been one of tremendous growth and learning. Each of you has played a pivotal role in this. Today, let's review our progress and set our objectives for the next year. Minister Lorne, let's start with agriculture. How are the new cooperatives doing?"

Minister Lorne nodded, shuffling his papers before speaking. "Your Majesty, the agricultural cooperatives have been a success, particularly in terms of increasing crop yields and farmer incomes. For next year, we propose expanding these cooperatives into more regions and integrating smart technology to further enhance productivity."

"That sounds promising," Serena responded. "It's crucial that we continue to support our rural communities. What about the infrastructure improvements we discussed last quarter?"

"We are on track with the rural road improvements," Minister Lorne continued. "We've also initiated several water conservation projects that will begin in the spring. These will be crucial for the dry seasons."

Turning her attention to healthcare, Serena addressed Minister Halen. "Minister Halen, the healthcare improvements in rural areas have been one of this year's highlights. What steps are we taking to ensure these improvements are sustained?"

Minister Halen, looking prepared and eager, replied, "We're enhancing our training programs for rural healthcare workers and expanding our telemedicine services. Additionally, we plan to increase our mobile health clinics to reach the most isolated communities."

"Excellent, ensuring that every citizen has access to healthcare is a priority," Serena affirmed. "And the feedback from the communities?"

"Very positive, Your Majesty," Halen answered. "There is a noticeable improvement in community health, and the accessibility has been life-changing for many."

Serena then focused on education, her gaze settling on Minister Tala. "Minister Tala, the integration of technology in education has been revolutionary. How do we plan to build on this progress?"

Minister Tala smiled, clearly passionate about the topic. "Next year, we'll expand the digital classroom program. We also plan to introduce coding and digital literacy into the curriculum, starting as early as primary school."

"Preparing our children for the future is essential," Serena nodded approvingly. "And the cultural studies program?"

"Growing stronger, Your Majesty," Tala replied. "We're developing partnerships with cultural institutions to provide students with hands-on learning experiences. It's vital they understand and appreciate their heritage."

As the meeting progressed, Serena listened, interjected, and guided the discussions with a keen sense of duty and vision. Each minister presented their sector's achievements and projections, with Serena ensuring alignment with the broader goals of her administration.

Finally, as the meeting drew to a close, Serena stood and addressed her council. "Your dedication and hard work have been the backbone of this year's successes. Let's move forward with the same commitment, ensuring that the policies we implement are not only effective but also sustainable."

The ministers nodded in agreement, inspired by her leadership and the clear direction she had set. As they left the room, the warmth from the fireplace lingered, a metaphor for the enduring efforts that would continue to light their way forward.

Serena remained a moment longer, reflecting on the discussions. The winter outside might bring cold and stillness, but within the walls of the palace, the plans and preparations promised a vibrant and dynamic new year. Each conversation, each decision taken today, was a step towards a future where Eirene not only prospered but also became a model of sustainable and inclusive growth.

Chapter 13
Gathering Forces

The dawn of the new year brought a fresh blanket of snow to the kingdom of Eirene, transforming the landscape into a serene tableau of white. Within the warm confines of the palace, Queen Serena convened the first meeting of the year, aimed at ensuring the swift implementation of the initiatives planned in the previous months. Gathered in the vibrant Sun Room, where the morning light spilled over the colorful tapestries and illuminated the faces of her ministers, the mood was one of optimism and determination.

"Good morning, everyone," Serena began, her voice echoing the bright promise of the day. "As we stand at the threshold of a new year, our focus must be on action and impact. Minister Lorne, let's start with the expansion of the agricultural cooperatives. Where do we stand?"

Minister Lorne, ever organized, laid out his documents before replying. "Your Majesty, we've successfully identified three additional regions for the cooperative expansion. The local communities have been briefed, and we're seeing enthusiastic participation from the farmers. We are on schedule to launch these cooperatives by the spring planting season."

"That is excellent to hear," Serena responded with a nod. "What measures are we putting in place to ensure these cooperatives are as successful as the pilots?"

"We're implementing a mentorship program, where successful farmers from the pilot programs mentor the new participants," Lorne explained. "Additionally, we're integrating technology for better crop monitoring and management."

"Very well," Serena said, satisfied. "Now, turning to healthcare—Minister Halen, how are we progressing with the mobile health clinics?"

Minister Halen, looking upbeat, answered, "The mobile clinics are set to deploy next month, Your Majesty. They are equipped with the necessary medical technology to provide comprehensive care. We've also partnered with local healthcare providers to ensure continuity of care."

"And the training programs for healthcare workers?" Serena inquired further.

"We've increased the frequency of our training sessions, focusing particularly on emergency care and disease prevention," Halen detailed. "The feedback has been very positive, and we're seeing improved healthcare outcomes as a result."

"That's heartening," Serena remarked. "Education is next. Minister Tala, please update us on the integration of coding and digital literacy into our curriculum."

Minister Tala, enthusiastic about the progress, shared, "The new curriculum modules are ready, Your Majesty, and will be introduced this semester. We've trained our teachers over the winter break, and they're equipped to deliver these modules effectively."

"And the cultural studies program?" Serena probed, knowing its importance in maintaining the kingdom's heritage.

"It's expanding, Your Majesty," Tala replied. "We've developed interactive modules that include virtual tours of historical sites and collaborations with local artisans. The program now also includes a student exchange component to promote cultural appreciation and understanding."

"Excellent," Serena smiled. "I believe these programs will not only educate but inspire our youth."

As the meeting continued, each update bolstered Serena's confidence in her team and their shared vision for the future. The dialogue was not just about reporting but a vibrant exchange of ideas and strategies, reflecting the dynamic spirit that Serena had always envisioned for her council.

As the session drew to a close, Serena concluded, "This year is crucial for us. We need to ensure that our initiatives not only take root but flourish. I trust in each of you to lead your sectors with integrity and innovation."

The ministers left the meeting energized, ready to tackle the year's challenges. Serena lingered for a moment, looking out at the snowy landscape, a symbol of the blank slate they were given each year to redraw the contours of Eirene's future.

With a deep sense of responsibility and anticipation, she prepared for her next engagement, carrying with her the steadfast belief that together, they were building a legacy of prosperity and resilience for Eirene. Each step forward was guided by thoughtful planning and the collective will of her devoted council.

Later in the year, with the kingdom in the full bloom of spring, Queen Serena turned her focus towards Eirene's youth, the future stewards of her realm. She organized a summit specifically for young leaders from across the kingdom, held in the lush gardens of the royal estate, where the vibrant colors and fresh air provided a perfect backdrop for fresh ideas and youthful enthusiasm.

The summit attendees were a diverse group: students, young entrepreneurs, artists, and community activists. Each was eager to share their vision and to learn how they might contribute to the ongoing development of Eirene. Serena, dressed in a simple yet elegant gown that mirrored the informal yet earnest nature of the event, initiated the discussions with a welcoming speech.

"Thank you all for joining this summit," Serena began, her voice imbued with genuine excitement. "Today is about your voices, your ideas, and how you envision the future of our kingdom. Let's share, discuss, and inspire each other."

A young woman, a recent graduate in environmental science, was the first to speak. "Your Majesty, I appreciate this opportunity. I believe Eirene can lead in sustainable living. Could we consider expanding the environmental curriculum in schools to include hands-on projects that not only teach but also actively contribute to our communities?"

"That's an excellent suggestion," Serena responded warmly. "Education that connects directly with real-world applications is powerful. Minister

Tala, could we integrate this proposal into the existing curriculum reforms?"

Minister Tala, present at the meeting, nodded. "Absolutely, Your Majesty. Practical, project-based learning can be highly effective. We'll explore partnerships with environmental organizations to create these opportunities."

Another participant, a young man who had started a tech cooperative in his hometown, chimed in. "Your Majesty, for many young entrepreneurs like myself, access to early funding and mentorship is a huge barrier. Can the kingdom support a program to connect young innovators with experienced mentors and potential investors?"

Serena considered the idea thoughtfully. "Supporting young entrepreneurs is crucial for our economy's growth and diversity. Let's establish a royal grant program specifically for young entrepreneurs, and set up events where you can pitch your ideas to investors. Minister Lorne, please take the lead on this initiative."

"I will begin the preparations immediately, Your Majesty," Minister Lorne confirmed, jotting down notes.

The dialogue continued, with another young leader discussing the potential for cultural exchanges that could broaden international understanding and bring global perspectives to Eirenean youth. Serena listened intently, her eyes reflecting her appreciation for the innovative ideas being presented.

"International exchanges are a cornerstone for building global relationships and understanding," Serena acknowledged. "Let's expand our current exchange programs to include more countries and disciplines."

As the summit progressed, the discussions deepened, covering topics from healthcare innovation to the arts. Serena facilitated the conversations, ensuring every voice was heard, every suggestion considered.

As the meeting drew to a close, Serena stood and addressed the group once more. "Today has been incredibly insightful. Your energy and commitment to our kingdom's future are inspiring. Let's continue this dialogue and turn these ideas into actions. Together, we will shape an Eirene that is vibrant, sustainable, and inclusive."

The young leaders applauded, motivated by the queen's engagement and the tangible outcomes of their discussions. They left the summit with a sense of purpose and a commitment to contribute positively to their communities.

Serena remained in the gardens for a while after everyone had departed, contemplating the promising future shaped by the young minds she had just engaged with. She felt reassured that the future of Eirene was in capable hands, as each young leader returned to their corner of the kingdom, energized to enact the change they wished to see. The discussions of today were planting the seeds for the innovations of tomorrow, ensuring that the kingdom's progression was as perennial as the spring around her.

As the days grew longer and the air warmer, Queen Serena continued her steadfast work, overseeing the various initiatives that had begun to transform the landscape of Eirene. It was a period of profound growth and subtle challenges, each day bringing with it the promise of progress and the necessity for vigilance. The initiatives born from the youthful summit were now taking root, and Serena was keen to ensure they grew strong and viable.

In the heart of Eirene's capital, a new cultural center, initially proposed at the youth summit, was nearing completion. Its architecture—a blend of traditional Eirenean styles with modern design—symbolized the fusion of heritage and innovation that Serena had championed. This center was intended not just as a hub for the arts but also as a space for community learning and interaction, reflecting the dynamic spirit of the kingdom's youth.

One afternoon, Serena visited the site to review its progress. Walking through the spacious atrium, she could envision the exhibitions and performances that would soon fill the space with life and color. She discussed with the project manager the final preparations needed before the grand opening, emphasizing the importance of accessibility so that all citizens, regardless of background or ability, could enjoy the facility.

"Accessibility is key," Serena affirmed, as the manager noted her directives. "Let's ensure that everyone who visits feels welcomed and valued."

The discussion was brief but productive, with both parties satisfied with the course of action. Serena's visit was a reassurance to the workers and planners alike that their efforts were recognized and appreciated at the highest levels.

Meanwhile, the royal grant program for young entrepreneurs, another outcome of the summit, was in full swing. Serena received regular updates on the program, which had already funded a dozen new startups, ranging from sustainable farming initiatives to digital education tools. Each report detailed the progress and challenges faced by these burgeoning companies, and Serena read each one with a keen interest, aware that the success of these ventures was a critical measure of her policies' effectiveness.

On one particular evening, Serena hosted a small reception at the palace for the first cohort of grant recipients. The event allowed her to engage directly with the young entrepreneurs, listening to their stories and sharing in their early successes and obstacles.

"I am truly inspired by what you are achieving," Serena told them. "Your innovations are the seeds of Eirene's future prosperity."

The dialogue was limited but meaningful, with each entrepreneur expressing gratitude for the support that had turned their visions into reality. They spoke of the impact of their work on their communities and their hopes for the future.

As summer approached, Serena's attention also turned to the expansion of the health and education initiatives. She made several unannounced visits to the new healthcare facilities in remote areas, ensuring that the services provided met the high standards promised by her administration.

Each visit was an opportunity to speak with both patients and healthcare providers, gaining insights into the effectiveness of the new programs and facilities.

In education, the expanded digital classroom program was under review. Serena attended a series of virtual classes, observing firsthand how teachers and students interacted with the new technology and curriculum. Her presence was a quiet but powerful reminder to all involved that the queen herself was deeply invested in the educational future of her kingdom's children.

Each day ended with Serena reviewing her notes and plans, often late into the night. The weight of her crown was a constant reminder of her duty to her people, but it was a weight she bore willingly and with honor. For Serena, these were not just projects to be managed but commitments to be nurtured, each one contributing to a tapestry of national vitality that would cover and protect all Eireneans.

As she prepared for another day, Serena felt a profound connection to the rhythm of her kingdom's life—its challenges and its triumphs. Her leadership, guided by both wisdom and the willingness to listen, continued to steer Eirene toward a future bright with possibility. Each initiative, each policy, each day was another stitch in the fabric of a resilient, thriving society.

As the summer sun set slowly behind the hills, casting long shadows across the land, Queen Serena decided it was time to revisit the communities to see the impact of her policies. The queen, alongside her advisors, planned a tour of various projects, beginning with the newly established cultural center in the capital. Her aim was to gather feedback and understand firsthand the successes and areas needing improvement.

At the cultural center, Serena was met by the director, Mr. Eldric, who was eager to show her around and discuss the facility's impact on the community. They walked through the bustling halls, filled with visitors of all ages engaged in various workshops and exhibitions.

"Your Majesty, the response has been overwhelmingly positive," Mr. Eldric began, leading Serena into a vibrant gallery. "Our workshops have been particularly popular, providing both young and old with a place to learn and express themselves creatively."

Serena smiled, observing a group of children focused intently on their painting. "It's wonderful to see such engagement. What are the challenges you've encountered so far?"

"We've seen a greater demand than anticipated, which is fantastic, but it does stretch our resources," Mr. Eldric replied. "Particularly, we're looking at needing more facilitators for our programs."

"Let's explore partnerships with local universities and art schools. Students could gain experience teaching here, and we could meet the demand," Serena suggested thoughtfully.

"A splendid idea, Your Majesty," Mr. Eldric agreed enthusiastically. "I will initiate discussions with educational institutions immediately."

Their conversation continued, with Serena taking notes and asking detailed questions about the center's operations and future plans. Each answer provided her with insights into how well her vision was being translated into reality.

Next, Serena visited a small town that had benefited from the agricultural cooperative initiatives. She met with a group of farmers who shared their experiences and the changes they had noticed.

"Your Majesty, the cooperative has changed our lives," one farmer, a middle-aged woman named Mara, explained. "We have better access to markets now, and our profits are more stable."

"I'm pleased to hear that, Mara," Serena responded, genuinely relieved. "What improvements would make the cooperative even more beneficial for you?"

"If we had more storage facilities, we could manage our produce better and reduce waste," another farmer chimed in.

Serena nodded, making a note. "I will ensure that the expansion of storage facilities is considered in our next budget review."

The tour continued, with Serena visiting several more sites, including a new healthcare clinic in a remote village. Here, she spoke with healthcare staff and patients, who shared their appreciation for the improved access to medical services.

"The new clinic has been a blessing, Your Majesty," a nurse told her. "Especially for our elderly patients who struggled to travel far for care."

"How can we improve our services here?" Serena asked, her tone inviting honest feedback.

"Perhaps more specialist visits? Some conditions still require our patients to travel to the city," the nurse suggested.

"Let's look into a schedule for specialists to visit monthly. I want everyone to have access to the care they need, regardless of where they live," Serena decided, her commitment unwavering.

With each visit, Serena deepened her understanding of the impacts of her policies. The feedback was invaluable, not just in affirming the success of many initiatives but in highlighting areas where additional resources or adjustments were needed.

As the tour concluded and Serena returned to the palace, she felt a renewed sense of purpose. The discussions of the day had not only strengthened her resolve to continue her work but had also reinforced the bond between her crown and her people. Each conversation, each site visit was a reminder of her commitment to serve and uplift every citizen of Eirene. Her reign, defined by these moments of connection and progress, continued to shape a kingdom that was not only prosperous but also compassionate and united.

Chapter 14
The Siege of the Forgotten Palace

As the vibrant hues of autumn once again draped themselves over the kingdom of Eirene, the air was crisp with the scent of change and the rustle of falling leaves. This season marked not only the turning of the year but also the nearing completion of Queen Serena's first comprehensive five-year plan—a plan designed to fortify the kingdom's infrastructure, enhance its educational systems, and enrich the lives of all its citizens.

Throughout her reign, Serena had focused on creating a sustainable future for Eirene, one that balanced growth with conservation, innovation with tradition. Now, as she walked through the royal gardens, reflecting on the years past, she was keenly aware of the milestones achieved and the challenges that still lay ahead.

The new network of roads linking remote villages with major cities was nearly complete. This infrastructure project, the largest undertaken during her reign, was crucial for fostering economic growth and ensuring that no part of her kingdom was isolated from the advancements of the era. As Serena reviewed reports from her ministers, she noted the increased trade activity and the improvements in emergency services that the new roads facilitated.

Education reform had been another pillar of her plan. Digital learning hubs established across the kingdom had become centers of innovation and learning. The hubs not only provided students with access to global knowledge and digital skills but also connected Eirenean educators with international experts. Although the transition had not been without its hurdles, the overall feedback was overwhelmingly positive. Parents appreciated the new opportunities available to their children, and young learners thrived under the updated curriculum that prepared them for a rapidly changing world.

However, the journey was not merely about building roads or enhancing educational facilities. Serena's vision included strengthening the cultural fabric of Eirene, ensuring that progress did not erode the rich heritage that defined her people. To this end, the cultural centers established in major towns had started hosting monthly festivals, celebrating everything from traditional Eirenean music and dance to contemporary arts and theater. These centers had become hubs of community life, places where the old and the young could share stories and skills, weaving a tapestry of shared identity and mutual respect.

Serena's commitment to healthcare also saw significant strides with the establishment of regional healthcare centers equipped with the latest medical technology. These centers had significantly reduced the travel time for medical care for many rural citizens and introduced preventive healthcare programs that helped catch potential health issues before they became emergencies.

As autumn deepened, Serena knew that the true measure of her policies' success would be their longevity and their ability to adapt to future needs. She planned a series of town hall meetings to gather direct feedback from her citizens, intending to understand their perspectives and experiences firsthand.

One cool evening, as she prepared her notes for these upcoming engagements, Serena pondered the weight of her crown and the responsibilities it entailed. Each decision she made, each initiative she launched, was with the hope of leaving behind a legacy of a stronger, more connected Eirene.

Tomorrow, she would travel to the northern provinces to see the effects of the new agricultural programs designed to increase sustainability in farming practices. Her heart was set on hearing directly from the farmers and landowners about the impacts of these programs.

As the night drew in and the stars began to dot the sky, Serena felt a quiet confidence in the path she had chosen for Eirene. The challenges were many, but the achievements were real and tangible. As she retired for the evening, her thoughts lingered on the faces of the people she served— faces that mirrored hope and gratitude, faces that inspired her to continue her journey of service and stewardship. Each step she took, each policy she crafted, was a brick in the foundation of a thriving kingdom that she hoped would withstand the tests of time and change.

With the golden hues of autumn painting the landscape, Queen Serena embarked on her visit to the northern provinces, an area of Eirene that had seen some of the most significant changes due to her agricultural initiatives. The purpose of her visit was multifaceted: to observe the harvest, to engage with the local farmers, and to assess the sustainability of the new practices that had been implemented over the past year.

The morning was brisk as Serena, dressed warmly, arrived at the first of many farms on her itinerary. Here, innovative methods of crop rotation and organic farming had been introduced, transforming what had once been tired soil into fertile ground teeming with life. The farm's owner, a middle-aged man named Eron, greeted her with a proud smile and a firm handshake.

"Your Majesty, it's an honor to welcome you," Eron began, his voice rich with the pride of a seasoned farmer. "Let me show you the fruits of our labor."

As they walked through the fields, Eron pointed out the different crops that were now part of the rotation—legumes, grains, and root vegetables. "This rotation has not only improved yield but also soil health," he explained. "We've seen a significant decrease in the need for chemical fertilizers."

"That's exactly what we hoped for," Serena replied, examining a handful of rich earth. "Sustainability is key. How have the other farmers adapted to these changes?"

"It was challenging at first, but the results speak for themselves. Now, many are enthusiastic about adopting these methods," Eron answered. "The support from your advisors and the training workshops have made a big difference."

Serena nodded, pleased with the progress. "Continued education and support are crucial. We must ensure everyone who wants to adopt these methods has the resources and knowledge to do so effectively."

As the tour continued, Serena met with other farmers, each sharing stories of success and the occasional setback. The discussions were candid, providing Serena with invaluable insights into the real-world impacts of her policies. The farmers expressed gratitude for the changes but also pointed out areas where additional support could make a difference, such as more localized seed banks and further advancements in irrigation technology.

In the afternoon, Serena visited a newly established cooperative where farmers pooled their resources to buy equipment and sell their produce collectively. The cooperative's manager, a dynamic young woman named Lila, shared her perspective.

"We've been able to negotiate better prices and reduce our costs significantly," Lila explained. "It's empowering. We're retaining more profits and reinvesting in our community."

"I'm delighted to hear that," Serena said. "Empowering communities to take charge of their economic future is a cornerstone of our agricultural policy."

The visit concluded with a roundtable discussion at the local community center. Here, Serena listened more than she spoke, taking notes as various stakeholders—farmers, local business owners, and representatives from the agricultural ministry—discussed the ongoing challenges and opportunities.

The dialogue was constructive, with many expressing a hopeful outlook on the future. They discussed the potential expansion of organic markets and the integration of technology in farming, from soil health sensors to data-driven crop management systems.

As the sun began to set, casting long shadows over the fields, Serena felt a deep sense of accomplishment mixed with the responsibility of continuing to support these initiatives. The feedback from today would inform further enhancements and funding allocations to ensure the longevity and success of the agricultural reforms.

Leaving the northern provinces, Serena looked back at the sprawling fields, now ready for harvest. The journey back to the palace was a time for reflection. Each visit, each conversation had not only strengthened her resolve but had also deepened her understanding of the practical application of her policies.

Tomorrow would bring more challenges, more decisions, but for now, Serena was content in knowing that her efforts were bearing fruit, changing lives for the better and weaving a stronger, more sustainable future for all of Eirene.

Queen Serena's commitment to her kingdom's flourishing future brought her next to the bustling city of Veridian, where she planned to inspect urban development projects and discuss urban planning with city officials and community leaders. The meeting was held in the city hall, a building as historic as it was grand, reflecting the city's vibrant past and its dynamic future.

As Serena entered the large conference room, she was greeted by Mayor Elden, along with his team of urban planners and several community leaders. The atmosphere was charged with anticipation, everyone prepared to share insights and seek guidance on enhancing the city's infrastructure and livability.

"Good morning, everyone," Serena started, settling into her seat at the head of the table. "I'm here today to discuss how we can further support Veridian's growth and ensure that our urban planning aligns with both our environmental goals and the well-being of its citizens."

Mayor Elden nodded, appreciative of her proactive approach. "Thank you, Your Majesty. One of our main concerns is the integration of green spaces within the city. As Veridian expands, we want to ensure that we're not just building upwards but also creating breathable, livable spaces for our residents."

"That's a priority for us as well," Serena agreed. "Green spaces are essential for the health and happiness of our citizens. What specific initiatives are you considering?"

"We are planning to convert several abandoned industrial sites into parks and community gardens," the Mayor explained. "However, funding and maintaining these spaces are our main challenges."

"Perhaps we could explore partnerships with private businesses for the development and upkeep of these parks," Serena suggested. "Corporate sponsorships could be a way to fund these projects, with companies benefiting from tax incentives."

"That's an excellent idea," a senior urban planner added. "We could also incorporate community involvement in the maintenance of these gardens, fostering a sense of ownership and community spirit."

"I like that approach," Serena said, nodding. "Engaging the community not only eases maintenance burdens but also strengthens communal ties. What about public transportation? How are we addressing the growing needs of Veridian's population?"

"We're in the process of extending our metro lines and adding more eco-friendly buses to our fleet," another planner responded. "Yet, funding remains a hurdle, and ensuring efficient connectivity between new and old parts of the city is a complex challenge."

"Let's consider applying for international green grants," Serena proposed. "There are funds available for cities taking innovative steps towards sustainability. We should leverage our environmental initiatives to access these resources."

"That would be invaluable," Mayor Elden agreed. "We'll need your support to navigate the application process."

"You'll have it," Serena assured him. "Improving our city's infrastructure is a critical component of our national development. Also, how are we incorporating technology in managing city services?"

"We've started using smart technology to improve our waste management systems," a technology advisor chimed in. "Sensors in bins that alert management when full and optimized routes for collection are reducing operational costs and environmental impact."

"Expanding that technology to other utilities could yield similar benefits," Serena noted. "Energy management, for example, could be significantly optimized."

"The potential is enormous," the advisor agreed. "We'll prepare a proposal on how we can expand these technologies to other sectors."

As the meeting drew to a close, Serena expressed her satisfaction with the progress and the collaborative spirit of the discussion. "This has been a productive meeting. Let's continue to push forward with innovative and sustainable solutions to urban development. Veridian is not just a city; it's a reflection of our kingdom's progress."

Grateful nods and smiles filled the room as the meeting adjourned. Serena left City Hall feeling confident in the path Veridian was on. Each step taken in this city, under her guidance, was a blueprint for the future, ensuring that as Eirene grew, it did so thoughtfully and sustainably, setting a standard for cities everywhere.

Serena's day concluded with a quiet stroll through one of Veridian's oldest parks, contemplating the discussions of the day. Each conversation, each decision, formed part of the intricate mosaic of her reign, each piece essential to the whole, each effort a step toward a prosperous future.

As autumn's crispness began to soften into the colder embrace of early winter, Queen Serena convened a roundtable discussion focused on enhancing community engagement across Eirene. The meeting was held in the newly established community center in Veridian, which had become a symbol of civic pride and involvement. The participants included community leaders, local government officials, and representatives from various non-governmental organizations (NGOs).

Serena opened the meeting with a welcoming smile, acknowledging each attendee before beginning. "Thank you all for joining this discussion. Today, we focus on how we can further catalyze community engagement in our civic projects and local governance. I believe that for our initiatives to be truly successful, they must be supported and propelled by the community."

A seasoned community leader, Mr. Harrow, took the lead. "Your Majesty, we appreciate your commitment. One challenge we often face is the lack of consistent participation. People are initially enthusiastic but maintaining that interest over time can be difficult."

Serena nodded thoughtfully. "What strategies do you think could help sustain engagement?"

"We need to create more inclusive platforms where community members feel their contributions are valued," Mr. Harrow suggested. "Perhaps regular feedback sessions and visible implementation of community-sourced ideas could reinforce their involvement."

"That's a vital point," Serena agreed. "Inclusivity is key. Let's plan to establish these feedback mechanisms. We could use this very community center as a pilot model for regular town hall meetings."

Ms. Tiller, a representative from an NGO focused on civic education, added, "Education plays a crucial role as well. Many citizens feel disconnected because they don't fully understand how local government works or how they can influence it."

"Indeed," Serena responded. "Let's expand our civic education programs. We could partner with schools and community centers like this one to offer workshops and courses that demystify governance."

"That would be incredibly beneficial," Ms. Tiller said, making a note. "Empowered citizens are engaged citizens."

As the discussion progressed, a young community organizer, Lena, highlighted the potential of digital platforms. "With many young people engaged online, creating digital forums and apps for civic participation could bridge the gap between the government and younger generations."

"That's an excellent suggestion, Lena," Serena said, visibly excited by the idea. "Digital engagement could indeed be a game-changer. Minister Lorne, could we explore the development of a digital civic engagement platform?"

"Certainly, Your Majesty," Minister Lorne replied. "We can start by consulting with tech experts and young people to understand what features they would find most useful and engaging."

The conversation turned towards volunteerism, with another leader, Mr. Fen, discussing how rewarding volunteer efforts can strengthen community bonds. "If people see the tangible results of their volunteerism, not just in their environment but in social recognition, it encourages continued participation."

"Recognition is important," Serena acknowledged. "Perhaps we could institute an annual celebration of volunteers, with awards and public acknowledgment of their contributions."

As the meeting drew to a close, Serena summarized the key points discussed. "Today's insights have been invaluable. By fostering education, creating inclusive and responsive engagement platforms, and recognizing our citizens' efforts, we can strengthen our communities."

Everyone left the meeting energized and optimistic, ready to take the discussed ideas back to their communities and start implementing them. Serena stayed behind for a few moments, speaking individually with several attendees, reinforcing her commitment to the initiatives discussed.

Walking through the community center once the room had cleared, Serena felt a renewed sense of connection with her people. Each conversation and each shared idea was a step towards a more engaged and cohesive community. The winds of winter might be cold, but the seeds of community engagement planted today promised to yield a warm and vibrant civic life for all Eireneans.

Chapter 15
The Power of the Crown

As winter draped its silvery cloak over the kingdom of Eirene, Queen Serena turned her attention to a project that resonated deeply with her heart: the restoration of historical landmarks. This initiative was not just about preserving architecture but about revitalizing the stories and heritage that these landmarks represented. To discuss the progress and planning, she convened a meeting with historians, architects, and cultural preservationists in the royal library, a fitting venue surrounded by tomes of Eirenean history.

The room was filled with the soft glow of oil lamps, casting gentle light on the ancient books that lined the walls. As the participants gathered around a large oak table, Serena initiated the discussion with a tone of reverence for the task at hand.

"Thank you all for joining me this evening," Serena began. "Our historical landmarks are not only treasures of architectural beauty but also repositories of our shared past. How are we progressing with the restoration of the Old Fortress?"

Dr. Merek, the lead historian, was the first to speak. "Your Majesty, the restoration is well underway. We've managed to preserve much of the original stonework, and the archaeological finds have been quite remarkable. They tell us more about the fortress's role in our history."

"That's wonderful to hear," Serena replied. "It's crucial that we not only restore but also interpret these sites correctly for future generations. What challenges are we facing?"

"The main challenge," noted Engineer Thorne, responsible for the physical restoration, "is integrating modern preservation technology without compromising the integrity of the original structures. We're working closely with conservation experts to ensure that our methods are both effective and respectful of the past."

"I appreciate that meticulousness," Serena said. "Preservation is delicate work. What about public engagement? Are we planning exhibitions or educational programs around these landmarks?"

"Yes, Your Majesty," responded Ms. Lirette, a cultural preservationist. "We're developing a series of exhibitions that will rotate through the restored sites. Each exhibition will focus on different aspects of Eirene's history, accompanied by interactive educational programs designed to engage both schools and the general public."

"Engagement is key," Serena affirmed. "We want our citizens to feel connected to their heritage. What support do you need from me to enhance these efforts?"

"Funding for multimedia resources would greatly enhance the visitor experience," Ms. Lirette suggested. "Virtual reality experiences, for instance, could bring historic battles or daily life in ancient times to vivid life for visitors."

"That's an excellent idea," Serena enthused. "Let's allocate resources for that. I want these sites to be places where history comes alive, where every Eirenean can walk through the echoes of their ancestors' lives."

As the conversation continued, each participant contributed ideas and expertise, weaving together a comprehensive plan that bridged the past with the present. The discussions were rich with enthusiasm and a shared sense of purpose, reflecting the collective commitment to heritage and education.

"Lastly," Serena concluded as the meeting drew to a close, "let's ensure these sites are accessible to all. No one should be barred from exploring their own country's history. We'll include paths for those with mobility issues and sign language guides for the hearing impaired."

The group agreed wholeheartedly, and as they departed, each was buoyed by the meaningful work ahead. Serena lingered in the library, surrounded by the whispers of ages past, feeling a profound connection to the work they were undertaking. These landmarks were not just stone and mortar; they were the soul of Eirene, and through their preservation, she was keeping the spirit of her people alive and vibrant.

As she left the library, the snow outside seemed to sparkle a little brighter under the moonlight, mirroring the renewed sparkle of Eirene's historical legacy that she was determined to illuminate. Each step taken in this project was a step towards reconnecting her people with their roots, ensuring that the kingdom's history would continue to inspire and guide its future.

Queen Serena's dedication to preserving Eirene's cultural heritage brought her to the ancient town of Marlowe, home to one of the oldest theaters in the kingdom, which had recently been restored. Today, she was attending its grand reopening, a celebration not just of the theater's physical restoration but of its historical and cultural significance to Eirene.

As the curtains parted, revealing the beautifully restored interior, the crowd, including Serena, was visibly moved. The theater's ornate carvings and vibrant frescoes had been meticulously restored, each detail telling a story of artistic endeavors spanning centuries.

After the initial ceremony, Serena, accompanied by the Minister of Culture, Mr. Caelan, and the theater's director, Ms. Elara, walked through the foyer where historical displays had been set up.

"Your Majesty, this theater is more than a venue; it's a testament to our artistic heritage," Ms. Elara began, her voice echoing slightly in the high-ceilinged space.

"It's magnificent," Serena responded, admiring a display of original playbills. "Tell me, how have you planned to integrate the community with this wonderful space?"

"We've scheduled a series of plays and concerts that reflect Eirene's history and diversity," Ms. Elara explained. "Additionally, we are introducing workshops and talks by historians and playwrights to educate our visitors about the theater's significance and the broader context of Eirenean arts."

"That's excellent," Serena nodded in approval. "Engagement with the arts is essential for fostering a well-rounded society. How can we further support these initiatives?"

"Perhaps by establishing a fund to support local playwrights and artists who wish to present their work here," suggested Mr. Caelan. "Such a fund could help ensure that the theater remains a lively and dynamic part of our cultural landscape."

"I like that idea very much," Serena agreed. "Let's set that up. I believe supporting our artists is key to keeping our cultural heritage alive."

As they continued their tour, the conversation turned to the challenges of maintaining such a historic site. Ms. Elara voiced a concern, "While the restoration has brought this theater back to life, ongoing maintenance will be crucial to preserve its beauty and structural integrity."

"Let's ensure we have a dedicated team for that," Serena said thoughtfully. "Preservation is as important as restoration. We must keep this place as splendid as it is today for future generations."

The conversation flowed into the logistics of such maintenance, with Mr. Caelan outlining a preliminary plan for regular reviews and conservation efforts.

As the tour concluded and they prepared to enjoy a performance of a classic Eirenean play, Serena addressed the theater staff and the restoration team. "Your hard work and dedication shine through in every corner of this theater. Thank you for helping preserve our cultural treasures. This place is a bridge from our past to our future, and you have all played a part in building that bridge."

Applause filled the room, and as the lights dimmed to signal the beginning of the performance, Serena took her seat, reflecting on the day's discussions. Each dialogue had reinforced her commitment to cultural preservation and had highlighted the community's role in sustaining these efforts.

As the actors took the stage, the magic of the theater enveloped the audience. For Serena, this was a vivid reminder of why her work mattered: it was about creating moments like this, where history and art came alive, touching the hearts and minds of her people. This theater, restored to its former glory, was now ready to host countless such moments, each one weaving the rich tapestry of Eirene's cultural identity, now and into the future.

As the restoration of historical sites across Eirene progressed, Queen Serena dedicated a day to visit the Royal Archives, a repository of the kingdom's most treasured documents and artifacts. The Archives, housed in a grand stone building that had stood the test of time, were undergoing a significant digital transformation project, aimed at preserving the delicate pages of history for future generations.

On a crisp morning that hinted at the coming of spring, Serena, cloaked against the chill, made her way through the cobblestone streets of the capital to the Archives. The air was filled with the promise of renewal, and as she entered the hallowed halls of the building, she was greeted by the Archivist, Master Toren, whose life's work had been dedicated to the preservation of Eirenean history.

"Your Majesty, welcome to the Archives," Master Toren began, his voice a soft echo in the vast, book-lined corridor. "Let me show you the advancements we've made in digital preservation."

As they walked through the dimly lit corridors, Serena observed the meticulous process of digitizing ancient texts. Each page was carefully photographed using state-of-the-art equipment that ensured no further wear on the fragile documents.

"It's impressive," Serena remarked, watching as a particularly old manuscript was gently placed on the scanner. "How are we ensuring that these digital copies remain safe for the long term?"

"We're using multiple redundancies in our storage solutions," Master Toren explained. "Each document is stored in several digital formats and across multiple secure locations. Additionally, we are constantly updating our storage technology to keep up with the latest advancements in digital preservation."

Serena nodded, satisfied with the thoroughness of the approach. "It's vital that these documents are preserved not just physically but also in a format that will be accessible for centuries to come."

Their walk took them next to a section of the Archives that had recently been restored. Here, ancient maps and treaties were displayed, each piece a testament to Eirene's rich and complex history. Serena paused before a map depicting Eirene as it was two centuries ago, tracing the borders with her finger.

"Seeing our history laid out like this, it truly brings into perspective the journey we've been on as a kingdom," she mused.

"Yes, Your Majesty," Master Toren agreed. "These maps are not just geographical representations; they are stories of our ancestors' lives and struggles."

As they continued their tour, Serena's thoughts turned to the broader implications of the Archives' work. Preserving history was more than just a duty; it was a bridge to the past that informed the future. She considered the impact of making these digital archives available to the public, particularly to educational institutions.

"Master Toren, once the digitization project is complete, I would like to initiate a program to integrate these resources into our schools' curricula," Serena proposed. "Our students should have access to these documents, to learn directly from the primary sources of their history."

"That would be most wise, Your Majesty," Master Toren replied, his eyes brightening at the idea. "Education is the key to appreciation and preservation."

The visit concluded with Serena reaffirming her commitment to the Archives and their work. As she stepped out of the building, back into the sunlight that now streaked through the clearing clouds, her mind was filled with the day's discoveries. The work done here was a critical piece of the kingdom's cultural puzzle, ensuring that the threads of history would continue to weave through the fabric of Eirenean society, connecting past, present, and future in an unbreakable chain of knowledge and legacy.

As winter's grip loosened and the first signs of spring whispered through the kingdom of Eirene, Queen Serena's focus shifted towards enriching the kingdom's educational landscape with the vast historical knowledge now digitally preserved from the Royal Archives. It was a project close to her heart, believing firmly that a nation's future is shaped by understanding its past.

One crisp morning, Serena convened a meeting with her educational advisors and key historians in the palace's sunlit conservatory, where the scents of blooming flowers were beginning to permeate the air. Here, amidst the burgeoning signs of spring, they discussed integrating the kingdom's rich history into school curriculums across Eirene.

"Good morning, everyone," Serena started, her tone imbued with a sense of purpose. "Today, we lay down a plan to bring our history to the classrooms of Eirene. Our children must grow up knowing the stories of those who walked these lands before them."

Minister Tala, overseeing the kingdom's education, was quick to respond. "Your Majesty, we've begun to outline a curriculum that includes interactive lessons based on the digitized documents. These lessons will allow students to explore Eirenean history through primary sources, offering them a more engaging and immersive learning experience."

"That sounds wonderful," Serena replied, clearly pleased. "How will we ensure that these lessons reach all students, regardless of their location?"

"We plan to use a combination of digital access and physical materials. For schools in remote areas, we'll provide tablets loaded with the digital archives," Minister Tala explained. "Additionally, we're scheduling traveling exhibitions that will visit these schools, bringing with them artifacts and replicas from the Archives."

Serena nodded thoughtfully, her mind considering the logistical challenges and the opportunities this plan presented. "And what about training for our teachers? They will need to be familiar with these materials to effectively teach them."

"We are scheduling a series of workshops for teachers over the summer," the head of the Teacher Training Program interjected. "These will not only cover the new material but also instructional techniques for engaging students with digital and physical historical resources."

"Excellent," Serena acknowledged. "Engaged learning is effective learning. It's crucial our teachers feel prepared and supported."

As the meeting progressed, the dialogue delved into specifics—budget allocations, potential partnerships with technology firms, and the involvement of historians as guest lecturers. Each point was meticulously discussed, ensuring the initiative's success.

Before the meeting concluded, Serena addressed the group once more. "This project is more than just an educational initiative; it's a way to honor our heritage and inspire our future leaders. Let's proceed with enthusiasm and diligence."

After the meeting, Serena decided to visit a local school that was piloting an interactive history module. As she entered the classroom, she was greeted by a group of lively students, eager to show their projects based on the battles of ancient Eirenean warriors.

A young student, barely twelve, approached her with a tablet in hand, showing a map he had created based on an old battle plan from the Archives. "Your Majesty, look what I made! I can tell you all about the Battle of Elden Hill now!"

Serena listened intently as the boy explained his project, her heart swelling with pride and hope. It was moments like these that reinforced the value of her initiatives—seeing young minds excited about their history and heritage.

Leaving the school, the fresh spring air felt invigorating. Serena walked back to her carriage, her steps light, her resolve firm. This day had been a reaffirmation of her commitment to education and heritage—a commitment that would continue to shape the cultural and intellectual landscape of Eirene for generations to come. Each student like the boy with his battle map was a testament to the lasting impact of her work, weaving new threads into the enduring tapestry of Eirenean legacy.

Chapter 16
The Battle of Wills

As the gentle warmth of spring began to chase away the last chills of winter across Eirene, Queen Serena's vision for a more interconnected kingdom took a significant step forward with the inauguration of the new cross-kingdom highway—a project that promised to enhance trade, improve access to services, and unite various parts of the kingdom like never before.

The grand opening was held at the central junction of the highway, where paths from the northern mountains and southern coastlines converged. Political dignitaries, local leaders, and citizens from across Eirene had gathered to witness this historic event. As Serena arrived, she was met with applause and cheers, a testament to the popular support for this transformative project.

"Thank you, everyone, for such a warm welcome," Serena began, addressing the crowd from a dais adorned with the flowers of spring. "Today is not just about a new road. It's about forging new connections, opening new opportunities, and bringing our kingdom closer together."

Minister of Transportation, Lord Garren, stood beside her, his eyes bright with the success of his department's efforts. "Your Majesty, this highway is a testament to your vision. It will not only decrease travel times but also facilitate quicker emergency responses and boost local economies by improving access to markets."

Serena nodded, her gaze sweeping over the gathered crowd. "Lord Garren, what challenges did we overcome in this project? It's important for everyone to understand the effort that goes into such undertakings."

"Indeed, Your Majesty," Lord Garren replied. "One of the biggest challenges was ensuring minimal environmental impact. We worked closely with environmental experts to design a route that would preserve our natural landscapes and wildlife. Additionally, securing the cooperation of all the local jurisdictions to agree on the route was crucial and required extensive negotiations."

"I appreciate everyone's efforts and cooperation," Serena said. "Now, let's talk about safety. With the increase in traffic that this highway will bring, how are we ensuring that it remains safe for all travelers?"

"We have implemented several measures," the Minister responded. "Apart from state-of-the-art road safety designs, we are launching a public education campaign about road safety. We are also increasing highway patrols to ensure compliance with traffic laws and to provide assistance in emergencies."

"That's excellent," Serena acknowledged. "Public safety is our utmost priority. And what about maintenance? How do we plan to maintain this highway to ensure it serves our kingdom for generations to come?"

"We have established a dedicated Highway Maintenance Fund," Lord Garren explained. "This fund will ensure that we have the resources necessary to maintain the highway in top condition. Regular inspections and repairs are scheduled, and we have the latest technology to monitor the highway's condition in real time."

Serena smiled, pleased with the thoroughness of the planning. "This highway symbolizes our commitment to the future, to ensuring that our kingdom remains vibrant and accessible for everyone. It is a lifeline, connecting our people and places in ways that were once just a dream."

As the ceremony concluded and the ribbon was cut, the first official vehicles—a convoy of cars representing each region of Eirene—rolled onto the highway. Serena watched them disappear into the distance, each vehicle a bearer of new possibilities.

The rest of the day was spent in discussions and celebrations. Serena engaged with local business owners who were enthusiastic about the prospects of increased trade and tourism. She listened to their plans and challenges, offering support and encouragement.

As the sun began to set, casting long shadows across the new asphalt, Serena felt a deep satisfaction in the completion of this project. She knew that while today marked the end of one journey—the building of the highway—it also marked the beginning of another. This new road was a path forward, not just in terms of geography, but in economic growth, community building, and national unity.

With the cross-kingdom highway now open, communities across Eirene began to feel its impact. Queen Serena, determined to ensure that the benefits of this major infrastructure project were fully realized, scheduled a series of follow-up visits to various towns and cities that bordered the highway. Her goal was to engage with local leaders and citizens to understand their experiences and address any emerging issues directly.

The first of these visits took her to the town of Dellridge, situated near a critical junction of the new highway. The town, known for its artisanal crafts and small-scale manufacturing, had the potential to expand its market significantly due to the increased accessibility the highway provided. As Serena arrived, she was greeted by Mayor Benson, along with a group of local business owners and community leaders.

"Welcome, Your Majesty," Mayor Benson began as they started their walk through the town's bustling market area, where local products were on proud display. "The new highway has already started to bring more visitors to Dellridge. Our local businesses are seeing increased foot traffic, and there's a renewed energy in town."

"That's wonderful to hear, Mayor Benson," Serena responded, stopping to admire a stall laden with handmade textiles. "How are the townspeople adapting to the increased traffic and the changes it brings?"

"There are challenges, of course," the mayor admitted. "With more visitors, we've had to think about expanding our local infrastructure— more parking, better signage, enhanced local roads."

Serena nodded thoughtfully. "It's important that the benefits of the highway do not become burdens. What support can the crown offer to help manage these changes?"

"We would appreciate expertise and funding in urban planning and traffic management," suggested the mayor. "Help in planning for sustainable town expansion would ensure that our growth does not compromise the charm and character of Dellridge."

"Let's arrange for a team of urban planners to work with you," Serena decided. "It's crucial that Dellridge grows in a way that preserves its heritage and enhances its future."

As the tour continued, Serena met with several business owners who shared their stories and aspirations. One young entrepreneur, who had recently started a craft brewery, shared his excitement and concerns.

"Your Majesty, the highway has opened up new markets for us," he said, offering Serena a sample of his latest brew. "But we're struggling to scale up production safely and sustainably."

"Let's explore specific training and mentorship programs for small business owners like yourself," Serena proposed. "Supporting your growth ensures the highway serves as a catalyst for economic development, not just a quicker route through it."

The conversation was constructive, with each participant bringing forward both positive impacts and practical concerns about the rapid changes. Serena listened, asked questions, and provided direct feedback, ensuring that her responses were not just immediate reassurances but actionable promises.

Before departing Dellridge, Serena addressed a gathering of the town's residents. "This highway is yours as much as it is Eirene's. It brings opportunities and challenges, but I am committed to ensuring that it serves as a bridge to prosperity for all. Together, we will navigate these new pathways."

Leaving Dellridge, Serena felt reassured that while the highway's construction was complete, her work to integrate it into the lives of her citizens was just beginning. Each visit, each conversation was a step towards understanding and addressing the multifaceted impacts of this significant development. As she planned her next visit, Serena was determined to keep these lines of communication open, aware that her journey along this new highway would be one of continual engagement and adaptation.

Continuing her journey along the newly inaugurated highway, Queen Serena's next stop was the city of Crestwood, a hub that had historically served as a gateway between the northern and southern regions of Eirene. With the highway promising to enhance its role as a pivotal economic and cultural crossroad, Serena was keen to understand the city's adaptation to its expanding influence.

Upon her arrival, she was welcomed by Mayor Irwin, along with representatives from various sectors of the community, including commerce, education, and public health. They gathered in the city hall, a grand building with a view of the bustling city center.

"Mayor Irwin, it's good to be here," Serena began, her voice echoing slightly in the spacious hall. "I am eager to hear how Crestwood is harnessing the potential brought by the highway."

"Thank you, Your Majesty," Mayor Irwin replied, offering a smile. "The highway has already significantly impacted our city. There's increased traffic—both vehicular and pedestrian—which has boosted local businesses. However, with this growth, we also face new challenges, particularly in managing the increased demand on our public services."

"How are you addressing these challenges?" Serena inquired, her expression showing both concern and interest.

"We are currently expanding our public transport network to reduce road congestion and making significant upgrades to our healthcare facilities to accommodate the growing population," the mayor explained. "Yet, we need to enhance our urban infrastructure further to keep pace with development."

Serena nodded thoughtfully. "What specific areas would benefit most from immediate attention?"

"Public safety and housing, Your Majesty," responded the chief of police, who had joined the discussion. "With the population growth, ensuring safety and providing affordable housing are becoming increasingly challenging."

"Let's explore funding for these areas specifically," Serena suggested. "Safe and affordable housing is foundational to a stable community. Additionally, perhaps we could initiate a community policing program to enhance public safety."

"That would be most beneficial," the chief agreed, visibly relieved.

The conversation shifted as a local school superintendent brought up the topic of education. "Your Majesty, our schools are experiencing overcrowding due to the population boom. We need more classrooms and more teachers to maintain the quality of education."

"Education cannot be compromised," Serena affirmed. "Let's prioritize an expansion of educational facilities in our budget discussions. Perhaps we can also partner with private organizations to develop programs that can alleviate some of the immediate pressures."

"That sounds like a practical approach," the superintendent replied, grateful for the support.

As the meeting progressed, various community leaders voiced their perspectives, discussing potential solutions and strategies. Serena listened, responded, and proposed ideas, actively engaging in the dialogue to ensure that the responses were not only immediate but sustainable.

Before concluding the meeting, Serena addressed the group, "Your insights today have been invaluable. Crestwood's success is critical to the success of our entire kingdom. We will take proactive steps to support your city's growth and ensure it remains a vibrant and safe community."

With a round of applause from the participants, the meeting adjourned. Serena stayed briefly to speak individually with some of the community leaders, reaffirming her commitment to supporting their efforts.

As she left city hall, Serena felt a renewed sense of purpose. The challenges were significant, but the collaborative spirit she had witnessed promised that together, they could turn these challenges into opportunities. Crestwood, with its strategic position and dynamic community, was on the brink of a new era of prosperity, and Serena was determined to ensure it had the support needed to thrive. As she walked back to her carriage, her thoughts were already turning to the next steps, planning, and policies that would continue to foster growth not just in Crestwood but across all of Eirene.

As the tour along the highway concluded, Queen Serena organized a strategic session back at the palace to ensure that the momentum gained from the recent infrastructural improvements was sustained. The session was attended by key ministers, city mayors including Mayor Irwin from Crestwood, and representatives from various sectors impacted by the highway. The goal was to create a cohesive plan that would address the immediate successes and challenges while laying groundwork for long-term benefits.

In the palace's grand strategy room, with maps and economic data displayed around, the group assembled around a large oval table. Serena initiated the discussion with a tone of constructive focus.

"Thank you all for joining this crucial discussion," Serena began. "We've seen firsthand the immediate impacts of the new highway on local communities. Now, we must strategize on how to sustain and enhance these benefits. Mayor Irwin, let's start with you. Based on our last discussion in Crestwood, what are the key areas you believe we need to focus on immediately?"

Mayor Irwin nodded, acknowledging the queen's directive. "Thank you, Your Majesty. The primary areas are housing and public safety, as discussed. We need a strategic plan to develop affordable housing quickly to prevent a potential crisis due to our rising population. Additionally, enhancing our public safety measures to keep pace with our growth is crucial."

"Indeed," Serena replied. "Minister of Housing, could you outline what initiatives we could launch in the short term to address the housing issue?"

The Minister of Housing adjusted his papers before speaking. "Your Majesty, we can expedite the process of identifying suitable land for housing development. Additionally, implementing tax incentives for developers to build affordable housing could accelerate the construction. We're also exploring modular housing as a quicker solution."

"That sounds promising," Serena said approvingly. "And for public safety?"

The Minister of Public Safety interjected, "We propose increasing funding for local police forces and integrating more advanced surveillance technologies in key areas. Community policing initiatives, as you suggested earlier, would also bridge the gap between the police and the community, enhancing safety through cooperation."

"Let's ensure those initiatives are implemented efficiently," Serena directed, her gaze then shifting to other areas impacted by the highway. "What about the economic impacts? How do we ensure that the growth we are seeing translates into long-term prosperity?"

The Minister of Economy spoke up, "Leveraging the increased traffic and accessibility, we should promote local businesses and tourism. Creating 'business hubs' near highway exits could provide necessary services for travelers and employment for local residents. Additionally, marketing campaigns to attract tourists to our scenic and historic sites along the highway could boost local economies."

"That's an excellent approach," Serena agreed. "We need to consider the environmental impact as well. How do we balance development with sustainability?"

The Environmental Advisor added, "Continuous environmental monitoring is essential. We should consider impact assessments for all new developments and perhaps look into establishing green belts around new business hubs to maintain ecological balance."

As the meeting progressed, Serena led the discussion with a keen eye on integrating all suggestions into a unified plan. Each point was debated, refined, and recorded, with Serena ensuring that every decision aligned with the broader goals of economic growth, community well-being, and environmental sustainability.

"Thank you, everyone, for your contributions today," Serena concluded as the meeting neared its end. "This strategic session has laid the foundation for a comprehensive approach to maximizing the benefits of our new highway. Let's proceed with these plans with diligence and foresight."

With the strategy session wrapped up, each participant left with clear actions and responsibilities. Serena remained briefly, looking over the notes and plans that covered the table. Her commitment to Eirene's prosperity was as steadfast as ever, each decision made with the future of her people in mind.

The day's work affirmed the queen's role not just as a monarch, but as a visionary leader poised to guide her kingdom through challenges and opportunities alike. As she left the strategy room, her thoughts were already on the next steps, ready to continue driving Eirene toward a future as promising as the roads that now connected it more closely than ever before.

Chapter 17
Morana's Fall

With the cross-kingdom highway fostering newfound connectivity, Queen Serena turned her focus towards innovation in technology and its integration into everyday life in Eirene. Recognizing the potential to significantly advance the kingdom's infrastructure and public services through technological innovation, she convened a summit at the Royal Tech Hub, a newly inaugurated center dedicated to fostering technological development and collaboration across various sectors.

The Tech Hub, located in the heart of the capital, buzzed with activity as developers, entrepreneurs, and government officials gathered under its modern, glass-paneled roof. The day was bright, mirroring the mood inside the hub where the air was electric with ideas and the promise of progress.

Queen Serena opened the summit with a welcoming address, standing confidently at the podium with a digital screen displaying the day's agenda behind her. "Welcome to the Royal Tech Hub," she began, her voice clear and resonant. "Today, we come together to explore how technology can not only enhance our infrastructure but also improve the daily lives of our citizens. We are here to turn potential into action."

Minister of Technology, Adrian, was the first to respond, stepping up to join Serena. "Your Majesty, thank you for spearheading this initiative. One of the key areas we can immediately impact is our public transportation system. With the data we've gathered since the opening of the highway, we can use machine learning to optimize traffic flows and reduce congestion."

"That's an excellent starting point, Minister Adrian," Serena replied. "How do you propose we implement this?"

"We're developing an app that drivers can use which will not only guide them on the best routes in real-time but also provide data back to our traffic management system to improve its accuracy," Adrian explained.

"An integrated approach, I like it," Serena nodded. "It's essential that these technological solutions are accessible to all. What steps are we taking to ensure widespread adoption?"

"We plan to make the app free and are considering pre-installing it on devices sold in Eirene. Additionally, we will launch educational campaigns across all media platforms to ensure our citizens understand the benefits and how to use it effectively," Adrian detailed.

"Very well," Serena said thoughtfully. "Let's also discuss how we can use technology to enhance healthcare services, especially in remote areas."

Dr. Helena, the Chief Medical Officer, took the cue. "We are looking to expand our telemedicine services, which have become increasingly vital. By using satellite technology, we can ensure that even the most isolated communities have reliable access to healthcare professionals."

"Ensuring health equity is crucial," Serena agreed. "What support do you need from the government to roll this out successfully?"

"Funding for the necessary satellite infrastructure and training for healthcare providers to effectively use telemedicine platforms will be critical," Dr. Helena responded.

"Consider it done," Serena assured her. "We must guarantee that no citizen is left behind in our quest for advancement."

The discussions continued, with other leaders contributing their ideas on enhancing educational tools through technology, improving agricultural practices with smart farming techniques, and increasing the efficiency of renewable energy sources.

As the summit drew to a close, Serena addressed the assembly once more. "Today, we have laid the groundwork for a technologically advanced Eirene. Let us proceed with these initiatives with the same spirit of innovation and collaboration that has brought us here today."

With applause echoing in the large hall of the Tech Hub, the participants left feeling energized and committed to the tasks ahead. Serena lingered, speaking individually with several attendees, her mind as active with plans and possibilities as the technology they were discussing.

Leaving the hub, Serena felt confident in the progressive path Eirene was on, her leadership steering the kingdom into a future where technology and tradition merged to create a society that was not only more connected but more capable. Each conversation at the summit was a seed planted for future innovations, each project a step towards a more prosperous and efficient kingdom.

Continuing her commitment to embedding technology across Eirene, Queen Serena next attended a workshop focused on the implementation of smart farming technologies in rural areas. Held in the fertile valley of Greendale, known for its sprawling farms and now, its innovative approaches to agriculture, the workshop aimed to equip local farmers with the knowledge and tools to enhance productivity and sustainability.

The day was bright and clear as Serena arrived at the workshop venue, a large barn converted into a meeting space for the occasion. Inside, farmers gathered around various displays showcasing the latest in agricultural technology—from soil sensors to drone technology for crop monitoring.

Serena was greeted warmly by the Minister of Agriculture, Lucas, who was already deep in discussion with a group of farmers. Joining the conversation, Serena expressed her enthusiasm for the project.

"It's wonderful to see so many of you here today," Serena began, addressing the group. "Minister Lucas, could you share how these technologies are being received by our farming communities?"

"Absolutely, Your Majesty," Minister Lucas replied. "There's a lot of interest, especially in technologies that can make farming more efficient and less resource-intensive. For example, the soil sensors help farmers understand their soil's needs better, preventing overuse of water and fertilizers."

A farmer named Dara, who had been using the sensors, chimed in. "The difference is remarkable, Your Majesty. We can see exactly what the soil needs, and it's saving us time and money. It's also better for the land, which feels good."

"That's excellent to hear, Dara," Serena responded with a smile. "Are there challenges that you face in adopting these technologies?"

"Some of us are not as tech-savvy, Your Majesty," another farmer, an older gentleman named Harold, admitted. "It can be daunting to learn all this new stuff."

"I understand that," Serena acknowledged. "What support can we provide to help overcome these challenges?"

"We're rolling out training programs, Your Majesty," Minister Lucas interjected. "We're also considering a mentorship system where tech-savvy farmers like Dara could help others in the community adapt."

"I think that's a fantastic idea," Serena said, nodding approvingly. "Building community support systems is key to successful integration."

The discussion then moved on to the potential for expanding the market for these tech-enhanced agricultural products. Serena listened intently as a young farmer named Ella spoke about organic markets.

"With these technologies, we can produce truly organic products more reliably. If we could market our goods under a certified organic Eirene brand, I think it would attract a lot of buyers, both locally and internationally," Ella suggested.

"That's a brilliant point, Ella," Serena responded. "Minister Lucas, let's explore how we can support our farmers in obtaining organic certifications and marketing their products effectively."

"Absolutely, Your Majesty," Lucas agreed. "There's potential here to create a niche market that could benefit our economy greatly."

As the workshop continued, Serena moved between groups, engaging in discussions and noting down ideas and concerns. Her presence not only uplifted the spirits of those attending but also reinforced the importance of government support in technological adaptation.

Before leaving, Serena addressed the gathering once more. "Thank you all for sharing your insights and embracing these new opportunities. Together, we are not only improving our agricultural practices but also ensuring a sustainable future for the next generation of Eirenean farmers."

With a final round of applause, the workshop concluded. Serena left Greendale feeling optimistic about the future of Eirenean agriculture. Each conversation had reinforced her belief that through collaboration and innovation, the kingdom could address not only its immediate needs but also pave the way for long-term prosperity.

After the success of the smart farming workshop in Greendale, Queen Serena's focus shifted toward urban sustainability, specifically how technological innovations could enhance the living standards in Eirene's bustling cities. Her next initiative aimed to integrate smart technology in urban infrastructure to create smarter, more sustainable urban environments. This initiative was to be showcased in the city of Meridian, a growing metropolitan area known for its vibrant culture and now, its burgeoning tech scene.

The project in Meridian involved the introduction of smart street lighting systems that would not only provide energy-efficient lighting but also integrate sensors to monitor air quality and traffic. This dual function was expected to not only enhance public health and safety but also gather valuable data that could inform future urban planning decisions.

On a clear morning, Serena visited Meridian to observe the early stages of this implementation. She walked through the city streets with Mayor Jensen and several engineers, discussing the impact and potential of these smart technologies. Mayor Jensen, enthusiastic about the project's scope, detailed the immediate benefits.

"Your Majesty, these smart lights adjust their brightness based on the natural light available, which significantly reduces energy consumption," Mayor Jensen explained as they watched a technician program one of the lights. "They also collect data on traffic patterns, which helps us manage congestion more effectively."

Serena, interested in the practical applications of the technology, inquired about the integration of the data collected into broader city management systems. "How are we ensuring that the data these sensors collect is used effectively?"

"We're developing a centralized management system that will allow us to analyze the data in real time," an engineer from the project team answered. "This will enable us to make immediate adjustments to traffic light timings and dispatch public safety resources more efficiently when needed."

The discussion underscored the multifaceted benefits of the smart street lighting project, from enhancing citizen safety to contributing to environmental sustainability. As they continued their tour, Serena was pleased to see not only the technological advancements but also the public's positive response to the improvements.

The visit to Meridian also included a public forum where Serena heard from local residents about their experiences and suggestions regarding the ongoing technological upgrades. While the feedback was largely positive, some residents expressed concerns about privacy and data security.

Serena addressed these concerns directly. "Ensuring your privacy and the security of your data is paramount. We are implementing stringent security measures and transparency protocols to ensure that all data collected is protected and used responsibly."

The rest of her visit was spent in strategic meetings with city officials and technology experts, discussing how to replicate Meridian's successes in other urban areas across Eirene. These discussions were crucial in shaping a scalable model for urban technology integration that could be adapted to different cities with varying needs and characteristics.

As Serena left Meridian, her commitment to fostering a technologically advanced but sustainable and humane urban future was stronger than ever. The integration of technology in urban planning was not just about making cities smarter but making them better places to live. It was about creating environments that supported their residents' well-being while preserving the resources for future generations.

Reflecting on the day's achievements and the road ahead, Serena felt a deep sense of responsibility and optimism. The successful merging of technology and urban life in Meridian was a blueprint for the future, demonstrating that with thoughtful implementation and community involvement, technology could significantly enhance the quality of life. Each step forward in this city was a step towards realizing her vision for a modern, connected, and sustainable Eirene.

With the implementation of smart technology initiatives across Eirene gaining momentum, Queen Serena turned her attention to ensuring these technologies were not only embraced but effectively integrated into the social fabric of the kingdom. Her next step was to oversee the deployment of a kingdom-wide digital network designed to enhance communication and data sharing between cities, towns, and rural areas alike. This network, termed the Eirene Connectivity Grid, aimed to ensure that every citizen had access to digital resources and communication tools, regardless of their geographic location.

On a brisk autumn morning, Serena visited the central control facility of the Connectivity Grid located outside the capital. The facility, a marvel of modern engineering and architectural design, was equipped with state-of-the-art servers and data processing units that managed the vast flows of information across the kingdom.

Upon arrival, Serena was greeted by Minister of Digital Infrastructure, Ethan, who led her on a tour of the facility. The walls of the center were lined with large screens displaying real-time data and analytics of network usage across different regions.

"Your Majesty, this facility is the heart of our digital infrastructure," Minister Ethan began, pointing to a map that highlighted various network nodes. "From here, we can monitor and manage the health of the

Connectivity Grid, ensuring that data flows seamlessly and securely across Eirene."

Serena, observing the complex systems at work, inquired about the security measures in place to protect the network. "With such a comprehensive grid, security must be a top priority. How are we safeguarding against potential threats?"

"We have implemented multiple layers of security protocols, including advanced encryption, intrusion detection systems, and continuous monitoring," Ethan explained. "Additionally, we conduct regular audits and drills to ensure our defenses remain robust against evolving threats."

Satisfied with the response, Serena shifted the discussion towards the impact of the Connectivity Grid on rural communities, a particular concern of hers. "It's crucial that this technology serves not just our urban centers but also supports our rural populations. How are we ensuring that these communities are not left behind?"

"We've prioritized extending high-speed internet connections to rural areas first," Ethan replied. "We're also deploying mobile tech units in areas where permanent infrastructure is not yet feasible. These units provide temporary access points to the grid, ensuring that no community is disconnected."

As they continued their tour, Serena and Ethan discussed potential future enhancements to the grid, including integrating it with public services such as healthcare, education, and emergency services to improve response times and resource allocation.

Before leaving, Serena spoke briefly to the facility's staff, expressing her gratitude for their dedication. "Your work connects not just our lands but our people. You are weaving a tapestry of connectivity that will hold our kingdom together."

Leaving the facility, Serena felt a profound appreciation for the complexities and capabilities of modern technology. She recognized that the Eirene Connectivity Grid was more than just a project; it was a lifeline that tied the corners of her kingdom into a closer, more unified entity.

The day concluded with Serena reflecting on the broader implications of her initiatives. As she looked over documents outlining further technological projects on the horizon, her thoughts were on the balance between advancement and accessibility, ensuring that as Eirene grew more connected, it also grew more inclusive.

Every initiative, every project under her rule was a thread in the larger narrative of Eirene's progress. Through her leadership, she was crafting a legacy of not just technological achievement but of a truly interconnected society, ready to face the future as one cohesive, resilient kingdom.

Chapter 18
Healing the Land

As the leaves began to display their vibrant autumnal hues, signaling a time of renewal and reflection, Queen Serena convened a high-level meeting with her environmental council. The focus was on assessing the impact of the kingdom's environmental policies and expanding initiatives that had been successful. The meeting was held at the serene Lake Avon Retreat, a site that exemplified natural beauty and the benefits of environmental preservation.

Upon arrival, Serena was greeted by Minister Elaine, head of the Environmental Council, along with various experts and advisors. They gathered in a conference room overlooking the lake, where the tranquility of the surroundings underscored the importance of their discussions.

"Thank you for joining me in this beautiful setting," Serena began, her eyes taking in the view. "It reminds us of what we're striving to protect. Let's start with our current initiatives. Minister Elaine, could you provide an overview of our successes and the areas where we need to focus more attention?"

"Absolutely, Your Majesty," Minister Elaine responded. "One of our notable successes has been the Clean Water Initiative. We've seen a significant improvement in water quality in our rivers and lakes, including here at Lake Avon. However, we face ongoing challenges with air quality in some of our more industrialized cities."

"That's concerning," Serena noted. "What steps can we take to address this issue?"

"We might consider expanding our green zones and imposing stricter emissions regulations on industries," suggested an environmental scientist on the council. "Additionally, investing in public transport can reduce the number of vehicles on the road, which is a major contributor to air pollution."

"Implementing stricter regulations requires careful consideration and support from various stakeholders," Serena acknowledged. "Let's initiate a series of discussions with industry leaders to find a balanced approach. We must ensure our economic activities do not compromise our environmental responsibilities."

"Agreed, Your Majesty," Minister Elaine said. "On another note, our reforestation projects have not progressed as expected. We need to revitalize these efforts."

"What seems to be the bottleneck?" Serena inquired, genuinely concerned.

"Funding and manpower are our primary constraints," another council member chimed in. "We also need to improve community engagement to ensure the sustainability of these projects."

"Let's allocate more funds from our environmental budget and explore partnerships with local universities and NGOs to boost volunteer participation," Serena proposed. "Engaging local communities will be key to our long-term success."

"Absolutely, Your Majesty. I believe more educational campaigns about the benefits of reforestation could also spur public involvement," the Minister added.

As the discussion unfolded, various ideas and strategies were proposed, from enhancing renewable energy usage to improving waste management systems. Serena encouraged creativity and practical solutions, emphasizing the importance of action over deliberation.

"Before we conclude," Serena said as the meeting neared its end, "let's talk about our wildlife conservation efforts. How are we doing in that area?"

"We've had successes with our protected species programs, but habitat encroachment is an ongoing issue," replied a wildlife specialist. "Increasing the size and legal protection of wildlife reserves could help, as well as implementing more rigorous monitoring systems to prevent poaching and illegal activities."

"I support strengthening our legal frameworks and enforcement mechanisms," Serena stated firmly. "Protecting our biodiversity is not negotiable. We will make the necessary adjustments to our policies and enforcement strategies."

With a final round of discussions focused on setting timelines and responsibilities, the meeting concluded with a renewed sense of purpose. Serena thanked everyone for their contributions and dedication. As the group disbanded, she took a moment to gaze out over Lake Avon, its waters a mirror reflecting the sky above and the surrounding foliage. This serene vista was a reminder of the delicate balance her policies sought to maintain, ensuring that Eirene's natural beauty and resources endured for future generations.

Walking back to her quarters, Serena felt invigorated and ready to tackle the environmental challenges ahead. Each decision made today was a step towards a greener, more sustainable kingdom, aligning with her vision of a harmonious coexistence between nature and civilization.

Following the productive discussions at Lake Avon, Queen Serena's next focus was on harnessing and advancing green technologies to combat environmental challenges and promote sustainable development. A key element of this initiative was the introduction of a new green technology hub in the capital city, designed to be a collaborative space for innovators, scientists, and entrepreneurs.

In a spacious conference room within the newly inaugurated hub, flooded with natural light and adorned with indoor plants demonstrating sustainable design, Serena convened a meeting with the leading figures in green technology and innovation. Her aim was to discuss potential breakthrough technologies and strategies for their implementation across Eirene.

"Welcome, everyone," Serena greeted, as the attendees settled into their seats around a large, oval table made from recycled materials. "This hub represents our commitment to environmental sustainability and our faith in technology as a tool to achieve it. I'm eager to hear your ideas on how we can use green technology to further our environmental goals."

Dr. Fiona Kemp, a leading expert in renewable energy, was the first to speak. "Your Majesty, thank you for this opportunity. One area where we can make significant advances is in solar energy. We've developed a new type of photovoltaic cell that's much more efficient than current models and uses less rare material."

"That sounds promising, Dr. Kemp," Serena responded. "How can we facilitate the adoption of these new cells across the kingdom?"

"We would need to set up manufacturing facilities here in Eirene," Dr. Kemp explained. "Additionally, incentives for businesses and homeowners to switch to solar power would accelerate adoption. Grants, tax rebates, or even low-cost financing options could be effective."

"I see," Serena nodded thoughtfully. "Minister of Finance, could you explore funding options for these incentives?"

"Certainly, Your Majesty," the Minister of Finance replied. "We can allocate funds from our environmental budget and possibly seek partnerships with private investors who are interested in sustainable projects."

Next, the conversation turned to water conservation, an issue critical to Eirene's agricultural sectors and growing urban populations. Dr. Marcus Tiller, a hydrologist, outlined a proposal for a new water recycling system designed for urban environments.

"Your Majesty, our proposal involves using advanced filtration and purification technologies to recycle greywater for non-potable uses," Dr. Tiller detailed. "This could reduce the water consumption of urban areas by up to forty percent."

"Reducing water usage is crucial, especially in our drier regions," Serena acknowledged. "What are the implementation challenges we might face?"

"The main challenge is public perception and acceptance of recycled water," Dr. Tiller admitted. "Educational campaigns and transparent reporting on safety and benefits will be key to overcoming these challenges."

"Education will indeed play a vital role," Serena agreed. "Let's ensure we have a robust plan to educate our citizens about the benefits and safety of these technologies. Public trust is essential."

As the meeting progressed, other innovations were discussed, including advancements in electric vehicle infrastructure and biodegradable materials to reduce plastic waste. Serena encouraged a holistic approach, emphasizing the interconnectedness of these technologies with Eirene's overall environmental and economic health.

"We must think of these technologies not just as solutions to environmental issues but as opportunities for economic growth and improved quality of life," Serena concluded. "Let's continue to push the boundaries of innovation while ensuring that these technologies are accessible and beneficial to all our citizens."

With a round of affirmative nods, the meeting concluded, leaving the participants inspired and motivated. Serena lingered for a few moments to speak individually with some of the innovators, offering personal words of encouragement and reiterating her commitment to supporting their work.

Stepping out of the hub, Serena looked back at the building, a symbol of Eirene's green future, feeling a profound sense of responsibility and hope. Her leadership in driving these initiatives was not just about adopting new technologies but about fostering a culture of sustainability that would define Eirene for generations to come. Each conversation that day was another step towards a greener, more sustainable kingdom, aligned perfectly with her vision for a harmonious and prosperous future.

In the verdant outskirts of Eirene's capital, a large-scale project was underway that encapsulated Queen Serena's vision for a sustainable and self-sufficient future. The Green Corridor Project, an ambitious initiative to create a swath of land dedicated to sustainable agriculture, renewable energy, and conservation efforts, was approaching its first major milestone.

The corridor, a wide belt of land stretching several miles, was being transformed into a model of environmental stewardship. It included new installations of wind turbines and solar panels that dotted the landscape, working alongside carefully planned agricultural plots that utilized organic farming practices and state-of-the-art water conservation systems.

Queen Serena visited the site to assess the progress and to speak with the project managers and workers who were bringing her vision to life. As she walked through the site, her presence was a visible boost to the morale of everyone involved.

"This is remarkable progress," Serena remarked to the project lead, Mr. Alden, as they stood overlooking a newly completed section of solar panels. "How are the local communities adapting to the changes brought about by the Green Corridor?"

"They're very supportive, Your Majesty," Alden responded. "Many local farmers have embraced the training we've provided for organic farming techniques, and we've seen a lot of interest in the renewable energy programs as well."

"I'm pleased to hear that," Serena said, her gaze sweeping over the fields that were beginning to show the first signs of a bountiful harvest. "Engagement from the community is crucial. What are the main challenges we're currently facing?"

"The integration of the different technologies and ensuring they operate efficiently together has been a challenge," Alden admitted. "But we're learning and adapting as we go. The potential for energy production has exceeded our initial estimates, which is a promising sign."

"That is promising indeed," Serena nodded, pleased with the positive impact the project was having on the environment and the local economy. "It's essential that this project not only serves as a model of sustainability but also contributes tangibly to the community's welfare and the kingdom's energy needs."

As they continued their tour, Serena stopped to talk with a group of workers who were setting up an irrigation system designed to minimize water waste. She listened intently as they explained how the system collected rainwater and recycled greywater from nearby facilities, using it for irrigation.

"Your work here is vital to the success of this project," Serena told them. "It's innovations like these that will help ensure our kingdom remains lush and fertile for future generations."

The visit concluded with a brief meeting in the site's temporary command center, where Serena discussed with local officials and stakeholders about expanding the project's scope to include more areas and possibly replicating it in other parts of the kingdom.

Leaving the Green Corridor, Serena felt a profound connection to the project and its goals. The corridor was more than just a strip of land; it was a living, breathing testament to what could be achieved when innovation was guided by a commitment to the environment and the well-being of the people.

Driving back to the palace, the queen reflected on the day's experiences. The discussions, the faces of the people she met, and the green expanse stretching out behind her all reinforced the significance of her policies. Each element of the Green Corridor was a piece of a larger puzzle, representing a step towards a sustainable future. This initiative, like the seeds planted in its fields, was set to grow, flourish, and set roots deep into the fabric of Eirene, shaping a legacy of environmental consciousness and collective responsibility.

In the wake of the successes observed at the Green Corridor, Queen Serena turned her focus toward ensuring that these sustainable practices were not isolated triumphs but the groundwork for a broader environmental policy that would permeate all corners of Eirene. To this end, she convened a meeting at the palace with her environmental advisors and key cabinet members to discuss integrating the successful practices from the Green Corridor into national policy.

The meeting was held in the palace's west wing, overlooking the royal gardens—a constant reminder of the natural beauty they were committed to preserving. The room was set in a semi-circle, fostering an atmosphere of open dialogue, and as the participants gathered, the air was filled with a sense of purpose and anticipation.

"Thank you all for coming," Serena began, her voice resonant and clear. "The Green Corridor has set a benchmark for what we can achieve with dedicated effort and innovation. Now, we must discuss how we can apply these practices on a national scale. Minister Elaine, could you start us off by summarizing the main successes of the project?"

"Certainly, Your Majesty," Minister Elaine replied. "The Corridor's approach to integrating solar and wind energy has not only increased our renewable energy output but has also stabilized energy costs in the area. Furthermore, the organic farming initiatives have seen an increase in crop yields and a decrease in chemical runoff, improving local water quality."

"Excellent," Serena nodded. "How can we replicate these successes more broadly?"

"We need to consider a phased approach," suggested the Minister of Agriculture, who was also in attendance. "Starting with regions that are most similar to the Green Corridor in terms of climate and soil type could help ensure early successes that could encourage other regions to adopt similar practices."

"That sounds prudent," Serena agreed. "What about the funding mechanisms for such an expansion? Are our current budgets sufficient?"

"We may need to reallocate some resources," admitted the Minister of Finance. "Additionally, applying for international environmental grants could bolster our efforts without stretching our national budget too thinly."

"I urge us to pursue those grants aggressively," Serena said. "But let's also ensure we are not wholly dependent on external funding. Sustainability should be economically viable as well as environmentally sound."

The conversation then shifted to the educational aspect of sustainability, a topic Serena was particularly passionate about. "Educating our citizens on the importance of these initiatives is crucial. How can we enhance public awareness and education?"

"We could expand our partnership with schools and universities to include more on-site learning opportunities at projects like the Green Corridor," proposed the Minister of Education. "Additionally, running national awareness campaigns that highlight the economic and health benefits of sustainable practices could shift public perception and increase participation."

"I would like those campaigns launched by the next quarter," Serena decided, marking the urgency of the task. "It's vital that every citizen understands not just the how, but the why of our environmental policies."

As the meeting drew to a close, plans were made, tasks were assigned, and Serena's team left with clear directives and renewed motivation. Serena stayed behind, looking out over the gardens bathed in the soft light of dusk. Her commitment to transforming Eirene into a leader in sustainability was more than a policy objective; it was a personal mission, rooted in her deep love for her kingdom and her vision for its future.

Reflecting on the day's discussions, Serena felt a profound assurance that the path they were on was the right one. The strategies laid today would help Eirene not only adapt to the challenges of the present but lead the way into a sustainable, prosperous future. Each step forward was anchored in the lessons of the Green Corridor, guiding them towards a legacy of environmental stewardship that would benefit Eirene for generations to come.

Chapter 19
Rebuilding the Kingdom

As the year drew towards its close, Queen Serena was determined to ensure that the initiatives launched under her reign were not just temporary successes but sustained movements that would propel Eirene into a prosperous future. To achieve this, she convened a strategic planning session focused on the future of Eirene's economic development, particularly in sectors that had shown robust growth and innovation over the past year.

The session was held in the opulent conference room of the royal palace, with ministers and advisors gathered around a large mahogany table. Charts, maps, and digital displays provided a backdrop, ready to assist in their discussions.

"Good morning, everyone," Serena began, her tone both warm and authoritative. "This meeting is about ensuring the longevity and sustainability of our economic initiatives. We must craft strategies that not only address immediate challenges but also set a foundation for continued prosperity. Minister of Economy, what are the key growth sectors we should focus on?"

"Thank you, Your Majesty," the Minister of Economy replied. "Our technology sector has seen remarkable growth, particularly in green technologies and digital infrastructure. Additionally, the tourism sector has benefited greatly from our cultural preservation efforts and infrastructure improvements."

"Excellent," Serena said. "Let's start with technology. What specific actions can we take to foster further growth in this sector?"

"We could consider establishing more technology hubs across the kingdom, similar to the Royal Tech Hub in the capital," suggested the Minister of Technology. "These hubs could serve as incubators for startups and innovation centers for more established tech companies."

"That's a viable strategy," Serena nodded. "And how can we ensure these hubs are accessible to innovators across Eirene?"

"Incorporating virtual components and satellite locations in smaller towns could bridge the geographical gap," the minister proposed. "We could also offer grants and scholarships to potential innovators from underrepresented regions to help them bring their ideas to these hubs."

"Moving on to tourism," Serena transitioned, "how do we build on our current successes?"

"The recent interest in our historical sites presents a significant opportunity," the Minister of Culture and Tourism interjected. "We could develop themed travel packages that not only highlight these sites but also incorporate local festivals and arts, creating a comprehensive cultural experience for tourists."

"I like that idea," Serena replied. "It celebrates our heritage while also boosting local economies. What challenges do we anticipate with this approach?"

"Ensuring that the influx of tourists does not negatively impact the sites or local communities is crucial," the minister acknowledged. "We need to manage visitor numbers carefully and invest in maintaining and possibly expanding local infrastructure."

"We must balance growth with preservation," Serena affirmed. "Let's draft a detailed plan on how we can achieve this balance effectively."

The dialogue continued, with discussions on enhancing the agricultural sector through technology, expanding international trade by leveraging new market opportunities, and investing in education to ensure a skilled workforce ready to meet future challenges.

"As we conclude," Serena said as the meeting neared its end, "I want to emphasize the importance of integration across all these sectors. Our strategies must be interconnected, supporting not just economic growth but also social and environmental sustainability."

With a plan taking shape, the meeting wrapped up with tasks delegated and follow-up sessions scheduled. Serena felt reassured that the strategies discussed were not just pathways to immediate gains but were stepping stones to a sustainable and thriving future for Eirene.

As the participants left, Serena stayed behind, contemplating the detailed models and forecasts displayed around the room. Each figure and graph not only represented her kingdom's potential but also the responsibility she bore. With careful planning and dedicated implementation, she was setting the stage for a future that would benefit all her subjects.

Following the strategic economic discussions, Queen Serena shifted her focus to another crucial pillar of Eirene's future: education. Recognizing that the kingdom's long-term prosperity was inherently tied to the quality of its educational systems, she organized a roundtable with the nation's top educational leaders, including university chancellors, school superintendents, and experts in educational technology. The meeting was designed to forge a path forward in revolutionizing Eirene's educational landscape to better prepare students for the challenges of a rapidly changing world.

The roundtable took place in a sunlit room at the Royal Academy, where portraits of esteemed educators adorned the walls, serving as a reminder of the kingdom's rich academic heritage. As the participants gathered around the large oak table, the atmosphere was one of anticipation and collaborative spirit.

"Thank you for joining me today," Serena began, addressing the assembly. "Education is the cornerstone of our kingdom's future. We are here to discuss how we can innovate our educational system to not only foster academic excellence but also to cultivate critical thinking, creativity, and civic responsibility among our students."

Dr. Halverson, a prominent figure in curriculum development, was the first to speak. "Your Majesty, to achieve these goals, we need to integrate more interdisciplinary studies into our curriculum. By breaking down the silos between subjects, we can encourage students to think more broadly and apply their knowledge in innovative ways."

"I agree," Serena responded thoughtfully. "How can we practically implement this interdisciplinary approach across all schools?"

"We can start by training our teachers in these methods," suggested a superintendent from the northern region. "We also need to revise our assessment methods to reward critical thinking and problem-solving, not just rote memorization."

"That's a valid point," Serena noted. "Let's ensure our teacher training programs are equipped to handle these changes. We might also consider partnerships with international educational institutions to bring diverse perspectives and expertise."

As the discussion continued, the topic shifted to technology's role in education. "We have made strides in digital infrastructure," Serena said. "How can we further leverage technology in our classrooms to enhance learning?"

Professor Linn from the Royal University took up the question. "Your Majesty, interactive and adaptive technology can personalize learning, helping students progress at their own pace and according to their own style. However, we must ensure that technology complements, rather than replaces, the essential human elements of teaching."

"Absolutely," Serena agreed. "We must balance technological integration with personal interaction. Perhaps we can pilot a program that combines both elements in a few schools and study the outcomes."

The conversation also touched on vocational training and lifelong learning. "In addition to our academic institutions, we need to bolster our vocational schools and adult learning programs," said another educator. "Lifelong learning is becoming a necessity in the modern economy."

"Let's explore how we can expand these programs," Serena suggested. "Making education accessible throughout one's life is indeed essential in today's ever-evolving career landscape."

As the meeting drew to a close, Serena expressed her gratitude and optimism. "Today's discussions have laid a robust framework for the future of Eirenean education. Let's move forward with these initiatives with determination and foresight."

The educators left the roundtable energized and ready to implement the ideas that had been discussed. Serena remained for a moment, looking over the notes that had been compiled. Each idea, each proposal, was a seed that could grow into a transformative educational practice, potentially changing the lives of countless Eireneans.

Walking back to her study, Serena felt a profound commitment to these educational reforms. She knew that the decisions made today would ripple through generations, crafting a smarter, more capable, and more compassionate citizenry. Each step taken was a step toward a future where education opened doors not just to personal success but to a better, more understanding world.

Having addressed the foundational elements of economic and educational advancement, Queen Serena next turned her focus towards the realm of public health. The kingdom had made substantial progress in healthcare access and technology, yet continuous improvement was essential to meet the growing and changing needs of her people. To propel these advancements, Serena convened a critical meeting with healthcare policymakers, hospital administrators, and leading medical researchers at the Eirene Health Symposium.

The symposium took place in the newly opened Health Innovation Center in the capital. As healthcare professionals gathered in the modern conference hall, the atmosphere was charged with the anticipation of making meaningful strides in healthcare.

"Welcome, esteemed colleagues," Serena opened the session with a firm yet warm tone. "Today, we gather to discuss and design the future of healthcare in our kingdom. We aim to address the challenges and seize the opportunities to enhance the health and wellbeing of every Eirenean."

Dr. Marek, a leading public health expert, was the first to speak. "Your Majesty, thank you for bringing us together. One of our primary successes has been the integration of telemedicine, which has drastically increased access to care. However, we need to ensure that the quality of care through these platforms matches that of in-person visits."

"I appreciate that point, Dr. Marek," Serena responded. "What steps can we take to maintain and possibly enhance the quality of care provided via telemedicine?"

"We need to standardize the training for telemedicine across all healthcare providers," Dr. Marek suggested. "Additionally, investing in better diagnostic tools that can be used remotely will significantly improve the care we can provide online."

"That sounds like a practical approach," Serena acknowledged. "Minister of Health, can we explore partnerships with technology firms to develop these diagnostic tools?"

"Certainly, Your Majesty," the Minister of Health replied. "We can issue a call for proposals from tech companies for innovations in remote diagnostics. This could also spur economic activity in our tech sector."

The discussion then shifted to preventive healthcare, a topic Serena was particularly passionate about. "Preventive care is crucial to reducing the long-term burden on our healthcare system," she noted. "What initiatives can we implement to improve our preventive care measures?"

Dr. Elina, a specialist in preventive medicine, took the floor. "We should consider expanding our community health programs. These include more widespread health screenings and vaccination campaigns, as well as public health education that encourages proactive health management."

"I support that wholeheartedly," Serena said. "Prevention is better than cure. Let's make sure these programs are accessible to all citizens, regardless of their socio-economic status."

As the symposium continued, the conversation covered a range of topics, including mental health services, which Serena identified as a growing concern that required immediate attention.

"Mental health has often been overlooked in public discourse," Serena pointed out. "How can we better integrate mental health services into our primary healthcare system?"

"A multidisciplinary approach is essential," a psychologist at the symposium recommended. "We need to train our primary care providers to recognize and treat common mental health issues and ensure that referrals to specialists are seamless."

"Let's also destigmatize seeking help for mental health issues," Serena added. "Public awareness campaigns could be very effective here."

As the symposium neared its end, Serena concluded with words of encouragement and action. "The discussions today have laid down a comprehensive path forward. Each of you plays a pivotal role in this journey. Let's move forward with the plans we've discussed, for the health and well-being of our people."

With that, the symposium concluded, leaving participants motivated and ready to implement the ideas that had been discussed. Serena left the meeting with a sense of accomplishment and a renewed determination to see these health initiatives come to fruition, knowing that the wellbeing of her people was fundamental to the kingdom's strength and prosperity. Each decision made and each policy implemented was a building block towards a healthier, stronger Eirene.

As the year neared its end, Queen Serena took a moment to reflect on the strides Eirene had made under her leadership. Her initiatives in technology, education, and health were not just pillars for her reign but beacons that would guide future generations. To ensure these initiatives would endure beyond her tenure and continue to flourish, she planned a final review session with her top advisors and ministers. The goal was to establish robust mechanisms for monitoring, funding, and expanding the successful programs that had been initiated.

The session was held in the serene setting of the palace library, a place steeped in knowledge and history, where decisions of the past had shaped the kingdom. The room was filled with the soft rustling of papers and the murmur of conversations as participants prepared to present their progress and plans.

"Let us begin," Serena stated, her voice carrying a calm authority. "This year has been one of formidable challenges and substantial achievements. Our task today is to ensure that the progress we have made is not transient. Minister of Finance, can you provide an update on the funding strategies for our key initiatives?"

"Yes, Your Majesty," the Minister of Finance responded. "We have secured stable funding for the next five years for all major projects, including the expansion of the Tech Hubs and the Green Corridor. We are also exploring new funding models, such as public-private partnerships and international grants, to support our health and educational reforms."

"That is reassuring," Serena noted, nodding her approval. "It is crucial that financial stability underpins our efforts. What about the mechanisms for monitoring these initiatives? How will we measure success and identify areas for improvement?"

The Chief of Staff, who had been instrumental in implementing a new data-driven approach to governance, took the floor. "We have established a series of metrics and benchmarks for each initiative, Your Majesty. Regular reports will be generated, providing data on outcomes versus our set objectives. These will enable us to adjust our strategies in real-time and ensure our resources are being used effectively."

"I am pleased to hear that," Serena said, acknowledging the forward-thinking strategy. "Transparency and adaptability will be key to our ongoing success."

As they delved deeper into the discussions, attention turned to education and health—sectors Serena was particularly passionate about integrating more fully with technological advancements. "How are we ensuring that the integration of technology in schools and hospitals is not only innovative but also equitable?" she queried.

The Minister of Health and the Minister of Education jointly addressed this concern. "We are closely monitoring the deployment of technology to ensure it reaches all corners of the kingdom, including the most remote areas," the Minister of Health explained. "Additionally, we are investing in training programs to ensure that both health and education professionals are equipped to use these technologies effectively."

"And from an educational perspective," added the Minister of Education, "we are developing online resources that are accessible to all students, regardless of their location or economic situation. This includes virtual classrooms and digital libraries."

As the session came to a close, Serena expressed her gratitude and encouragement. "Thank you all for your dedication and hard work. It is our collective effort that transforms visions into reality. Let us continue to push forward with determination and vigilance."

Leaving the library, Serena felt a deep sense of accomplishment and cautious optimism. She knew that the road ahead would require continuous effort and adaptation, but she was confident that the foundations laid were strong. Her policies had set in motion a wave of change that would ripple through Eirene for many years to come.

Each step taken in today's session was a step toward securing a resilient and prosperous future for Eirene, ensuring that the progress made under her guidance would continue to benefit her people, reinforcing her legacy of thoughtful, progressive leadership.

Chapter 20
The Council of Memories

As winter's first frost touched the windowpanes of the palace, Queen Serena reflected on the past year's achievements and challenges. It had been a period of significant transformation for Eirene, marked by the successful implementation of various initiatives that promised to shape the kingdom's future. Now, with the year drawing to a close, it was time to look ahead and ensure that the foundations laid would support sustainable growth and development.

One of Serena's primary focuses had been to solidify the kingdom's economic stability. The advancements in green technology and the expansion of the Eirene Connectivity Grid were pivotal achievements that had begun to influence the kingdom's economic landscape positively. However, Serena knew that true success lay in the long-term benefits these initiatives would bring. To this end, she planned a comprehensive review of the economic impact of her policies, aiming to adjust and expand them where necessary to meet the evolving needs of her people.

The review would take place at the annual Economic Summit, scheduled at the onset of the new year, but preparation began under Serena's watchful eye during the quieter days of winter. Reports from various ministers and departments were compiled, analyzed, and synthesized into a briefing document that detailed the current economic climate, the impact of each major initiative, and projections for the future.

Amidst this flurry of preparation, Serena also turned her attention to social policies, particularly those affecting the most vulnerable in her society. She had initiated several social welfare programs aimed at improving healthcare access, education, and housing. These programs were particularly close to her heart, as they reflected her deep commitment to ensuring that prosperity was shared throughout all levels of Eirenean society.

As she walked through the snow-dusted gardens of the palace, accompanied by her Chief Advisor, Lord Harwick, discussions about the effectiveness of these social policies unfolded. "The feedback on the healthcare initiatives has been overwhelmingly positive," Lord Harwick reported. "However, there are areas in education where the intended outcomes have not yet been fully realized, particularly in remote areas."

Serena paused beside a statue of one of her ancestors, a reminder of the enduring legacy each ruler hoped to leave. "We need to push harder, Harwick. Let's ensure that no part of Eirene feels neglected. Perhaps we should consider increasing our investment in mobile education units and training more teachers specifically for remote and underserved areas."

"An excellent suggestion, Your Majesty," Lord Harwick agreed. "I will arrange for the Minister of Education to prepare a detailed proposal on expanding these efforts."

As the cold wind tugged at her cloak, Serena's thoughts also wandered to the kingdom's cultural heritage—a legacy of arts and history that was an essential part of Eirene's identity. Her government had made substantial efforts to preserve historical sites and promote the arts, understanding that culture was not only a repository of the kingdom's past but also a beacon for its future.

In the coming weeks, Serena would open a newly restored historical museum in the capital, showcasing Eirene's rich history and artifacts. This project was not just about preservation but about making history accessible to all Eireneans, educating them about their past, and inspiring them for the future.

As she returned to the warmth of the palace, Serena felt a renewed sense of purpose. The tasks ahead were daunting but not insurmountable. With careful planning, committed execution, and a clear vision, she was ready to lead her kingdom into another year of prosperity and peace.

Each decision she made, each policy she implemented, was another brushstroke on the vast canvas of her reign, each with the potential to color the future of Eirene in hues of progress and resilience.

As winter deepened, Queen Serena focused her energies on reinforcing the social fabric of Eirene, particularly through enhancing public services that directly impacted her subjects' daily lives. An important aspect of this endeavor was the enhancement of the kingdom's emergency services, which had become crucial in light of recent natural events that had tested the kingdom's resilience.

Inside the grand conference room of the Ministry of Public Safety, Serena convened a critical meeting with the heads of emergency services, including the fire brigade, the police force, and medical emergency services. The walls of the room were adorned with detailed maps of the kingdom, and the table was strewn with reports and digital devices ready to display data at a moment's notice.

"Thank you all for joining me today," Serena began, her tone both earnest and commanding. "The safety and well-being of our citizens are paramount. I want to discuss how we can enhance our emergency services to not only respond more effectively to incidents but also to proactively prevent them wherever possible."

Chief Marlow, the head of the fire services, was the first to speak. "Your Majesty, one of our key challenges is the aging infrastructure of our emergency response systems. Updating our communication and response equipment is crucial for improving our efficiency."

"What specific upgrades are you suggesting, Chief Marlow?" Serena inquired, her interest piqued.

"We need to integrate our communication systems across all emergency services to allow for real-time data sharing and coordination. Newer technologies, including drones for aerial surveillance in fire situations, could significantly enhance our capabilities," Chief Marlow explained.

"That sounds like a critical upgrade," Serena acknowledged. "Let's ensure the budget reflects this necessity. Minister of Finance, please take note. Now, what about our medical emergency services?"

Dr. Linnea, overseeing medical emergency responses, took the floor. "Your Majesty, our ambulance fleets are in need of modernization to include not only advanced life-saving equipment but also better navigation systems to reduce response times. Additionally, training our personnel in the latest emergency care practices is essential."

"I agree," Serena said thoughtfully. "Rapid response can be the difference between life and death. We will allocate funds for both upgrading the fleet and for continuous training of our emergency medical teams."

The discussion then shifted to preventive measures. "We also need to focus on public education about safety and first aid," suggested Serena. "Educating our citizens can dramatically reduce the number of emergencies and the strain on our services."

"An excellent point, Your Majesty," Dr. Linnea agreed. "We can develop community workshops and school programs that teach basic first aid and emergency preparedness."

As the meeting progressed, Serena directed her advisors to create detailed plans for each initiative discussed, setting clear timelines and expected outcomes. She emphasized the importance of accountability and regular progress reviews to ensure that the plans would not falter.

"Let us proceed with urgency and diligence," Serena concluded. "The safety of our people must not be compromised. I trust each of you to prioritize these improvements and report back with developments regularly."

After the meeting, as Serena walked back through the corridors of the Ministry, she felt a renewed assurance that her kingdom was becoming safer, stronger, and more prepared for any challenges it might face. The discussions of the day had not only set in motion plans for improvement but had also reinvigorated the commitment of her team to uphold the highest standards of public safety.

Outside, the snow had begun to fall gently, blanketing the palace grounds in a quiet hush. Serena watched the flakes drift down, each one unique and yet part of a larger whole, much like the citizens of Eirene whom she served with steadfast dedication. Each policy, each initiative, like the snowflakes, was part of a greater effort to protect and enhance the lives of all her people.

As the year waned, the snow enveloping Eirene seemed to usher in a period of introspection and planning for Queen Serena. With the foundational systems of her kingdom—economic, educational, and healthcare—strengthened and invigorated under her rule, she now turned her focus toward the broader vision of Eirene's future. The cornerstone of this vision was sustainable development, encompassing environmental conservation, technological advancement, and cultural enrichment, all intertwined to shape a resilient and prosperous future for all Eireneans.

In the quiet solitude of her study, with the winter landscape visible through her window, Serena drafted the principles of a long-term sustainability plan. She envisioned a kingdom where natural resources were not only utilized but revered and protected, where technology served to enhance quality of life without detracting from the beauty of the world around, and where culture and heritage were celebrated as the lifeblood of societal identity.

Later, at a small, carefully arranged meeting with her closest advisors, Serena shared her vision. "We must see beyond the immediate horizon and lay down a pathway for sustainable prosperity. This involves robust environmental policies that protect our natural heritage and ensure that our technological and economic advancements are sustainable."

Her Minister of Environment, who had been instrumental in expanding the national parks and improving waste management systems, responded with a thoughtful nod. "Your Majesty, with your support, we can enhance our conservation efforts and integrate them more closely with community development projects. This would not only preserve our environment but also educate and involve our citizens in these efforts."

Serena appreciated the affirmation and expanded on the idea. "We should also consider how our cultural initiatives can support this sustainable vision. Perhaps integrating traditional Eirenean practices and crafts into our educational curriculums and tourist attractions could foster a deeper connection with our heritage and promote sustainable tourism."

The ideas continued to flow, and plans began to take shape for integrating sustainability into every facet of national policy. This included proposals for green public transportation options, incentives for businesses adopting eco-friendly practices, and research into renewable energy sources that could further reduce the kingdom's carbon footprint.

As the meeting drew to a close, the quiet confidence in the room was palpable. Each advisor was tasked with refining the ideas into actionable plans, and Serena felt a deep sense of responsibility and hope. She knew the path would not be easy, and the challenges were significant, but the rewards of a sustainable, prosperous future for Eirene were worth every effort.

Leaving the meeting, Serena walked back to her private chambers, her thoughts filled with the work ahead. The winter might be cold, and the nights long, but they provided a perfect backdrop for planning and reflection. The stillness of the season seemed to give space for thoughts to grow and ideas to germinate.

Before retiring for the night, Serena stood by her window, looking out at the quiet beauty of the snow-covered gardens. The serene white landscape, undisturbed and pristine, reminded her of the blank slate of the future—full of potential, awaiting the imprint of wise leadership and thoughtful policies. Each decision she would make, like the snowflakes gently settling on the ground, would layer upon each other to form the foundation of tomorrow's Eirene.

This vision for the future, balanced and bright, was a testament to her commitment to her people and to the legacy she aimed to leave. It was a vision that would require continued dedication and vigilance to bring to fruition, but Serena was resolute. The work done today was just the beginning, and the true measure of her success would be seen in the sustainability and vitality of Eirene in the years to come.

As the year drew to a close and the kingdom of Eirene prepared to usher in a new year, Queen Serena found herself in the throes of finalizing her most ambitious project yet: the Future Eirene Initiative. This comprehensive plan aimed to intertwine the various threads of policy and innovation that had been discussed throughout the year into a cohesive strategy that would guide Eirene well into the future.

On a crisp, clear morning, Serena convened a meeting with her cabinet in the ornate conference room adorned with maps and portraits of past rulers—each a guardian of Eirene's storied past. Today's discussion was to integrate and finalize the initiatives, ensuring they were not just independent actions but parts of a greater whole.

"Thank you all for being here," Serena began, her voice steady and assured. "Today, we weave together the various strands of our initiatives to form a strong, unified fabric that will cover and protect Eirene in the years to come. Minister of Planning, please start by summarizing how our economic and environmental plans align with the broader goals of the Future Eirene Initiative."

The Minister of Planning, a seasoned official with a deep understanding of policy interconnections, responded, "Your Majesty, our economic plans have been designed to fuel sustainable growth. This includes supporting green technology startups through tax incentives and creating new jobs in the renewable energy sector. These actions align with our environmental goals of reducing carbon emissions and promoting sustainable resource use."

"Excellent," Serena replied. "It's crucial that economic growth does not come at the expense of our environment. What about our social policies, particularly in education and healthcare? How are they integrated into this initiative?"

"The education reforms you championed earlier this year," the Minister of Education interjected, "are geared towards producing a workforce that is not only skilled but also deeply aware of environmental and technological issues. This educational foundation is vital for sustaining long-term economic and environmental health."

"And in healthcare," added the Minister of Health, "we are focusing on integrating digital health technologies that improve patient care and also promote environmental health through better disease surveillance and response systems."

Serena nodded thoughtfully, pleased with the integration but aware of the challenges that lay ahead. "These plans are sound, but their success hinges on robust implementation and public support. How do we plan to engage our citizens and ensure they understand the benefits of these initiatives?"

The Minister of Communication, who had been preparing a national campaign, took the cue. "We are launching a series of community engagements and public information campaigns. These will not only inform but also involve citizens in the execution of these initiatives, making the public active participants in shaping the future of Eirene."

"I cannot stress enough the importance of public involvement," Serena emphasized. "Our plans must be lived, not just enacted. They must resonate with the people of Eirene, for their roots to grow deep and their impacts to be lasting."

As the meeting drew to a close, each minister was tasked with overseeing the integration of their department's initiatives into the broader Future Eirene Initiative. Serena, feeling a blend of anticipation and responsibility, knew that the coming year would be pivotal.

Stepping out onto a balcony overlooking the kingdom, Serena watched as the first snow of the season began to fall, each flake a silent promise of renewal. The cold air was invigorating, and as she wrapped her cloak tighter around her, she reflected on the intricate tapestry they had woven today. Each thread, each color, was necessary; each had a purpose and a place in the grand design of Eirene's future.

The decisions made today, shaped by wisdom and foresight, were her legacy—an enduring testament to her devotion to her kingdom and her people. As she turned back inside, her heart was steadfast, ready to lead Eirene toward a future as promising as the dawn of a new day.

Chapter 21
The Return of the Elders

With the dawn of the new year, Queen Serena decided to address another crucial aspect of Eirene's heritage and future—its rich cultural tapestry. Believing strongly in the power of arts and culture to unify and inspire her people, she organized a summit dedicated to revitalizing and expanding the kingdom's cultural initiatives. The event was held at the historic Eirene Theatre, a symbol of the kingdom's artistic legacy and a beacon for its cultural future.

As cultural leaders, artists, and policymakers gathered in the ornate lobby of the theatre, the air buzzed with anticipation and the murmur of excited conversations. Serena opened the summit with a speech that highlighted the intrinsic value of culture to the kingdom's identity and international reputation.

"Welcome to this gathering of Eirene's finest minds in arts and culture," Serena began, her voice echoing softly through the grand space. "Today, we stand at a pivotal point where we decide not only to preserve our rich heritage but also to ignite a renaissance that will carry our cultural legacy forward."

The Minister of Culture, the first to respond, shared his vision. "Your Majesty, thank you for this initiative. We propose the expansion of our national arts funding program, not just to support existing institutions but also to encourage grassroots cultural expressions across all regions of Eirene."

"That is a commendable start," Serena replied. "How do we ensure that these funds are accessible to all forms of artistic expression and not just the traditional arts?"

"We could establish a tiered funding system," suggested the minister. "One tier for established institutions and another for emerging artists and cultural projects. Additionally, a special committee could be set up to ensure representation from various artistic communities in the decision-making process."

"I like that approach," Serena noted. "It ensures diversity and inclusivity in our cultural promotion. What about our cultural heritage sites? How do we integrate them into this renaissance?"

The Director of Cultural Heritage, who had been overseeing the restoration of several ancient sites, joined the conversation. "We are developing interactive visitor experiences that combine technology with storytelling. This approach not only educates visitors about our history but also makes the experience memorable and impactful."

"Engaging our youth in these experiences is crucial," Serena emphasized. "Can we collaborate with schools to incorporate visits and interactive sessions into the curriculum?"

"Absolutely, Your Majesty," replied the Director of Education, who was also present. "Integrating cultural education into our schools will help foster a deep appreciation for our heritage from a young age. We can work with the Ministry of Culture to develop programs that are both educational and engaging."

As discussions unfolded, ideas flew about nurturing international cultural exchanges, investing in digital platforms for Eirenean artists, and creating cultural festivals that could attract global audiences.

Serena, pleased with the direction of the conversation, added, "Let us also think about how our cultural policies can support economic growth. Cultural tourism, for example, can be a significant economic driver if we market our arts and heritage effectively."

The Minister of Tourism supported this idea enthusiastically. "Integrating our cultural assets into our tourism marketing strategies can indeed boost our economy. We can create packages that showcase our diverse cultural landscape alongside our natural beauty."

The summit continued with breakout sessions, each focused on different aspects of the cultural renaissance Serena hoped to inspire. As the discussions drew to a close, there was a shared sense of excitement and a collective commitment to making these plans a reality.

Serena concluded the summit with words of gratitude and encouragement. "Today, we have laid the groundwork for a cultural renaissance that honors our past, celebrates our present, and anticipates our future. Let us move forward with creativity and passion."

As the attendees dispersed, energized by the day's fruitful discussions, Serena felt a profound connection to the cultural vibrancy of Eirene—a connection that reaffirmed her commitment to seeing this renaissance flourish. Her leadership had sown the seeds for a renewed cultural identity, one that would enrich her people and inspire the world.

Following the cultural summit, Queen Serena shifted her focus back to one of her key policy areas: education. Her next objective was to ensure that the education system in Eirene not only met the contemporary needs of its students but also prepared them for future challenges. To this end, she convened a workshop with top educational strategists, school leaders, and innovators in educational technology. The workshop was held at the Royal Educational Academy, a hub of learning and innovation that had become the center of educational reform under her reign.

As the participants gathered in the well-appointed conference room, equipped with the latest in digital presentation tools, Serena opened the session with a clear directive. "Thank you all for joining me today. Our goal is to forge educational frontiers that equip our students with not only knowledge but also with the critical thinking and creative skills they need to thrive in a rapidly changing world."

Dr. Elmore, a leading educational theorist, was the first to speak. "Your Majesty, our first step should be to integrate more problem-solving and project-based learning into our curricula. These methods encourage critical thinking and apply learning to real-world situations."

"That's a vital point," Serena responded. "How can we implement this across all schools, especially in more remote areas?"

"We can develop a train-the-trainer program," suggested another participant, the Superintendent of the national school district. "We train a core group of educators in these methods, who then can train others in their respective regions. Additionally, we can utilize technology to reach remote classrooms, perhaps through virtual workshops and online resources."

"I like that approach," Serena noted. "It ensures consistency in the quality of education and leverages technology effectively. Speaking of technology, how can we further utilize it to enhance learning?"

A tech entrepreneur, who had been developing educational software, chimed in. "Your Majesty, we have been working on adaptive learning platforms that adjust to the individual learning pace and style of each student. By integrating these platforms into our schools, we can personalize education and make it more effective."

"That's intriguing," Serena remarked with interest. "Can these platforms also be used to train our teachers, perhaps to familiarize them with new teaching methodologies?"

"Absolutely," the entrepreneur replied. "The same technology can be used for professional development, making it a versatile tool for our education system."

As the discussion evolved, the topic shifted to inclusivity and accessibility in education. "We must ensure that our advancements benefit all students," Serena emphasized. "What measures are we taking to address this?"

The Minister of Education responded, "We are expanding scholarship programs and updating our schools' infrastructure to be more inclusive, including facilities for students with disabilities. We're also looking into more bilingual education options to accommodate our diverse population."

"I am pleased to hear that," Serena said approvingly. "Education is a right, not a privilege. We must ensure it is accessible to every child in Eirene."

As the workshop drew to a close, Serena tasked each leader with developing actionable plans based on the strategies discussed. "We have charted a course today that promises to transform our educational landscape. Let's continue to work with dedication and creativity to bring these plans to fruition."

The participants left the workshop inspired and ready to take on the challenge. Serena, too, felt a renewed sense of purpose as she looked over the Academy's grounds, bustling with the energy of students and teachers. Her vision for an education system that nurtured intelligent, thoughtful, and creative individuals was slowly becoming a reality. Each step taken in the workshop was a step toward a future where education was the cornerstone of personal and national growth—a legacy that would endure for generations.

As the initiatives from the education workshop began to take root, Queen Serena turned her attention towards bolstering Eirene's public health infrastructure. Recognizing that the well-being of her subjects was a cornerstone of national strength and prosperity, she convened a focused group of health policy experts, medical professionals, and community health advocates. The goal was to discuss enhancements to the public health system that would not only address current needs but also anticipate future health challenges.

The meeting was held at the National Health Services Headquarters, where the walls were adorned with portraits of pioneers in medicine— reminders of the legacy that the current health policies would build upon. Around a large, oval table equipped with interactive digital displays showing health statistics and projections, the group assembled, ready to shape the future of health in Eirene.

"Thank you for joining me today," Serena began, her tone imbued with the gravity of their task. "Our public health system has served us well, but as we move forward, we must adapt and expand our services to ensure that they remain robust and responsive to our people's needs."

Dr. Maren, a leading public health expert, was the first to speak. "Your Majesty, our first priority should be to integrate mental health services more fully into our primary care offerings. Mental health is often overlooked, yet it is crucial to overall well-being."

"I agree," Serena replied. "Mental health should be as readily addressed as physical health. How do you propose we integrate these services?"

"We can start by training primary care providers in basic mental health care and ensure that referrals to specialized services are seamless," Dr. Maren suggested. "Additionally, establishing mental health awareness programs within communities can help reduce stigma and encourage more people to seek help."

"Those are sensible steps," Serena nodded. "What about our rural areas, where health services are not as readily accessible?"

"We need to expand our mobile health clinics," suggested another participant, a community health organizer. "These clinics are vital for reaching remote areas, and they can be equipped to provide a wide range of services, from vaccinations to chronic disease management."

"Let's also leverage technology," added Serena, thinking of the digital advances discussed in previous meetings. "Telemedicine can be a powerful tool in these areas, offering consultations and follow-up care remotely."

As the discussion unfolded, it also covered the need for improved health education in schools, the expansion of elderly care services, and the enhancement of emergency response systems to better handle public health crises.

"Let's ensure our emergency preparedness is robust," Serena emphasized. "We must be able to respond swiftly and effectively not just to natural disasters but also to health emergencies."

The meeting concluded with a comprehensive list of action items, each assigned to specific members of the group for follow-up. Serena was satisfied with the depth and breadth of the strategies they had outlined.

Leaving the headquarters, she felt reassured by the proactive steps they were taking to ensure the health of her people. The discussions had been thorough, covering the spectrum of public health from preventive care to emergency response.

As she rode back to the palace, Serena reflected on the interconnectedness of all the initiatives she had championed—from education and technology to health and culture. Each was crucial, feeding into the others, and together, they formed a cohesive strategy to lift and sustain her kingdom.

The health of her people was more than a policy agenda; it was a reflection of her commitment to their well-being and her determination to see Eirene thrive. As the carriage rolled through the streets, past bustling markets and quiet parks, Serena felt a deep connection to her people and a renewed commitment to their future—a future where health and happiness were not aspirations but assurances.

As the year's cycle neared completion, Queen Serena reflected on the vast landscape of progress Eirene had traversed under her guidance. Each initiative, from enhancing educational frameworks to embedding technological advancements into the fabric of everyday life, was a thread in the intricate tapestry of her reign. Now, as the kingdom prepared to step into another year, Serena focused on tying these threads together, ensuring that the progress made was not only sustainable but also irreversible.

The setting for this reflection and planning was the serene Winter Garden within the palace grounds, where Serena often found clarity amid its meticulously tended plants and tranquil water features. Here, with the crisp air of late winter swirling around her, she walked the stone paths, accompanied by her trusted advisor, Sir Cedric. They discussed the ongoing projects and the strategies for the upcoming year.

"Your Majesty, the initiatives you've set in motion have gained substantial momentum," Sir Cedric remarked, scanning the list on his tablet. "However, ensuring their sustainability is crucial. We must integrate these initiatives deeply into the societal structure to withstand the tests of time and policy changes."

Serena nodded, her gaze lingering on a frozen fountain, its stillness belying the flowing vitality it showed in spring. "We need to establish strong institutional frameworks, Cedric. For instance, our cultural renaissance must continue to be nurtured through continuous funding and public engagement. How do we solidify this?"

"Legislation could be key, Your Majesty," Sir Cedric suggested. "Enacting laws that protect and fund these cultural initiatives can ensure they endure beyond your reign. Additionally, establishing independent councils to oversee these projects could help maintain their integrity and direction."

"That's a sound approach," Serena acknowledged. "And what of our advancements in public health and education? These sectors are vital to our kingdom's well-being and must be fortified against future challenges."

"Perhaps establishing endowments for health and education, funded by both public and private sectors, could provide ongoing support," Sir Cedric proposed. "Also, embedding technology further into these fields could enhance efficiency and outreach, making these services more resilient and adaptable."

As they rounded a bend in the path, the conversation turned toward the economic strategies that had propelled Eirene into a new era of prosperity. Serena was particularly interested in ensuring that the economic growth was not only sustained but also equitable.

"We must continue to foster an environment where innovation is rewarded and entrepreneurship is supported," Serena mused. "Creating more opportunities for small businesses and startups, especially in the green technology sector, could drive our economy forward sustainably."

"Indeed, Your Majesty," Sir Cedric agreed. "Perhaps expanding our network of tech hubs and increasing grants and scholarships for aspiring entrepreneurs could spur further growth. Also, enhancing our trade relationships could open new markets for our burgeoning industries."

As the meeting concluded, Serena felt a profound connection to the tasks ahead. The paths of Eirene's garden were much like the paths of her policies—each turn and twist meticulously planned, leading to a vision of beauty and harmony. Her commitment to Eirene's future was as steadfast as the ancient trees that stood sentinel around the garden.

Walking back to the palace, Serena's thoughts were clear. The work done was substantial, but the journey ahead was longer still. Each decision, each policy enacted, was a step toward a future where Eirene was not only a kingdom of wealth and knowledge but also a beacon of culture, health, and equitable prosperity.

The winter might be receding, but the preparations for spring's renewal were already underway. Serena's vision for Eirene, a tapestry rich with the colors of progress and tradition, was gradually becoming a reality. With careful stewardship, this tapestry would hang in the halls of history, a testament to a reign that wove together the past and the future into a vibrant present.

Chapter 22
A Kingdom of Memory

As spring heralded new beginnings, Queen Serena turned her attention beyond the borders of Eirene, aiming to strengthen international relations and forge new alliances. Her first step was to host a diplomatic summit at the palace, inviting ambassadors and dignitaries from neighboring kingdoms and allied nations. The purpose of the summit was to discuss mutual concerns, explore new trade opportunities, and reinforce commitments to peace and cooperation.

The summit was held in the opulent Grand Hall of the palace, which had been splendidly decorated for the occasion. The long, ornate table was set with the flags of the attending nations, creating a colorful display of unity and diversity. As the guests arrived, the air was filled with the murmur of various languages, each a melody of diplomacy and tradition.

"Welcome, esteemed guests," Serena began, once everyone was seated. "It is an honor to host you all here in Eirene. This summit reflects our shared desire for a peaceful and prosperous future. Let us begin by discussing how we can enhance our economic ties."

The ambassador from the neighboring kingdom of Altheria took the lead. "Your Majesty, thank you for your warm welcome. Altheria is keen to expand our trade relations. We are particularly interested in Eirene's advancements in green technology. Perhaps we could explore a partnership in this sector?"

"Indeed, Ambassador," Serena responded with a nod. "Eirene has made significant strides in green technology. We are open to sharing our knowledge and exploring joint ventures that would benefit both our nations. Minister of Trade, perhaps you could elaborate on potential opportunities?"

"Certainly, Your Majesty," the Minister of Trade interjected. "We can offer expertise and investment in solar and wind energy projects.

Additionally, we could consider setting up a bilateral trade agreement that reduces tariffs on green technology goods and services."

"That sounds promising," the Altherian ambassador replied. "I believe such initiatives could serve as a model for sustainable development in our region."

As the discussion continued, the ambassador from the maritime nation of Corallis raised a concern about maritime security, which was vital for their trade routes. "Your Majesty, Corallis appreciates Eirene's commitment to regional stability. We would like to propose a cooperative framework for maritime security to protect our trade routes and ensure safe passage for all."

"I agree that security on the seas is crucial for our collective prosperity," Serena acknowledged. "We would be pleased to participate in a regional maritime security alliance. Admiral, could you provide some insights into how we might structure such an initiative?"

The Admiral, dressed in his ceremonial uniform, leaned forward. "We could establish joint patrols and share intelligence on potential threats. Such cooperation would not only enhance security but also build trust among our nations."

The conversation shifted towards cultural exchanges, with the ambassador from the artistic powerhouse of Lorien suggesting more robust cultural ties. "Your Majesty, Lorien would treasure the opportunity to host a cultural festival featuring artists from Eirene. We believe that cultural exchange strengthens the bonds between nations and enriches our societies."

"That is a wonderful idea," Serena replied with genuine enthusiasm. "Cultural diplomacy can indeed bridge gaps and deepen understanding. We would be honored to participate and can reciprocate by hosting Lorien artists in Eirene."

As the summit drew to a close, agreements were reached on several fronts, from economic collaborations to security partnerships and cultural exchanges. Serena felt a deep satisfaction as she watched the delegates converse amiably, their earlier formalities giving way to a shared sense of purpose and friendship.

"Thank you all for your constructive dialogues today," Serena concluded. "The agreements we've reached will undoubtedly lead to stronger bonds and shared prosperity. Let us continue to work together, with respect and mutual benefit guiding our way."

As the guests departed, the positive atmosphere of the summit lingered in the Grand Hall. Serena knew that the success of today's discussions would not only enhance Eirene's international standing but also contribute to a more stable and interconnected world. Each conversation, each agreement, was a step toward a future where nations not only coexisted but cooperated for the greater good.

Following the successful diplomatic summit, Queen Serena was invigorated by the possibilities that lay ahead for Eirene. Strengthened alliances and new partnerships had opened doors to opportunities that promised to enhance the kingdom's prosperity and global standing. One of the most promising outcomes was the initiation of a collaborative research project in green technology with Altheria, which Serena believed could set a precedent for international cooperation in sustainable development.

In the days following the summit, Serena organized a visit to Eirene's leading research institute, where this pioneering project was to be headquartered. The institute, a sprawling complex surrounded by lush gardens and equipped with state-of-the-art laboratories, was a symbol of Eirene's commitment to innovation and progress.

Upon her arrival, Serena was greeted by Dr. Fenwick, the head of the institute, who was eager to discuss the details of the new project. "Your Majesty, we are honored to lead this initiative. By combining our expertise with Altheria's resources, we aim to develop new methods of energy production that are not only more efficient but also more environmentally friendly."

Serena, while touring the facilities, observed the researchers at work, their focus and dedication a testament to the kingdom's intellectual wealth. "Dr. Fenwick, could you explain how this project will benefit not just our two nations but also set an example for others?"

"Absolutely, Your Majesty," Dr. Fenwick replied, leading her towards a display of the project's blueprint. "The technologies we develop here could drastically reduce carbon emissions worldwide. We're not just creating new products; we're fostering a new approach to how nations can collaborate on environmental challenges."

As they walked through the laboratories, Serena met several researchers, each working on different aspects of the project. The conversations she had were enlightening, reinforcing her belief in the power of shared knowledge and cooperative endeavor.

Back in the palace, Serena convened a meeting with her economic council to discuss leveraging the new international partnerships to boost Eirene's economy. The council, composed of her top economic advisors and business leaders, was tasked with finding ways to ensure that the economic benefits of these international projects were felt throughout the kingdom.

"Let's identify key industries that could benefit from these collaborations," Serena proposed during the meeting. "For instance, our manufacturing sector could expand its capacity to produce parts for green technology. Additionally, we should consider how our education system can align with these advancements to ensure our workforce is well-prepared."

Her Minister of Economy, Mr. Corvin, was quick to support the idea. "Your Majesty, by aligning our educational programs with these emerging industries, we can ensure a steady pipeline of skilled workers. Additionally, we can incentivize businesses to invest in related sectors through tax breaks and grants."

Serena, pleased with the proactive strategies being proposed, emphasized the importance of communication and public engagement. "We must ensure our citizens understand the importance of these projects and how they contribute to our national interests. Let's develop a communications strategy that highlights the tangible benefits of these international collaborations."

As the council meeting concluded, plans were put into place to expand industrial capacities, realign educational curricula, and enhance public awareness about the kingdom's strategic directions.

Walking through the palace gardens later that day, Serena felt a deep sense of responsibility and optimism. The seeds planted through international cooperation were just beginning to sprout, and she was determined to nurture them into strong, enduring trees that would shelter future generations.

Each step taken, each agreement forged, was a part of a larger vision—a vision of a world where nations worked together to overcome challenges, a vision where Eirene led by example. With careful planning and committed execution, the future looked bright, promising a legacy of prosperity, stability, and innovation.

Inspired by the positive strides in international relations and committed to fostering sustainable economic growth, Queen Serena organized a follow-up meeting with her economic council and representatives from the newly allied nations. The focus was to draft a sustainable trade framework that would not only boost Eirene's economy but also ensure that trade practices aligned with environmental and ethical standards.

The meeting was held in the stately Blue Room at the palace, where large windows offered views of the sprawling palace gardens, serving as a constant reminder of the natural beauty they were committed to preserving. The room buzzed with the low hum of discussions as delegates from Altheria, Corallis, and other partner nations mingled with Eirene's top economic strategists.

"Welcome, everyone," Serena began, as the attendees took their seats around the massive oak conference table. "Today, we gather to build upon our recent diplomatic successes by creating a trade framework that reflects our shared values of sustainability and mutual prosperity. Minister of Trade, please outline the initial proposal."

The Minister of Trade, a seasoned diplomat with a keen understanding of international economics, responded, "Thank you, Your Majesty. Our proposal focuses on creating trade agreements that prioritize environmental sustainability, including tariffs on goods that meet green manufacturing standards and incentives for companies that adhere to environmentally friendly practices."

"That's a solid foundation," acknowledged the ambassador from Altheria. "In Altheria, we've seen significant interest in importing Eirenean green technologies. Perhaps we could explore a reduced tariff rate for these products, which would make them more accessible in our markets."

"That aligns perfectly with our objectives," Serena agreed. "What are your thoughts on joint ventures in research and development, particularly in areas like renewable energy and sustainable agriculture?"

The Corallis representative chimed in, "Corallis would value collaboration in renewable energy research. We have ample maritime resources that could be better utilized with Eirene's technological advancements. Joint R&D projects could lead to innovations that benefit not just our nations but also set a standard globally."

"I see great potential in this," Serena responded with enthusiasm. "Let's consider establishing a bi-national innovation fund to support these projects. It would facilitate the pooling of resources and talent."

As discussions continued, the focus shifted to ensuring that trade practices supported not only economic growth but also social equity. "It's crucial that our trade agreements also consider the impact on local communities and small producers," Serena emphasized. "How can we ensure that they are not disadvantaged by these international agreements?"

The Minister of Social Equity suggested, "We could implement fair trade clauses that require international operations to adhere to labor and wage standards that protect workers. Additionally, supporting small producers through cooperative models could help them compete on a larger scale."

"That's an excellent point," the ambassador from Lorien noted. "Lorien would support initiatives that promote fair trade and worker rights. It aligns with our national values and international commitments."

As the meeting drew to a close, Serena felt optimistic about the collaborative spirit and shared commitment to creating a trade framework that was both innovative and conscientious. "Thank you all for your valuable insights and contributions today," she concluded. "Let's move forward with drafting these agreements, ensuring they embody our shared principles and aspirations."

The delegates left the meeting with a sense of accomplishment and a clear roadmap for the future. Serena remained briefly in the Blue Room, looking out over the gardens, contemplating the intricate web of relationships and agreements that was forming. Each conversation and decision at today's meeting was a stitch in the broader tapestry of Eirene's future, weaving together prosperity, sustainability, and equity into a cohesive whole.

With the foundational discussions on creating a sustainable trade framework advancing positively, Queen Serena convened a final meeting to finalize the agreements. The meeting brought together the key diplomats and trade representatives from Eirene and its allied nations. The atmosphere was one of cautious optimism as they gathered in the palace's diplomatic hall, a place where many of Eirene's historic treaties had been signed.

"Thank you all for coming back together to finalize what we have diligently worked on these past weeks," Serena began. "Our goal today is to seal our pact of prosperity—a commitment to each other that our future trade will not only bring economic benefits but will also uphold our deepest values of sustainability and fairness."

The Minister of Trade took the lead, laying out the draft of the trade agreement on the large mahogany table. "We have structured the agreement to include specific clauses that address environmental sustainability, fair trade practices, and mutual economic growth. Each nation represented here has the opportunity to review these clauses today before we proceed to signing."

The representative from Altheria, Minister Varick, leaned forward, perusing the document. "We appreciate Eirene's leadership in integrating environmental considerations so prominently. Altheria is particularly supportive of the clause that encourages technology transfer to facilitate green energy projects. However, we suggest adding a review mechanism to monitor the environmental impact regularly."

"That's a constructive suggestion," Serena replied, nodding to her secretary to note the amendment. "Regular reviews will ensure that our commitments translate into real benefits and allow us to adjust our strategies as needed. What are the thoughts from Corallis on the maritime cooperation clause?"

Ambassador Lin from Corallis responded, "Corallis agrees to the proposed joint maritime patrols and shared environmental monitoring. We believe this will strengthen not only our security but also our ability to manage and protect our shared marine resources. However, we would like to expand the cooperative research initiatives to include marine biodiversity."

"Indeed, marine biodiversity is crucial, and expanding research in this area is in all our interests," Serena agreed. "We will include this in the agreement. Moving on, does Lorien have any further input on the cultural exchange programs?"

Ambassador Toren of Lorien, always an advocate for cultural integration, smiled. "Lorien is delighted with the cultural exchange proposals. We see a lot of potential in these for deepening understanding and bonds between our nations. We propose establishing annual cultural festivals that rotate between our countries, showcasing not only traditional arts but also contemporary cultural expressions."

"A wonderful idea, Ambassador Toren," Serena said with genuine enthusiasm. "Such festivals will indeed celebrate our diversity and strengthen our connections. We will incorporate this into the agreement."

As each representative contributed and consensuses were reached, the final document began to take shape—a comprehensive pact that balanced economic ambitions with environmental stewardship and cultural respect.

Once all points were agreed upon, the representatives prepared to sign the agreement. "This document," Serena addressed the room, "is more than a treaty. It is a testament to what nations can achieve when they come together with mutual respect and a shared vision for the future."

With a flourish of pens on paper, the agreement was signed, each signature binding the nations to a common path of prosperity. Applause filled the room, not just for the successful conclusion of negotiations but for the promise of what was to come.

As the delegates exchanged handshakes and pleasantries, Serena stood by the window, looking out over the palace gardens. The agreement they had just signed was a significant achievement, and while it was an end to their negotiations, it was just the beginning of a greater journey. A journey that promised to bring prosperity and unity, guiding their nations through the challenges of the present and into the possibilities of the future. Each step they would take from here on out would be a step made stronger by their newfound unity.

Chapter 23
The Legacy of the Mist

Queen Serena, having successfully fostered international relationships and set a path toward sustainable prosperity, now turned her focus inward to her own kingdom—specifically, to the preservation and celebration of Eirene's rich cultural heritage. Recognizing the importance of connecting the younger generation with their history, she initiated the Heritage for Tomorrow project, a comprehensive program designed to engage youth with Eirene's traditions and history through modern and interactive means.

The project was launched at the National Museum of Eirene, a place where the past met the present amid ancient artifacts and cutting-edge digital exhibitions. Serena, accompanied by her Minister of Culture and the Director of the National Museum, hosted a roundtable discussion with educators, historians, and young leaders to discuss the integration of the kingdom's history into the lives of its youth.

"Welcome everyone," Serena greeted her guests warmly as they settled into the plush chairs of the museum's conference hall. "Today, we embark on a journey to bring our history to life for the younger generation. We want them to feel a deep connection to our past, as it will inform their future. Minister, perhaps you could start by outlining the main components of the Heritage for Tomorrow project?"

"Certainly, Your Majesty," the Minister of Culture replied. "The project includes three main components: an interactive digital archive accessible online, a traveling historical exhibit that will visit schools across the kingdom, and a series of workshops and seminars led by historians and cultural experts."

"That sounds excellent," Serena said, nodding in approval. "How will we ensure that these resources are engaging for young people, who might find traditional methods a bit dry?"

The Director of the National Museum, an enthusiastic supporter of using technology to educate, chimed in. "We are collaborating with digital artists and game developers to create virtual reality experiences that allow users to 'step into' historical events. We believe this immersive approach will captivate our youth and make learning about history an exciting adventure."

"I love the sound of that," Serena smiled. "Involving young people in these experiences is crucial. Do we have representatives from the youth council here today?"

A young woman, the president of the national youth council, spoke up. "Yes, Your Majesty. We are very excited about this initiative. It's important that young people not only learn about history but also see its relevance to their own lives. We would like to suggest incorporating interactive forums where students can discuss how the historical events relate to current issues."

"That's a valuable suggestion," Serena agreed. "Engaging young minds in discussions about history's impact on present-day challenges can provide them with a deeper understanding and appreciation of our heritage."

As the conversation continued, ideas were shared on how to integrate these historical programs into the school curriculum and public broadcasting, ensuring that children and young adults across Eirene could access and benefit from them.

"Let's also ensure that this isn't just about looking back," Serena added thoughtfully. "We should use our history to inspire future leaders and thinkers. Can we include leadership training in our workshops that draw on the lessons from our past?"

"That's an excellent idea, Your Majesty," replied the Minister of Education, who had been listening intently. "Incorporating leadership lessons into our history workshops can empower our youth to think critically about how they can shape the future."

As the meeting drew to a close, Serena felt encouraged by the enthusiasm and innovative ideas that had been shared. "Thank you all for your contributions today. The Heritage for Tomorrow project is not just about preserving the past; it's about inspiring our future. Let's proceed with creativity and passion."

Leaving the museum, Serena felt a deep connection to her kingdom's past and a renewed commitment to its future. She knew that by bridging generations through heritage, she was helping to weave a richer, more cohesive societal fabric—one that would support Eirene's prosperity and unity for many years to come.

In the verdant heart of Eirene, the Royal Botanical Gardens served not only as a sanctuary of natural beauty but also as an educational resource, illustrating the kingdom's commitment to both environmental preservation and public education. Inspired by the discussions at the National Museum, Queen Serena sought to extend the Heritage for Tomorrow project into a new domain: environmental heritage. She envisioned a program that would educate the youth about the kingdom's diverse flora and its importance to their natural heritage.

As spring unfurled its vibrant colors across the gardens, Serena walked the paths with her Minister of Environment and the Director of the Royal Botanical Gardens, planning an educational campaign that would intertwine botanical knowledge with cultural heritage, making the learning experience both enriching and engaging.

"Minister, Director, the botanical gardens are not just spaces of beauty but also of immense educational value," Serena began, her eyes reflecting the lush greens around her. "How can we integrate these gardens more deeply into our educational outreach, particularly focusing on students?"

The Director, an avid botanist, was quick to respond. "Your Majesty, we could start by developing a series of interactive workshops right here in the gardens. These could be tailored to different age groups and would include hands-on activities that teach children about plant biology, the importance of biodiversity, and the history of Eirene's native species."

"I like that approach," Serena said thoughtfully. "It's vital that our children understand and appreciate the richness of their natural environment. What about bringing the gardens to those who can't come to us?"

"That's an excellent point, Your Majesty," the Minister of Environment added. "We could develop traveling exhibits that visit schools, especially in more remote areas of the kingdom, with portable displays of native plants and interactive digital presentations about their ecological and cultural significance."

Serena nodded, pleased with the initiative. "Let's ensure these traveling exhibits also include materials that teachers can use to continue the education after the exhibit moves on. We want to spark ongoing interest and learning."

As they continued their walk, discussions turned towards integrating these environmental initiatives with the cultural aspects of the Heritage for Tomorrow project. They talked about creating a digital app that could allow users to virtually tour the gardens, learn about the plants, and understand their uses throughout Eirene's history, from medicinal purposes to their roles in public and private life.

"An app is a great idea," Serena acknowledged. "It could serve as a virtual extension of our gardens, accessible to anyone with a smartphone. This could be especially useful for our schools, integrating it into science and history curricula."

"Absolutely, Your Majesty," the Director agreed. "We can include features like augmented reality, where students can see the plants in their natural habitats and interact with them to learn about their ecosystems and conservation status."

The meeting concluded with a sense of accomplishment and a clear plan of action. Serena tasked the Minister and the Director to collaborate closely with the Ministry of Education to ensure that these new resources were well-integrated into schools and community centers.

As Serena left the Royal Botanical Gardens, she felt a refreshing sense of purpose. The gardens, with their myriad paths and hidden nooks, were much like the educational journey she hoped to cultivate—a journey of discovery, understanding, and respect for the natural world. By connecting the kingdom's youth with their environmental heritage, she was planting seeds not just of knowledge but of stewardship that would grow alongside them, ensuring that Eirene's natural and cultural legacies were cherished and preserved for generations to come.

Following the initiatives at the Royal Botanical Gardens, Queen Serena decided to address the next generation directly by hosting a youth summit at the Royal Palace. The summit, titled "Voices of Tomorrow," aimed to engage young leaders from across Eirene in shaping the future of their kingdom, particularly focusing on environmental and cultural sustainability.

As the young attendees gathered in the opulent assembly hall of the palace, decorated with banners proclaiming the summit's theme, the air buzzed with youthful energy and anticipation. Serena opened the summit with a welcoming speech that underscored her commitment to involving youth in the governance and future planning of Eirene.

"Welcome, young leaders of Eirene," Serena began, her voice resonating with warmth and authority. "Today, you are not just the future of our kingdom; you are its present. Your ideas, your passion, and your vision are crucial as we shape a sustainable future. I am here to listen and to work alongside you to bring those ideas to life."

A young woman, representing the national universities, was the first to speak. "Your Majesty, thank you for this platform. One critical area we need to address is the integration of environmental education at all levels of our schooling. Not just as a subject, but as a way of life that respects and preserves our natural resources."

"I couldn't agree more," Serena replied. "How do you propose we integrate this into our current education system?"

"We could start with 'green weeks' in schools where students participate in learning projects that involve local environmental issues," the young woman suggested. "These could be supported by workshops led by environmental experts and visits to places like the Royal Botanical Gardens."

"That's a fantastic idea," Serena nodded. "It brings the practical aspect of learning to the forefront. Minister of Education, could you take note of this suggestion?"

"Certainly, Your Majesty," the Minister of Education responded, jotting down notes.

Another young leader, a budding entrepreneur, then took the floor. "Your Majesty, as we talk about sustainability, we must also consider economic sustainability. Young entrepreneurs like myself often struggle with access to capital and mentorship. Creating more incubation hubs could foster innovation, particularly in sustainable technologies."

"That's an excellent point," Serena acknowledged. "Supporting young entrepreneurs not only drives economic growth but also fosters innovation in critical areas like sustainability. Minister of Economy, let's look into expanding our support for incubation hubs and linking them with universities and research centers."

"Will do, Your Majesty," the Minister of Economy confirmed.

The discussion then moved to cultural sustainability, with a young artist expressing concerns about the preservation of traditional Eirenean arts. "Your Majesty, while we embrace the future, we must also hold onto our artistic heritage. I propose creating digital archives of traditional Eirenean art forms and making them accessible to schools to ensure that this rich heritage isn't lost."

"A very thoughtful suggestion," Serena said. "Preserving our cultural identity in the digital age is indeed crucial. Minister of Culture, could we integrate this into the Heritage for Tomorrow project?"

"We certainly can, Your Majesty," the Minister of Culture replied. "It would be a valuable addition to our efforts in cultural education and preservation."

As the summit concluded, Serena felt a surge of hope and pride for the young leaders of Eirene. Their engagement and innovative ideas reinforced her belief in the bright future of her kingdom.

"Thank you, everyone, for your insightful contributions today," Serena concluded. "This summit is just the beginning. Together, we will ensure that the future of Eirene is vibrant, sustainable, and true to the spirit of our people."

As the young leaders dispersed, animatedly discussing their summit experiences, Serena stood for a moment, watching the future of Eirene embodying enthusiasm and intelligence. Today's dialogue had not only offered solutions but had also empowered the next generation to take the lead in their areas of passion, ensuring that the kingdom's future was in capable and committed hands.

After a series of impactful discussions and initiatives focused on youth involvement and environmental stewardship, Queen Serena dedicated the final session of the summit to solidifying the commitments made and establishing clear action plans. The goal was to ensure that the energetic discourse translated into tangible results that would benefit Eirene for generations to come.

The session took place in the Royal Palace's strategy room, where maps and charts adorned the walls, symbolizing the broad scope of the kingdom's aspirations. Gathered around a large oval table were young leaders, ministers, and advisors, all ready to commit to the future.

"Thank you all for the vibrant ideas and passionate discussions we've had so far," Serena began, her voice steady and inspiring. "Now, let's dedicate ourselves to turning these ideas into actions. Minister of Youth, could you start by summarizing the initiatives we are committing to today?"

"Of course, Your Majesty," the Minister of Youth responded, clearing his throat before continuing. "Based on our discussions, we are committing to several key initiatives. First, we will expand environmental education across all levels, incorporating practical learning experiences about sustainability into the national curriculum."

"That's an excellent start," Serena nodded. "What about support for young entrepreneurs?"

"We will enhance funding and support for incubation hubs, focusing particularly on those promoting sustainable technologies," the Minister of Economy interjected. "We also plan to link these hubs with academic institutions to facilitate knowledge exchange and innovation."

"I am pleased to hear that," Serena replied. "Now, turning to our cultural commitments. Minister of Culture, what are our steps to preserve and invigorate our heritage?"

"We will be launching a digital archive for Eirene's traditional arts, accessible to schools and the public," the Minister of Culture explained. "Additionally, we are organizing annual cultural festivals that will showcase both traditional and contemporary arts, celebrating our rich heritage and its evolution."

"Very well," Serena said, looking around the table, meeting the eyes of those present. "These are strong initiatives that will build a robust foundation for our future. How will we ensure that these plans are properly implemented and monitored?"

"The Office of Strategic Planning will oversee the implementation of these initiatives," Sir Cedric, her Chief Strategist, answered. "We will set up a quarterly review system to monitor progress and will adjust strategies as needed to ensure effectiveness and sustainability."

"I also propose we establish a youth advisory board," a young leader suggested. "This board could provide ongoing feedback and new ideas to keep our initiatives relevant and dynamic."

"A splendid idea," Serena agreed enthusiastically. "Engaging with our youth continuously will keep our policies and practices vibrant and forward-thinking. Let's ensure this board has a diverse representation from across the kingdom."

As the meeting drew to a close, there was a sense of accomplishment and anticipation. Documents were signed, hands were shaken, and commitments were made. Serena stood and addressed the room once more.

"Today, we have laid down a promise for the future—a promise to nurture our environment, support our young innovators, and celebrate our culture," she declared. "Let us move forward with determination and hope, for the work we begin today will shape the Eirene of tomorrow."

The session ended not just with a ceremonial conclusion but with the beginning of numerous projects that would carry the enthusiasm and commitments forward. As the participants exited the strategy room, the corridors of the palace buzzed with conversations about next steps and future meetings.

Outside, the palace gardens were in full bloom, a fitting metaphor for the seeds of change that had been planted over the past days. Serena walked among the flowers, her thoughts as much on the tasks ahead as on the young leaders who would one day continue the work she had begun. With each step, she was not just walking through a garden, but through the future she was helping to cultivate—a future that promised growth, sustainability, and unity.

Chapter 24
Festival of the New Dawn

With the vibrant energy of the "Voices of Tomorrow" youth summit still resonating through the halls of the palace, Queen Serena turned her attention to reinforcing the foundations laid by the various initiatives begun throughout the year. As the kingdom of Eirene blossomed into spring, she focused on strengthening the infrastructure that supported these projects, particularly in the realm of environmental conservation—a cause close to her heart and crucial to the kingdom's sustainability.

The queen convened a meeting with her environmental council in the lush setting of the Royal Conservatory, where the rich diversity of Eirene's flora was on splendid display. The glass-domed room, bathed in the soft light of the morning sun, served as a living reminder of what was at stake: the natural beauty and biodiversity of Eirene.

"As we continue to advance our environmental initiatives," Serena began, addressing the council, "it is crucial that we also strengthen the underlying systems that support these efforts. Our parks, wildlife reserves, and natural habitats must be protected and nurtured with more than just passion—they need robust infrastructure and sustainable management practices."

The Minister of Environment, who had been instrumental in expanding the national parks system, responded with a detailed update. "Your Majesty, we are currently enhancing our park infrastructures by integrating advanced ecological monitoring systems. These include sensor networks for tracking wildlife health and vegetation changes, which will help us manage these areas more effectively."

"I am pleased to hear this," Serena said, nodding appreciatively. "What steps are we taking to ensure that these technologies are used responsibly and that the data they collect is protected?"

"We are implementing strict data security protocols," the minister assured her. "Additionally, we are working with local universities to train the next generation of environmental scientists and park managers, ensuring that they are equipped to use these technologies ethically and effectively."

Serena was satisfied with the progress but knew that infrastructure was only part of the equation. "Let us also focus on community engagement. Our conservation efforts must be supported by the people of Eirene. How are we fostering a culture of environmental stewardship among our citizens?"

The Director of Environmental Outreach took up this question. "We are expanding our community outreach programs to include more educational workshops and volunteer opportunities. By involving communities in tree planting and conservation projects, we're not only improving our environment but also instilling a sense of ownership and responsibility towards these natural resources."

"Engagement is key," Serena agreed. "We must ensure that every citizen of Eirene feels connected to our natural heritage. This connection is what will sustain our efforts into the future."

As the meeting concluded, plans were set in motion to enhance both the physical and communal infrastructures supporting Eirene's environmental initiatives. Serena left the conservatory feeling confident in the council's direction and the steps being taken.

Walking through the gardens adjacent to the conservatory, the queen paused to observe a group of schoolchildren on a guided tour, their faces alight with curiosity and wonder as they learned about the different plants and ecosystems. This scene was a vivid illustration of the impact of her policies: young minds awakening to the importance of nature and conservation.

These moments reinforced Serena's commitment to ensuring that the beauty and diversity of Eirene's environment would endure. The policies and infrastructures being built were more than just mechanisms of governance—they were the guardians of the kingdom's future. With each policy refined and each system strengthened, Serena was weaving a resilient and sustainable tapestry that would shelter and sustain the generations to come.

As the initiatives for environmental conservation began to take root, Queen Serena shifted her focus to ensuring that Eirene's technological infrastructure could support and enhance these environmental efforts. Recognizing the potential of technology to revolutionize traditional practices, she convened a strategic meeting with her top technology advisors and environmental specialists. The meeting was set in the high-tech operations center of the Ministry of Technology, a hub of innovation that connected various parts of the kingdom through digital networks.

"Welcome, everyone," Serena began as the attendees settled around the sleek, holographic display table. "Our kingdom is at a pivotal moment where technology can dramatically amplify our conservation efforts. Today, I want us to explore how we can integrate advanced technologies to better monitor, protect, and manage our natural resources."

The Minister of Technology, a forward-thinking strategist, was the first to respond. "Your Majesty, we've developed a proposal for a smart network of sensors across our national parks. These sensors can monitor environmental conditions in real time, providing data that can preemptively inform us about issues like illegal logging, wildlife movements, and forest health."

"That sounds promising," Serena replied. "How would we ensure that this data is used effectively?"

"We propose setting up a dedicated environmental data analysis unit within the Ministry of Environment," the minister continued. "This unit would use AI to analyze the data, making predictive models that could help us not only react to environmental changes but also proactively manage them."

"An excellent idea," Serena acknowledged. "But how can we make sure this technology is accessible to local communities so they too can be involved in managing and protecting their environment?"

"We can develop community portals that allow local leaders and citizens to access relevant data," suggested the Director of Environmental

Technology. "These portals would provide not only data but also training modules on how to interpret and use the information for local benefit."

"I see tremendous value in that," Serena noted. "Empowering our communities to take an active role in conservation is essential. What about our younger citizens? How can we engage them in using these technologies?"

"We could integrate this technology into the educational curriculum," offered the Minister of Education, who had joined the discussion. "We can teach students how to use these tools through projects and competitions that encourage them to come up with their own conservation solutions."

"That's an innovative approach to education," Serena smiled, pleased with the holistic integration of technology and education. "Let's ensure these educational programs are well-funded and supported."

"As we advance these technologies," the Queen continued, turning to address a broader concern, "we must also consider the environmental impact of the technologies themselves. How do we mitigate the ecological footprint of deploying such a wide network of sensors and devices?"

"The devices we plan to use are designed to be low-impact," explained the Minister of Technology. "They require minimal power, which can be supplied by solar energy, and are made from environmentally friendly materials. Additionally, we are investing in recycling programs for electronic waste to ensure our tech advancements do not harm the environment."

"Very well," Serena concluded, nodding in approval of the thoughtful planning. "This meeting has laid out a clear path forward for integrating technology into our environmental strategies. Let's proceed with implementing these plans, ensuring that each step we take is in harmony with our commitment to the environment."

As the meeting adjourned, there was a shared sense of accomplishment and anticipation among the attendees. They were not just planning projects; they were paving the way for a future where technology and nature worked in seamless synergy. Serena, standing by the window overlooking the sprawling cityscape, felt reassured that these technological initiatives would indeed serve as vital tools in safeguarding Eirene's natural treasures. Each step was another stitch in the fabric of her kingdom's future, woven with the threads of innovation and care.

Following the integration of advanced technologies in environmental management, Queen Serena turned her focus toward fortifying Eirene's economic stability. She convened a high-level economic summit at the palace, aiming to align the kingdom's economic policies with the technological and environmental strides it had made. The summit brought together her economic advisors, business leaders, and representatives from various sectors, all gathered in the stately conference room designed to facilitate open and productive discussions.

"Welcome, everyone," Serena began, her presence commanding the room. "Our kingdom has made significant advancements in technology and environmental conservation. Today, we focus on ensuring that our economy not only thrives on these advancements but also promotes sustainable and inclusive growth."

The Minister of Economy was the first to speak. "Your Majesty, our first order of business should be to review our trade policies. With the new international agreements in place and our enhanced technological capabilities, we have a unique opportunity to position Eirene as a leader in sustainable trade."

"That's an excellent point," Serena replied. "How do you propose we enhance our trade framework to support this goal?"

"We could incentivize companies that engage in environmentally sustainable practices with tax breaks and grants," the minister suggested. "Additionally, establishing stricter environmental standards for products entering and leaving Eirene would not only uphold our commitment to sustainability but also encourage other nations to follow suit."

"I agree," Serena said, nodding thoughtfully. "It's important that our economic policies reflect our environmental values. What about internal economic stability? How do we ensure that our own industries are robust and capable of adapting to these changes?"

The Minister of Industry added, "To bolster our industries, we must invest in education and training programs that equip our workforce with the skills needed for the emerging green economy. Partnerships between educational institutions and industries will be crucial in this regard."

"Indeed," Serena acknowledged. "Education is key. Let's also explore how we can support small and medium enterprises during this transition. They are the backbone of our economy and need our support to adapt."

The conversation then shifted towards innovation in financial policies. The Treasurer of Eirene suggested, "We might consider developing green bonds and other financial instruments that can fund environmental projects. Such initiatives could attract investors who are interested in sustainable development."

"That's a forward-thinking approach," Serena said with approval. "Green bonds could indeed provide us with the necessary funds to further our environmental projects while also engaging the financial sector in our sustainability efforts."

As the discussion continued, the focus turned to integrating these economic policies with international economic relations. "We should ensure that our new economic policies align with the international agreements we have set," the Minister of Foreign Affairs noted. "This alignment will strengthen our position on the global stage and promote Eirene as a model of sustainable economic practices."

"Absolutely," Serena agreed. "Our foreign policy should reflect our domestic priorities. Let's ensure that our international economic engagements are consistent with our values and strategic goals."

As the summit drew to a close, there was a consensus on several strategic initiatives aimed at strengthening Eirene's economy in a way that was both sustainable and inclusive. Serena concluded the meeting with a call to action. "Thank you for your insights and contributions today. Let us proceed with these plans with diligence and foresight. Our collective efforts will ensure that Eirene's prosperity is both enduring and principled."

With the economic framework set, the participants left the summit with a clear direction and a sense of responsibility. Serena remained for a moment, looking over the notes and plans laid out during the discussion. Each decision made today was a step towards securing a stable and prosperous future for Eirene, one that harmonized with the kingdom's environmental and technological advancements.

The culmination of the economic summit marked the beginning of a pivotal phase for Eirene—a phase that would involve implementing the new economic strategies that Queen Serena and her council had meticulously planned. To oversee the deployment of these strategies, Serena organized a series of follow-up meetings with sector leaders and key stakeholders, held in the ornate Strategy Room at the palace, where the future of Eirene's economy would be shaped.

"Thank you all for gathering once more," Serena opened the meeting, her tone both resolute and encouraging. "Our summit laid the groundwork for transformative economic policies. Now, it's time to turn these plans into action. Minister of Economy, could you start by detailing the first steps for our green incentive program?"

"Certainly, Your Majesty," the Minister of Economy responded. "We have outlined the initial phase, which includes launching the tax break system for companies that achieve measurable environmental standards. We are finalizing the criteria for these standards and plan to roll out the program by the next quarter."

"That's a swift start," Serena noted. "How will we monitor and ensure compliance with these standards?"

"We are setting up an independent environmental audit body that will work closely with the Ministry of Environment," the minister explained. "This body will not only ensure compliance but also provide guidance to companies on how to meet the standards."

"Transparency and accountability are key," Serena affirmed. "What about our plans for green bonds? Treasurer, could you provide an update on that?"

"The framework for the green bonds is in place," the Treasurer added. "We are collaborating with international financial institutions to launch the bonds. This will not only fund our environmental projects but also signal to the global market that Eirene is serious about sustainable investment."

"I am pleased to hear this progress," Serena said. "Turning to our workforce, Minister of Education, how are we advancing the integration of green skills into our education system?"

"We are developing new curricula that incorporate sustainable practices and technologies," the Minister of Education replied. "These programs will start in vocational schools and extend to universities. We're also partnering with industry leaders to provide hands-on training and apprenticeships."

"Education is the foundation of sustainable development," Serena stated. "Now, let's discuss how we are supporting our small and medium enterprises during this transition. Minister of Industry?"

"We have established a support program that offers consultation and financial aid to small and medium businesses," the Minister of Industry explained. "This program helps them adapt to new technologies and business models that are environmentally friendly. Additionally, we are facilitating access to new markets for these businesses, especially in the green sector."

"Supporting local businesses ensures economic stability and job creation," Serena acknowledged. "Lastly, how are we aligning these initiatives with our international commitments, Minister of Foreign Affairs?"

"Our international agreements are being updated to reflect our new policies," the Minister of Foreign Affairs confirmed. "We are advocating for global environmental standards that align with ours, which not only strengthens our diplomatic stance but also promotes global sustainability."

"Excellent," Serena concluded, her gaze sweeping across the room filled with dedicated faces. "Each of you plays a crucial role in this transformative journey. Let's continue to work with integrity and innovation to ensure our policies not only promise but deliver a sustainable future for Eirene."

As the meeting adjourned, there was a clear sense of purpose and determination among everyone present. Serena stood by the window, watching the sunset paint the sky with hues of gold and amber—a daily reminder of the natural beauty they were all striving to preserve. Each policy implemented, each action taken, was a step toward a sustainable and prosperous future, cementing her legacy and Eirene's place as a leader in sustainable development.

Chapter 25
Whisper's Goodbye

As the initiatives to foster economic and environmental sustainability began to materialize across Eirene, Queen Serena shifted her focus to strengthening community resilience. Understanding that the well-being of her subjects was fundamental to the kingdom's prosperity, she planned a community engagement day, inviting leaders from various districts to discuss local issues and solutions. The venue chosen for this significant event was the open-air amphitheater in Eirene's largest public park, symbolizing transparency and openness.

Upon arrival, Serena greeted the community leaders warmly, each representing different facets of Eirene's diverse population. "Thank you for joining me today," she began, her voice carrying clearly across the amphitheater. "This gathering is about listening and learning from each other. It's about fortifying our communities to ensure they are not only resilient but thriving."

"Your Majesty," started Mr. Alton, a community leader from the northern district, "we appreciate your efforts in bringing us together. One of the pressing issues in our area is the lack of accessible healthcare facilities. Our residents have to travel long distances for medical services, which isn't always feasible."

Serena nodded thoughtfully. "Accessibility to healthcare is indeed a critical issue. Minister of Health, could you update us on the plans to address this?"

"Yes, Your Majesty," the Minister of Health responded. "We are in the process of expanding mobile health clinics that can travel to underserved areas on a scheduled basis. Additionally, we are exploring the establishment of a telemedicine service to provide consultations and prescriptions remotely."

"That sounds promising," Mr. Alton replied. "Remote services could be a game-changer for us. It's crucial that these plans are implemented swiftly."

"Absolutely," Serena agreed. "Speed is of the essence, and we are committed to rolling out these services as quickly as possible."

Next, Ms. Vera, representing the coastal communities, raised a concern about environmental degradation affecting local fisheries—a key livelihood in her region. "Your Majesty, our community depends heavily on fishing, but pollution and changing climate patterns are affecting our catches. We need support in adapting to these changes and in protecting our marine environment."

Serena turned to her environmental advisor. "What steps can we take to assist Ms. Vera's community?"

"We are working on several fronts," the advisor explained. "This includes strengthening regulations on pollutants entering our waterways and investing in marine conservation projects that help replenish fish stocks. Additionally, we're looking into alternative livelihood programs for communities most affected by these environmental changes."

"I'm relieved to hear there are plans in motion," Ms. Vera said. "Engaging our community in these conservation efforts and diversification programs will be crucial."

Another topic discussed was the integration of the younger population into the local economies. A young entrepreneur, Mr. Kendricks, highlighted the challenge. "While there's a focus on traditional employment, there's less support for young entrepreneurs who wish to innovate or start new ventures. We need more than just encouragement; we need concrete support like grants and mentorships."

"Your point is well taken, Mr. Kendricks," Serena responded. "Fostering a culture of innovation is essential. Minister of Economic Development, perhaps you could expand on how we might support our young entrepreneurs?"

"We're in the process of establishing a fund specifically for young entrepreneurs," the minister detailed. "This fund will provide the financial assistance you mentioned, along with access to a network of mentors who can guide you through the process of starting and running a business."

As the discussion drew to a close, Serena felt a renewed sense of connection with her subjects. "Today's conversations are just the beginning. We will continue to work together, listen to each other, and implement solutions that address your needs directly."

The community leaders left the meeting feeling heard and hopeful, energized by the tangible plans laid out and the queen's commitment to their well-being. Serena remained for a while, reflecting on the discussions, knowing that the strength of Eirene lay in the resilience of its communities, each unique yet united in their pursuit of a better future. Each conversation today was a step towards that resilient and vibrant future, a tapestry woven from the diverse threads of her beloved kingdom.

Following the productive community engagement day, Queen Serena was determined to ensure that the momentum gained would translate into actionable results. To facilitate this, she convened a task force specifically designed to oversee the implementation of the initiatives discussed. This task force included ministers, community leaders, and experts from various fields, reflecting a cross-section of Eirene's diverse society.

The first meeting of the task force took place in the Council Chamber at the palace, a room known for its long history of decision-making and strategic planning. As the members gathered around the large, circular table, the atmosphere was one of collaborative purpose.

"Thank you for assembling on such short notice," Serena began, addressing the group with a measured tone. "Our discussions during the community engagement day highlighted several critical areas needing immediate attention. Our task now is to ensure these areas are not just addressed but transformed into strengths for our communities."

The Minister of Health spoke first, detailing the progress on expanding healthcare accessibility. "Your Majesty, following our discussions, we have expedited the deployment of mobile health clinics to northern districts. Additionally, the telemedicine initiative is set to launch next month, which will dramatically increase access to medical consultations."

"That's excellent news," Serena responded with a nod. "How are we ensuring that these services reach the most isolated communities effectively?"

"We have coordinated with local leaders to identify the most suitable locations and times for the clinics," the Minister explained. "We are also utilizing local radio stations and community centers to disseminate information about the telemedicine services."

Turning the discussion towards environmental issues, Serena asked about the initiatives to support the coastal communities affected by environmental changes. The Environmental Advisor updated her on the progress. "We've initiated several projects aimed at marine conservation and pollution control. These include setting up artificial reefs and stricter monitoring of industrial waste disposal into water bodies."

"I am particularly interested in how we are engaging the local communities in these efforts," Serena said, emphasizing community involvement.

"We're organizing workshops to educate the community about sustainable fishing practices and involving them in the conservation projects as paid participants," the advisor detailed. "This approach not only helps the environment but also provides economic benefits to the community."

The conversation then shifted to economic development, particularly support for young entrepreneurs. The Minister of Economic Development provided an update. "We have launched the young entrepreneur fund, which has already begun to receive applications. We are pairing each approved project with a mentor from our network of experienced business leaders."

"Are we providing any specific support to help these young entrepreneurs navigate the complexities of starting a business?" Serena inquired, focusing on the practical challenges.

"Yes, Your Majesty," the minister replied. "We have set up a series of online seminars that cover everything from business planning and funding to marketing and legal compliance. These resources are designed to be easily accessible and are supplemented by regional workshops."

As the meeting drew to a close, Serena felt assured that the task force was not only addressing the immediate needs but also laying down a sustainable framework for the future. "I am pleased with the progress we have made in such a short time," she concluded. "Let us continue to push forward with determination and a clear focus on our goals. Our communities depend on the success of these initiatives."

The members of the task force left the meeting energized and ready to continue their work. Serena remained behind for a few moments, reflecting on the day's discussions. She knew that building community resilience was a complex challenge, involving myriad factors from health and environment to economic opportunities. However, the commitment shown by the task force gave her confidence that these challenges could be met with innovative and sustained efforts.

With each initiative set into motion, the fabric of Eirene's communities was being strengthened, woven tighter with threads of care, respect, and mutual support.

The initiatives set forth by Queen Serena were beginning to bear fruit across Eirene, yet she understood the importance of maintaining the momentum and ensuring that every sector of the society was aligned with the new policies. To gauge the progress and integrate feedback directly from the community, Serena arranged a series of town hall meetings across the kingdom. The first of these was held in Eirene's bustling central district, a melting pot of cultures and economic activities, where she could interact with a broad spectrum of her subjects.

The town hall was packed with citizens eager to voice their thoughts and hear directly from their queen. Serena opened the meeting with a brief overview of the initiatives and their intended impacts, then quickly turned the floor over to the attendees.

"Your Majesty, thank you for this opportunity," began a local shop owner. "The new health clinic on wheels visited our area last week, and it was a huge help, especially for those of us who can't travel far. What are the plans for making this a regular service?"

"Thank you for sharing that," Serena responded warmly. "I'm pleased to hear the clinic was helpful. The plan is indeed to make these visits regular, with at least two visits per month to each designated area. We are committed to ensuring that no one in Eirene lacks for basic healthcare due to location constraints."

A young teacher took the next question. "Your Majesty, the initiatives for integrating environmental education are wonderful, but we teachers need more training to effectively deliver this new curriculum. How will the Ministry of Education support us in this?"

"An excellent point," Serena acknowledged. "Minister of Education, could you address this concern?"

"Certainly, Your Majesty," the minister replied, addressing the crowd. "We are rolling out a comprehensive training program for all teachers, starting next month. This includes workshops and hands-on training sessions that will be held throughout the year. Additionally, we're developing online resources that you can access at any time to aid your teaching."

The discussion then shifted to environmental concerns, with a local fisherman raising the next question. "Your Majesty, the efforts to clean up our waterways have been noticeable, and I thank you for that. However, we're still facing challenges with overfishing. What more can be done?"

Serena nodded, understanding the gravity of the issue. "We are implementing stricter fishing quotas and increasing surveillance to prevent illegal fishing practices. Also, we're investing in aquaculture projects to reduce the pressure on wild fish populations. Our goal is not only to address the current decline but to ensure sustainable fishing practices for the future."

A young entrepreneur then spoke up, "I appreciate the new funding initiatives for startups, especially in green technologies. However, connecting with potential investors is still challenging. Can more be done to facilitate these connections?"

"Indeed, we can do more," Serena agreed. "Minister of Economic Development, perhaps you could expand on our efforts in this area?"

"Yes, Your Majesty," the minister responded. "We are initiating a series of networking events specifically designed to connect startups with investors interested in sustainable technologies. Additionally, we're enhancing our online platform to include features that allow entrepreneurs to showcase their projects to potential investors worldwide."

As the town hall meeting drew to a close, the air was thick with a sense of community and shared purpose. Serena concluded, "Thank you all for your insightful questions and suggestions. These meetings are crucial for us to understand your needs directly and to adjust our policies accordingly."

As the citizens dispersed, their conversations lingered in the air, a blend of hopeful tones and determined chatter. Serena stayed a moment longer, absorbing the atmosphere, pleased with the engagement and feedback. Each voice added depth to the ongoing narrative of Eirene's development, each concern addressed wove another thread into the rich tapestry of national progress. This direct interaction was vital in shaping a responsive and inclusive government, one that not only listened but acted on the voice of its people.

With valuable insights gathered from the town hall meetings, Queen Serena was committed to ensuring that the feedback translated into enhanced and sustained community actions. To solidify this commitment, she organized a concluding forum at the Royal Assembly Hall, bringing together community leaders, government officials, and key stakeholders to outline and pledge specific actions based on the community's feedback.

As the participants filled the grand hall, the anticipation was palpable. Serena opened the forum with a clear message of unity and action. "Today, we come together not just to discuss but to commit to specific actions that will ensure the prosperity and well-being of all Eirenians. Let us begin by addressing the top concerns raised and outlining our strategies for addressing them."

A community leader from the eastern district was the first to speak. "Your Majesty, our primary concern remains healthcare access. The mobile clinics are a great start, but we need more permanent solutions in remote areas."

"Thank you for raising this," Serena responded. "Minister of Health, could you share the steps we are taking to address this concern?"

"Yes, Your Majesty," the Minister of Health replied. "Based on the feedback, we are increasing the number of mobile clinic visits while simultaneously planning the construction of two new health centers in the most remote districts. These centers will be operational within the next year, fully equipped to meet the needs of their communities."

"That is reassuring," said the community leader. "What guarantees do we have that these centers will be adequately staffed?"

"We are currently in the process of training additional healthcare professionals and have partnerships with local universities to ensure a steady flow of medical staff to these centers," the minister assured.

Next, an educator from the central district addressed the assembly. "While the environmental education initiative is commendable, we need to ensure it is continuous and evolving with the environmental challenges we face."

"Absolutely," Serena agreed. "Minister of Education, please elaborate on how we intend to sustain and adapt this initiative."

"We are establishing a special task force to continuously update our environmental curriculum," the Minister of Education explained. "This task force will work closely with environmental experts and community leaders to ensure our educational content remains relevant and impactful."

The discussion then moved towards economic development, where a young entrepreneur highlighted the need for ongoing support for startups. "It's crucial that the support for entrepreneurs doesn't end with initial funding. Continued mentorship and market access are essential for long-term success."

"Indeed," Serena nodded. "Minister of Economic Development, what are our plans for ongoing support?"

"We are expanding our mentorship programs to include not just startup advice but also ongoing business development support," the minister detailed. "Additionally, we are launching an online marketplace by the end of the year, which will help startups by providing them direct access to national and international markets."

As each leader spoke and commitments were made, Serena ensured that every pledge was not only noted but also scheduled for review. "We will hold annual reviews to assess the progress of each initiative we've discussed today. This will ensure accountability and allow us to adjust our strategies as needed."

The forum concluded with a signing ceremony, where each leader and official signed a pledge to uphold their commitments to the initiatives discussed. The community leaders left the meeting with a sense of accomplishment and a clear understanding of the steps forward.

Serena stayed behind as the hall emptied, reflecting on the day's outcomes. The commitments made were more than just promises; they were the blueprint for a thriving Eirene. Each signed pledge was a testament to the collective dedication to the kingdom's future, a future that was being built on the solid foundation of community input and governmental action.

Conclusion

As the winds of change swept through Eirene, Queen Serena stood atop the newly restored walls of the royal palace, gazing out over the land that was once shrouded in both literal and metaphorical mists. Her journey, woven from dreams and determination, had rekindled the heart of a kingdom long lost to time and neglect. Below, the bustling sounds of a people rejuvenated filled the air—markets thrived, children's laughter echoed, and artisans of all crafts shared their wares with pride.

Whisper, the ethereal fox that had once guided her through the mists of uncertainty, now nestled comfortably at her side, a constant companion in both spirit and guidance. "We have done well, Whisper," Serena mused softly, her voice a mix of triumph and contemplation. "The mists have cleared, not just from our lands, but from our hearts."

"Yes, Serena," Whisper replied, its voice a melodious echo in her mind. "You have awakened more than just the echoes of old. You have ignited a flame of hope, a beacon that will guide Eirene into a new era."

Around them, the castle was alive with the preparations for the Festival of Renewal, a celebration Serena had instituted to mark the annual anniversary of Eirene's awakening. It was a festival that not only celebrated their past victories but also forged new connections and friendships among her people and their neighbors. Flags representing the diverse cultures of the kingdom fluttered in the gentle breeze, symbolizing the unity and diversity that now thrived under Serena's rule.

Turning her gaze towards the horizon, Serena could see caravans arriving from distant lands, bringing with them the promise of new alliances and shared knowledge. The roads, once dangerous and unkempt, now served as lifelines, connecting the heart of Eirene with the outer villages and beyond.

Her council, a diverse group drawn from all corners of the kingdom, approached her on the battlements, their faces wearing expressions of respect and admiration. "Your Majesty, the delegates from the Highland

Territories have arrived," announced the Minister of Commerce, a capable woman whose own village had been among the first to feel the benefits of Serena's reforms.

"Thank you, Minister. Please ensure our guests are comfortable and prepare them for the summit tomorrow. We have much to discuss and even more to share," Serena instructed, her voice firm yet warm.

As the sun dipped below the horizon, casting a golden glow over the land, Serena felt a profound peace settle over her. She had faced countless challenges, from unraveling the mysteries of her ancestry to rebuilding a kingdom from the ashes of its former glory. Each step had been a testament to her strength and vision, guided by the legacy of those who had come before her and fueled by the aspirations of those who would follow.

Tonight, as the stars began to twinkle in the twilight sky, the lights of the festival flickered to life below, mirroring the stars above. Music drifted up to the battlements, a melody made up of countless instruments played by hands united in celebration and hope.

Serena and Whisper stood together, watching the night unfold. "This is just the beginning, isn't it, Whisper?" she asked, her eyes bright with the reflection of the festivities below.

"Indeed, Serena. As long as you lead with kindness and courage, Eirene will continue to flourish. And remember, wherever the journey takes you, you are never alone," Whisper responded, its ethereal form shimmering with the same light that sparkled across the kingdom.

With her heart full and her resolve unwavering, Serena looked out over Eirene, her spirit intertwined with the land and its people. Here, in a kingdom reborn under her guidance, the tales of yesterday would weave into the hopes of tomorrow, crafting a legacy that would endure for generations to come.